The Watchers Trilogy

LEGIONS

KARICE BOLTON

ISBN: 10: 0615579930
ISBN- 13: 978-0615579931

DEDICATION

To all of the people in my life who always tell me to go for it!

Love you my dude! Jon, you are the best husband a girl could ask for...

Mom, thank you for always giving me encouragement and to my dad who is watching down over us all!

ACKNOWLEDGMENTS

I want to say a simple thank you to Amazon, Barnes & Noble, and all of the other avenues available for the indie publishing world. It allows the art of storytelling to continue to flourish in unexpected ways!

TO CONTACT THE AUTHOR
PLEASE VISIT HER WEBSITE AT

KARICEBOLTON.COM

OR
EMAIL

INFO@KARICEBOLTON.COM

OR
FOLLOW HER ON FACEBOOK or TWITTER

@KARICEBOLTON

Books by Karice Bolton

The WATCHERS TRILOGY
Taken
Awakening
Legions
Cataclysm

THE WITCH AVENUE SERIES
Lonely Souls
Altered Souls
Released Souls
Shattered Souls

BEYOND LOVE SERIES
Beyond Control
Beyond Doubt
Beyond Reason
Beyond Intent

AFTERWORLD SERIES
RecruitZ

Chapter One

I closed my eyes as tight as they could possibly shut, not wanting to see any of the images that were shoving their way into my psyche. I was hoping that the images I saw dancing in the smoke of the flames were nothing more than hallucinations. Seeing Athen's body that close to another's was more than I could comprehend. I didn't know how this was supposed to be connected to the Awakening or getting him back to us. With my body squirming and trying to get away from the visions, Cyril and Arie had to tie me down so I didn't disrupt the process. My body was going against everything I was supposed to be doing. My body and my mind were in a battle against each other. Neither wanted to accept the vision of Athen and the demon together. With my legs kicking, and arms flailing in all directions, all I wanted to do was to flee - but my soul knew better. If I disrupted the Awakening now, all hope was pretty much lost on getting Athen back soon.

My most intimate moments with Athen began being projected against the flames. The night was a perfect backdrop to highlight our images together as one. I didn't know if it was only me who was seeing that, but the amount of pain I was suffering made me not care. Cyril and Arie kept the flames tended while I did my best confronting the physical and emotional pain that was running through my entire body. When I thought there were no more tears to be had, the wetness continued streaming down my cheeks. I had no control over anything.

My lungs began to tickle. A cough began stirring in my abdomen. I wasn't in control of anything physical or mental. I tried to gesture towards the flames, turning my head the other direction thinking it was the smoke that was causing my lungs to twitch, but Cyril shook his head.

"It's not the smoke, Ana. It's the..." Before he could get the last word out, I was gasping for air. I tried to take breaths in, but it was as if my lungs were already full. Every gulp of air brought on another coughing fit.

I turned back to the fire only to be accosted by the very images I had been doing my best to avoid and never make a reality. One image flashed right after the other of the two of them together – holding hands, walking a beach, getting coffee. The serpent woman and Athen were participating in things that normal couples do, only they weren't a normal couple. I knew they weren't. They couldn't be. Couldn't Athen see that? She was a fraud. I didn't understand what I was witnessing. But, I did my best to take in every detail, no matter how small, just in case it was needed to hunt him down.

The physical pain writhing through every part of my body was nowhere near the emotional distress I was feeling. If I didn't know better, I would think I was hallucinating. Unfortunately, it was nothing of the sort. I had lost Athen because I refused to believe the images that were coming to me in my dreams. I jeopardized his safety because I didn't want to utter aloud what I was seeing in my mind. With every beat of my heart, a shot ran through my veins slicing up along some extremity making way for the next iron-hot rush of blood behind it. I found myself getting lightheaded time and time again because I'd suck in all the breath I could. So fearful any movement would make the pain worse. I tried letting out air, little by little.

I didn't know how much more I could take of this, but when I thought I could handle no more, I reminded myself that Athen, too, went through this very same process for me decades earlier. I, also, pushed out the one tiny fact that I didn't want to dwell on, which was that there was no one chasing after me to get in the way of my reintroduction process. There wasn't someone fighting for my attention. It seemed like I was going to have to fight for Athen's affections. He wasn't faced with those challenges. Closing my eyes tightly to shield out the burning sensation that was becoming overwhelming, my lungs let out a scream that I couldn't bottle up any longer. I needed Athen. We weren't meant to be apart.

Chapter Two

The Awakening had gone how it was supposed to from what I was told. I don't remember that much of it, except for the excruciating pain. My arms and hands still felt like they were on fire in every single one of my joints – even the little ones. I thought what I had gone through during my reintroduction process was horrible, but it was nothing compared to the excruciating pain that ripped through my veins during the Awakening. It took all of the strength that I had to endure the process – that and the thought of Athen. His images carried me through it. He had done the same for me half a century ago. Everything I was doing now was for him. I was determined to get him back with all of us, his family.

I still blamed myself for the events that took him from us. It was hard not to. The guilt riddled my every thought. My visions told me exactly what was going to happen, and I did nothing. He didn't have a chance in the attack. That many demons against one of us was almost impossible. The worst part, that eats at me every second of every day, was that the events that unfolded matched my nightmares almost perfectly. If I had only told him about the dreams I was having, maybe, none of this would have occurred. I just didn't want to believe that my nightmares could be real. That was my gift, seeing these visions. That was what my family told me. To me it felt more like a curse.

Once Athen was taken away, we immediately began the Awakening process. Thankfully, before the pain swept through my body, I was able to get a glimpse of him. He was doing okay - looked fine, but the beautiful, familiar green glow was missing from his eyes. His eyes looked like mine did before my family reintroduced me. He looked as if nothing ever happened, actually. I was thankful for that.

Not having him near me was the worst. It was hard even getting up and ready for the day – no laughter to begin my day in a wonderful way, no hug, no kiss. I longed for him beyond anything I ever thought possible - to just be touched by him one more time. I promised myself that we would get him back soon, not fifty years like it took for me. I don't think I could last fifty years without him. A shudder ran up my spine only to be met with an overwhelming amount of guilt and grief.

There was a gentle and familiar mist seeping through the air as I looked out our bedroom window onto Puget Sound. The water was calm this morning, only slightly moving with the breeze. At least there was something consistent and familiar I could grab onto. Anxiety began building as I heard the voices from downstairs become louder. The murmurs of the other families provided little comfort as I longed to be held by Athen. I knew this was the path that would get me to my true love once again, but every step felt like an enormous step backwards not forward. I was grateful to be back at our Kingston home but knew we would be headed to Victoria, B.C. where Athen appeared to be located. Thank goodness for our little homing beacon, Matilda. I missed her almost as much as Athen but knew she was the key to bringing us all back together with him. We were able to keep tabs on him since Matilda was with him. Not hearing her snorts and pants was really disheartening.

I let my mind wander off thinking of Athen, and I could feel tiny swells of excitement building at the prospect of being reunited. Being in the same city, that close in vicinity to Athen again, was something I needed and the sooner the better. I only hoped that I did everything correctly so that we could reunite quickly. I wasn't going to make the same mistakes he made.

I readied myself to greet everyone downstairs. I had come to know many of these fellow Fallen Angels and their descendants as the activity from the demons rose in frequency. Many of them had been through the same things as I. Some had their loved ones returned to them already, and others were still waiting, like me. Our family knew where Athen was, but it wasn't time to get him back yet. Knowing that Athen had endured this very feeling for decades - one that I had only known for mere weeks - was crushing. I don't know how he stayed so strong. I was just going through the motions trying the best I could to be of use to my family. Anything to bring Athen back in his true form.

I grabbed my grey wool sweater from the closet and shuffled down the hall to the gathering that was downstairs waiting for me. The chill wouldn't leave my bones no matter what I wrapped around myself. As I struggled to get my arms through the sweater, I realized how everything had become such an effort since Athen was taken. The grief had penetrated every fiber of my being.

All of the Christmas decorations had been put away by Cyril and Arie, for which I was eternally grateful. The New Year had begun and brought nothing except misery so far. Somehow I was sitting in the family room sipping a cup of coffee that Arie had brought me, just staring into oblivion. I don't even know how I got there. I noticed I did that quite a bit – arriving places, never remembering how I arrived. The fire was roaring, but the ice in the air was overwhelming. Part of our area rug was folded up on the corner, and I immediately thought about Matilda, our bulldog - our little homing beacon.

I pulled the sleeves of my sweater over my hands to warm up. There was far too much loss in the room to have the warmth of the flames penetrate the flesh of any of us. If I could only feel the warmth of Athen's touch. As I looked around the room, I could tell immediately which families were waiting for loved ones like I was, and which families had already experienced their return. A flash of envy appeared inside of me, which I squashed immediately. I'm sure that was all part of the demons' plan to have us turn against one another.

It had become apparent in the last few weeks, as we reached out to others, that we were under attack. This was our first opportunity to discuss our options as a group. We needed to find out as much information from around the area as possible. I only hoped I was up for it. I knew this was far too elaborate an undertaking for the dark demons to be concentrating on only us white demons. There was a more intricate plan laying in wait for us. We had to uncover it before it was too late.

I tried to focus on the task at hand, but my mind couldn't stop drifting to the images of Athen in the last weeks. His green eyes glimmering with hope as I remembered our past, the kindness in his touch as he would brush my cheek, the warmth of his body lying against mine. I tried to shake myself from going down that path. I needed to remain strong and focused. I glanced at one of the beautiful paintings near the sofa table. The vibrant reds splashed throughout made me focus on my fury that was beginning to build. Going down memory lane would only make it that much more difficult on me.

I heard Cyril's voice from the living room trying to gather everyone together. I felt the shift in movement as people began making their way towards me. Since I had been the last person to rephase from such a long time away from my family, I knew everyone was counting on my memories from the other side. They were hopeful that I'd somehow hold the key to how they would get their loved ones back as quickly as possible. Obviously, they didn't put two and two together that if it was that easy, Athen would be by my side right now.

I pushed my snide thoughts aside and concentrated on the good intent of everyone here. I felt a hand on my shoulder and turned around to see a stranger with tears in her eyes looking at me with the same level of desperation that I felt. I realized I had to get out of myself and look at the bigger picture. It wasn't just Athen I was going to be fighting for any longer. I held her hand briefly, and I stood up and went in front of the fireplace to speak to the group. I finally felt the warmth of the flames on the back of my legs soaking through the jeans that I was wearing. I looked around at everyone, all so welcoming and filled with anticipation. I was ashamed of myself for envying any of them. They were here to help. We were all in this together.

"Hi, everyone. I know many of you from my previous existence. At least, that's what I'm told. You'll have to forgive me for not being as quick as I should be with my memories," I said, trying to force a smile. Arie came up next to me to stand, grabbing my hand for support.

"As we all are coming to find out, there is change beginning to occur from the evil ones. We need to be vigilant in protecting the family members that remain, while still attempting to get our missing loved ones back. Don't be foolish and neglect the ones who are still with us. I have a feeling there will be evil creatures waiting for that very moment. We must not let our guard down. They're counting on us to be distracted, and since there are so many of us with those distractions, we must ensure the safety of each other. We can't create any larger openings for them. I get the feeling they are lurking where we might least expect them."

I had no idea where this confidence was coming from, but I felt empowered. I had the knowledge of my staged life, and the experience of the rephasing still a part of me, all within a breath away from each other. I felt very in tune with the feelings that were washing over me from fellow Fallen Angels in this room. I, also, realized I was able to sense most of their thoughts. I was thankful for these newly-developed skills. Quickly pausing on individuals, I was able to see where and how their family members were taken and the thoughts and worries of the families, as well as the darkness that was attempting to cloud over the room. It wasn't just me who had to squash the feelings of envy and jealousy. My heart started beating swiftly as I began to feel a change in the room. Hope and unity stirred in the room; the loss and despair was beginning to dissipate. I wondered if it was the words I spoke.

"We've divided everyone here into groups so that we can obtain as much information as possible. We need to uncover where, and how you lost your family member. Explain any abnormalities that might have occurred prior to them being taken away and any human anomalies that you may have noticed prior to the event or even after. Obviously, after the hikers and snowboarder incidents in Whistler, we know that the demons aren't afraid to pull from the human world to complete their tasks. The hikers are still on the loose. Unfortunately, now they're on the demons' side. My guess is since they were willing participants, they will be a crucial part of one of the Legions - so be on guard. I think we have about six groups carved out here, and Arie will give an iPad to each of your groups to start writing whatever you can outline for us. Write anything down no matter how small you think it may be. We are going to take all the iPads and compile everything. We'll be looking for any patterns or similarities that we can find. They aren't as smart as they think they are. After this exercise, we'll be able to compile some good information and send it out to everyone."

"We'll get our loved ones back. If there is one piece of advice I can give, it's to remember that it's harder on us than them. They don't know that anything is out of the ordinary. As of now, they don't know we exist." The words that escaped my lips made me choke up. I paused to regain my composure. I looked around the room seeing so many faces experiencing the loss I had in my heart, and I knew we all had to stay strong for each other.

"They don't know what they're missing, only we do. Their memories of us are gone. But remember the moment the process is ready to begin, the feelings will be rushing back to them like a wave crashing down on their souls. Make sure to be there for them the entire time and don't give up. The process is a long one. I'm still going through it." I was feeling stronger than I had in a long time. The thought that I could help the others gave me purpose.

"After tonight, we won't be able to meet here again," Cyril began. "We need to ensure that the demons can't detect our plans or any of our contact with each other. We must keep them thinking that we're all behaving as separate entities. When we do meet up, it'll need to be in smaller groups, always at someone's home, never in public, and we'll then have to figure out a system to spread the findings."

Arie had handed out the iPads to everyone, and the groups began working hard deconstructing the last few weeks of their lives. I was thankful Arie, Cyril, and I had already performed this act. I was able to sit in front of the fire, listening in on others, hoping I'd hear something that would piece everything together immediately. I waited earnestly for some such outcome as the thoughts and words came pouring over me, but my mind continued to drift to Athen, and I was unable to piece anything together. I excused myself and went up to our bedroom. As of now, I was an empty shell of a being. I was no longer whole.

Chapter Three

Everyone had left from the meeting. I had made sure of it before I made my way down to greet Arie and Cyril. I slowly puttered down the stairs hoping something had miraculously changed from the day before. I was sure they were feeling the same as I was - exhausted. It was a long night, and I never really felt like I got much sleep, if any. We had a few families who spent the night working on the project we had given them. I think they hoped that every second they stayed to help, it would bring them that much closer to finding their loved ones. I wished that was the case for us all.

The fire reflected off the glass coffee table in the family room, as I made my way to the sectional in front of it. Grabbing the red chenille throw, I covered myself as Cyril brought me a cup of coffee. Arie jumped on the cushion next to me almost spilling the beautiful brown liquid all over the couch.

"Well, since none of us can sleep, I say we get started. Does that work?" she asked, already handing us the iPads from the previous day's activities.

"Absolutely. Anything to get the show on the road," Cyril muttered, as he pulled up the ottoman.

"Alright, so let's scan over all the notes manually. Each of us can take a few, and then once we do that, we can compile them onto one iPad. I want to make sure that we all read enough to have things fresh in our memory," Arie instructed.

"Yeah, sounds good," Cyril and I spoke in unison.

I began scanning the first document. I noticed some similarities right off the bat between their situation and ours. I realized I needed to start taking notes on my findings immediately, so I opened up a new task list and began typing my observations. It looked like we were off to a good start.

The family who I was reviewing lived in Portland, Oregon. The Bullons started noticing suspicious activity among the locals who they knew. They had lived in Portland for about five years and had grown very fond of some of the humans in their little community, Arbor Lodge. There were quite a few independent boutiques, coffee shops, and bakeries where they got to know the locals very well. Because of this, they were able to quickly determine the changes that they were seeing as unnatural progressions.

Couples who had shown no outward signs of distress were suddenly dealing with infidelity. Drugs and alcohol had started entering conversations, and small thefts had been reported. The community was a tight knit one, but everyone started to become suspicious of one another, creating a tense environment that never existed before. Carson, their loved one, had been taken at the park when he was walking a dog for a neighbor who was on vacation. In hindsight, the family was able to pinpoint oddities that had occurred at their home that they dismissed as nothing.

"Hey, guys," Arie said, looking up at us with a very concerned look. "This one is pretty horrible."

"Where's the family from?" Cyril asked, moving over to look at Arie's iPad.

"The Romanos are from Coeur d'Alene, Idaho." She took a deep breath in. "There were four suicides in three weeks."

The color drained from my face. I knew demons meddled in all aspects of life, but I didn't fully grasp until this moment how they played with the lives of humans in such startling terms. It was as if humans were chess pieces being picked up and carelessly moved by either the good side or the bad side – just that easy. It was actually a lot simpler when I was a naïve girl, who thought she was a mere mortal, dealing with average nineteen year old type problems.

"That's not all," she continued, disrupting my thoughts. "There were two arsons, one murder, and a fight, which left the victim in a coma. This town hasn't seen even one of these events in years, let alone all of them in that short of a time frame. They think that these were all planned for quite some time, but the creatures must have gotten the go ahead to condense all the events to create the disturbances needed."

"Wow, how horrifying. I had no idea the havoc that could be created. Have you ever seen this before? I know my memory isn't up to par yet, but I don't recall anything like this, especially pocketed in so many areas. We haven't even gotten to all the groups." I was in complete shock.

"Well, considering these are only the families who we have relationships with, it makes me think that this is far bigger than we first realized. I only hope we can accomplish everything that we need to," Arie spoke softly, laying the iPad on the coffee table and walked over to Cyril. "This is building pretty fast, whatever it is."

"I know, but we'll figure it out." Cyril moved Arie's hair back from her face, and a twinge of sadness entered me quickly as I yearned for such affection again.

We'd spent a few hours compiling all the data, and we were able to come up with some pretty significant findings. My nerves were about fried, and I really wanted to get to Athen, even if that meant just living in the same city with him. I was told I couldn't contact him until the time was right. I was okay with that, but I needed to be near him. That I was certain of.

It turned out that Athen was the first one to be attacked. His attack seemed to set off a chain reaction. The demons had been stalking our family first, probably because I had barely been reintroduced. We were an easy target - plain and simple. After turning the snowboarder into a demon and introducing the hikers into the underworld, the demons left our area humans alone. It was pure luck that they found such eager participants with the hikers up in Whistler. There was the chance of infidelity with Karen, which was interrupted by me. Then there was an attempted kidnapping that was preempted by Cyril, unknowingly. Lastly, an arson was started at a boutique hotel. It was thwarted before it caused any real damage. It seemed that the demons got tired of failing and decided to take out Athen first to begin the process. The other families then began being picked off one at a time.

The timing of everything seemed to indicate that there were many factions being constructed. The Legions were dispersing and had no intent of stopping until they achieved their goal. We had to figure out what that was. That and, of course, get Athen back. From what we could gather, the demons had been traveling somewhat together as a group. The Masters had been teaching their followers and spinning off minions to stir up a little trouble in between major events. We needed to figure out who was orchestrating it and why. Azazel was definitely involved, but to what degree, we didn't know. The events and human tampering seemed too large scale to only be him unless there was something I didn't know. I had to get out of myself. I could sit and stew all day.

"What do you say we finish this on the road?" I asked in as innocent of a tone as I could pull off.

"Are you all packed?" Arie raised her eyebrows at me suspiciously.

My cheeks flushed instantly.

"I've been packed since the eve of that first night we had our ritual. I had no idea what to expect so I thought I'd better be prepared rather than be the one to hold everyone up. I thought that first night when we would summon him that he would..."

"Appear?" Cyril chimed in.

"Yep, foolish on my part," I whispered, shaking my head.

"No, we should have explained more. That step was crucial in locating him and creating a shield around him. Hopefully, we even placed some of our memories in there too. That's the key. Time will tell," Arie said, hugging me. "I'll go grab our bags as well." She gently squeezed my shoulder.

"Ha! So you've been ready too! That makes me feel better, not so desperate maybe," I said, trying my best to force a laugh.

"We are all desperate, Ana," Cyril said, beginning to lock things up.

Off to Victoria - I only hoped I wouldn't come back home empty-handed. I had to follow the rules. I would not mess up over some silly emotions and repeat the mistakes of the past. It was as if the more I chanted it to myself, the better my odds of sticking to it.

Chapter Four

We drove in silence to Anacortes, where we would catch the ferry to Victoria. The soft melody of *Between Two Lungs* hummed in the background, calming me to a certain degree. I loved Florence and the Machine. I hoped that I'd be able to share it again with Athen in this era and not another. A deep sadness began to crawl into everything. As I tried to take in the beauty of the car ride, it only made me wish Athen was with me to experience the beautiful Douglas firs towering over the road or to witness the jagged boulders that were whipping alongside the freeway as we drove. I thought of his green eyes glowing with anticipation, searching for my reactions. My soul ached. My life had been filled with so much happiness, and it had now been reduced to a loneliness that was indescribable.

A constant pursuit of someone who I was deeply in love with, who may not even remember me for centuries, created a gloom I couldn't shake. If my heart could shatter into a million little pieces, I knew this would be the moment. The dark green ferry signs, that fought with the moss, which was attempting to hijack the wording, pointed to the lane we needed to be in, and our car began to downshift. Soon I'd be near Athen; even if I wasn't allowed to see him.

As soon as our car was situated on the car deck, I hopped out of the car, running up the stark metal stairs, leaving an echo of footsteps in my wake. I wanted to enjoy the ride from the passenger deck and, possibly, pretend that Athen was here with me. I was determined to take in the view as much as I could. I was thankful for the latte that I'd gotten on the way to the ferry. I needed some comfort in my life, and for now, Starbucks would have to do. Hopefully, Athen would see the humor in him being replaced by coffee. I wondered if Matilda was enjoying her life with Athen because I sure missed her. The ferry window was beginning to steam up, and I did my best to secure a spot to look out by wiping the glass with my tissue that I always now carried in my pocket, for one of those moments when I was about to spontaneously burst into tears. My mood certainly matched the dullness in the air.

Arie and Cyril made their way through the line of people, who were waiting to get coffee, and landed in our booth with a thud.

"You know some things just work out. This is the last ferry ride to Victoria until Spring," Cyril announced grinning, eyes sparkling, reminding me just enough of Athen, and the smirk I missed so much.

"Is it a sign? I kind of hope not... I'd like to think that getting Athen back won't take until Spring." I noticed Cyril and Arie exchange glances.

"What faith you have," I said, trying to tease them a bit.

Arie reached across the table and grabbed my hand. The red vinyl seats squeaked as she moved forward. I began to chuckle. Athen wouldn't have missed the noise either, if only he were here. Our humor was so in tune.

"I know it's tough, but you should maybe try to prepare yourself for a little longer than a week up here, sweetie."

"I got it, really. I want to think positively. You know, take things in little steps. Otherwise, I don't think I can handle it." My throat started to constrict. Realizing how many emotions I'd been holding in, I paced myself with every breath so I wouldn't start crying again. I looked down at my lap, trying to get myself together before the other ferry passengers noticed.

Most of the ferry ride encompassed us staring gloomily out the glass window that now had glistening rain droplets rolling down in a steady stream, and Cyril walking to the cafeteria hoping that their food offerings had changed from the last time he was there, searching the sandwich cooler and coming back to our table empty-handed, time and time again.

The ferry ride was non-eventful, thankfully. The water was pretty calm. That was about the only thing in my life that appeared to be that way. The clouds loomed so low that it was almost difficult to see where the dark grey clouds stopped, and the dark ocean began. If it wasn't for our chugging through the water leaving plenty of suds, the water would be almost as smooth as glass, which was

21

extremely unusual for this time of year and in the rain no less.

My daydreaming was interrupted by the Captain's booming voice coming over the loud speaker announcing our arrival time. The crackle of the intercom kept echoing through the cabin as if to chase us all out. So we all scurried down to our car as fast as we could. I could tell that Cyril and Arie were equally as amped as I was. If nothing else, we could, at least, feel like we were close to Athen. The energy was running through every part of my body. I was ready for whatever battles might be ahead to get my love back. I wasn't going to stop until he was back in my arms.

"This is the beginning, guys. I know it. We will not leave here empty-handed," I announced emphatically, as we all piled into the Jeep.

"That's the spirit!" Arie exclaimed.

"Let's find a Starbucks first before we head to our abode," I pleaded.

"That's a deal. That tea I had didn't quite quench my caffeine need," Cyril said, shaking his head. "I don't know why I do that."

The traffic directors dressed in their orange vests and yellow flashlights signaled for us to start our engine and off we went into the unknown. Arie was looking at her iPhone getting more updates about the disturbances that were not letting up, as Cyril drove us to a rental home that he was able to secure on a week-to-week basis, which told me he was holding onto enough hope that we would get Athen back sooner rather than later as well.

We pulled off the ferry dock and headed into town. I noticed the Starbucks right away. I was a girl who knew how to get her caffeine fix, no matter how dire the situation.

"Right there, you guys!" I pointed, but Cyril kept driving, and then I felt it. Athen was in there. I wasn't expecting anything like this to happen. I immediately started hyperventilating. The waves of nausea hit next, creating a clammy shell over my entire body. Out of any of the rules that I was supposed to adhere to the first one was not to run into him or try to see him unless he was ready, and he wasn't ready.

"He's there, isn't he? He's there?" The butterflies in my stomach began fluttering double time. My arms became weak with hope and anticipation. Being this near to him was almost incapacitating.

"You guessed it." Cyril stared at me in the rearview mirror. "You can do this, Ana. Stay strong. Now isn't the time."

"Was he alone?" I muttered.

Arie flipped around in her seat. I could tell by her eyes.

"No."

My entire body stiffened. I had no idea that this could even be a possibility. I wasn't even sure why I had asked it, but I certainly didn't expect that response, especially so soon. I tried blocking out the images that began flooding my mind of the woman who I'd seen in my nightmares so often – the one with the serpent-shaped eyes. The wretched raven-haired demon, her hand grasping Athen's, with her eyes meeting mine. Her evil smile was dripping with a depravity that I couldn't stomach. I prayed with all my heart that it wasn't true.

"I guess that's going to complicate things?" I asked, trying to sound as strong and unworried as I could.

"Possibly." Was all I heard before I slumped back into my seat and went into a deep stirring of oblivion. I never should've asked the question. I already knew the answer. My dreams had told me.

Chapter Five

The rental home was a beautiful Tudor house. It was situated close to town, which was nice, but it wasn't nearly close enough to that particular Starbucks I had encountered earlier. I never expected to feel Athen on the first day of coming to Victoria. Now I was feeling as if I couldn't even concentrate on a simple task like emptying out my suitcases.

I looked around the room and began feeling the emptiness creep into my mind. The four walls staring back at me were beautifully wallpapered in a tiny floral print, but it wasn't the same as Kingston or Whistler where I last was with Athen, together. I yearned for Whistler or our home on Kingston – anything to be near Athen's last presence. The home did remind me of something I couldn't put my finger on though. Maybe, a home I'd see in Europe. Memories quickly began flooding in of Athen and I wandering the streets of London, and I realized it was one of the last trips we'd been on before I was taken away. I was filled with despair as I realized my thinly stretched images did nothing to satiate my need to be with him. If only I could remember us in more detail together.

I was doing so much better before we got off the ferry. Feeling him in such close proximity made me feel as if everything I was instructed to do completely vanished from my mind. I knew I needed to stay away from him until it was time. Yet, the pull I was feeling was overpowering common sense. Now, I could see how Athen may have disrupted the process so early on with me. It was going to take every ounce of strength I had to stay away from him. I wondered if I made a mistake coming here so soon. Only the tick of time would answer my question.

I opened the top drawer of the dark pine dresser to an eruption of squeaks from the slats of wood rubbing against each other and began slowly piling all my sweaters inside with not a happy thought to be had. I took a deep breath in, thankful that Arie and Cyril decided to go grocery shopping to get our kitchen stocked. I somehow doubted that was the only reason they left. At this point, I didn't really feel like hearing what they might be up to. I thought about Matilda again, which only made me feel more depressed. I missed her light snores and snorts. I understood the importance of her being with Athen, but she really was my partner in crime over the years. I wondered if she'd remember me.

I popped my iPhone onto the player and hoped that my usual playlist would brighten my spirits. I tried my hardest to let *Rill Rill* permeate my senses and bring a smile to my face but no such luck. Even Sleigh Bells, one of my favorite bands, couldn't help my mood. I opened the curtains to let a little light in, even though the city was covered in a thick layer of clouds. The naked maples lining the streets were a pretty sight. In the fall they would be gloriously blazed in reds, oranges, and yellows. I only hoped that I wasn't here long enough to see that.

On my way to the kitchen, I noticed that some of the photographs on the walls were pictures of Athen and myself. I immediately flipped on the hall light, staring in disbelief. It stopped me dead in my tracks. I couldn't figure out what was going on, or why in the world we would be on the wall. Was this supposed to make me feel better? It's not like we're staying at some long-lost family member's house. They would have told me that. I don't even think we can have long-lost family members in our situation... Or maybe we can. I don't know anymore. I put my thoughts aside and began taking in the photographs - anything to get another glimpse of Athen. Seeing his smile up close and the little creases around his eyes that formed when he was laughing, lit up my world.

My fingers began gently touching the photos as if that would make him real again. His eyes were so beautiful. The happiness radiated out from the images that were on the wall. The lump in my throat was getting bigger by the minute. I wasn't sure I'd be able to hold in my tears. I was so tired of crying. I wanted to be able to save my tears for a moment of happiness, not all this loss.

As I was getting lost in the maze of my own mind, I decided to not tip on the verge of insanity and, rather, wait for Arie and Cyril to come home and explain why in the world there were pictures of all of us on the wall. In the meantime, I'd continue to explore this supposed rental home for more possible treasures.

I wasn't disappointed during my scavenger hunt. I found letters that were written between us. It seemed that there were a few times where we were separated by our travels, but we were never far from each other's thoughts; that was proven. I had spread some of the most beautiful letters out in front of me in the dining room, rereading them over and over again, tracing his penmanship with my fingertips. His writing matched his personality – deliberate but with ease. I reached for matches and lit one of the cranberry candles on the hutch, which provided a wonderful aroma that reminded me of Whistler. This was one of my favorite candles that I'd always light when Athen was around. I felt a little closer to him through his words, his handwriting so old-fashioned, not the phone texts I was so used to seeing nowadays. I was on the verge of something. I didn't know what, however, which only left me frustrated.

***

Cyril and Arie were barely able to get into the door with their bags of groceries before I jumped them. I needed to know how in the world so many things that belonged to us were already here in this home.

"So you two want to tell me why on earth there are pictures of me and Athen everywhere, along with letters dated *back in the day* between us?" I cornered Arie as she was putting away chips in the cupboard.

"Easy enough." Arie smiled widely, moving me aside. "This was or is your house or, actually, your and Athen's home."

"What do you mean? From when?" I was completely baffled as to why no memories washed over me from being here.

"Well, there was a time when we all lived separately, that is until you were taken from us. It wasn't until then that we all begin living together.

Athen was distraught over losing you, and I was pretty worried about him. Also, we didn't know if they were finished with us or not. We thought it was probably better to be in a group for protection." Arie had finished emptying her bag and spun around waiting for my reaction. The only problem was that I didn't have one to give her. I didn't understand why this house was never mentioned before, or why they didn't tell me on the way over. There have been plenty of opportunities to fill me in.

"Will there ever be a time when I'll feel like things aren't being hidden from me?" I was incredulous.

"We didn't want to get your hopes up. You know? I don't know -just trying to protect you, I guess." Cyril said, folding up the reusable bags and stuffing them in a drawer.

I didn't want to admit it out loud, but I knew where they were coming from. I probably would've jumped to some random conclusion, like Athen would be hanging out in the living room waiting for us or something. Instead, all I could do was shake my head, and I wandered off to the living room.

"So are there any other hidden homes out in the world that I should know about?" I hollered to them.

"Nope!" They hollered back in unison.

I sat on the couch, closing my eyes, waiting for some sort of calm to wash over me, but instead, images of Athen and the serpent-eyed woman began creeping into my thoughts. I didn't know if they were figments of my imagination or truly visions. Cyril and Arie found their way into the living room, making themselves comfortable on the loveseat.

"Did Athen ever worry that I might become interested in someone else during all those years or is it just me who is plagued with those thoughts?"

Knowing I never really had much interest in other guys during my time away from him, I hoped that he was worried about that for no reason too.

"Of course he was. It was pretty unlikely, but he still worried about it - sure!" Cyril wrapped his arm around Arie's shoulder, grabbing the remote. "How could you not be?"

"Yeah, I guess... It feels like it could be a real possibility in this situation, though... You know, with my visions of that creature and Athen and all." I was thankful that I had revealed my dreams or, more pointedly, my nightmares to them. I was already keeping enough things bottled up inside.

"Well, we can't all mope around here for the next long while. We need to start getting some training going or something," Cyril announced out of the blue. Hearing those words made my stomach start to flutter a little in pure excitement. I knew there was so much left for me to learn, and I hoped that whatever he had planned would keep my mind occupied.

"It's true." Arie nodded her head quickly. "In addition to whatever may come up with Athen, the Legions are building quickly. I got word that there have been uprisings in Wyoming and Illinois. Whatever they've planned is moving pretty fast. We've got to hope that we can get Athen back soon, so we can begin the real fight and not fall into the obstacles they seem to have set up for us."

"So this is the real thing, huh?"

"Most definitely." Cyril pressed his lips together and reached for a lighter to light up the candle next to him on the end table. It was always kind of funny to watch him keep himself busy when he began worrying about things.

"What are we gonna start on? You know - for training?"

"I think we need to start off with some basic moves."

"You mean fighting, at last?" The grin began spreading across my lips. I've been feeling at such a disadvantage and vulnerable since all this began. I really wanted this. I wanted to destroy a certain someone too.

"Don't get ahead of yourself, Ana," Arie chided.

"Darn! I forgot to shut you people out!" I laughed. "Gotta get better at that." My mood was instantly improving. I felt like I was being proactive for once. I needed this.

"We were thinking of getting started tomorrow, if that works for you?" Cyril totally sensed my excitement.

"Uh, yeah!" I hopped off the couch and felt a sudden surge of energy. "You know? I'm gonna go on a quick walk." I darted out the front door, letting the energy pull me to a place I was never supposed to go.

Chapter Six

I noticed him from afar. My heart began beating a little faster. He was bent over a long, wooden table with books spread around him. He was touching his forehead the way he did when he was concerned about something. My mind flashed to the night that he came to pick me up from the bar when the stranger was lurking in Whistler. His beautiful eyes glistened, but they lacked that familiar, green glow. It was hard to not go running over to him and jump on his lap. Hiding as best I could, I slowly walked to a bookcase that had art history books stacked neatly.

I snuck another glance at him. His pull was so hard to resist. I couldn't jeopardize the process, being here was bad enough. Cyril and Arie would kill me if they knew I was even checking on him. We had a plan. I promised I would follow it, and apparently, my word didn't mean anything to me any longer. I didn't know how I got this close. I felt that I was in control of the situation - everything would be okay. Plus, after hearing he wasn't alone at the Starbucks made me think of all kinds of horrible scenarios. I just had to double check... Make sure she hadn't completely gotten to him yet.

He was taking notes feverishly. I was puzzled over what, in the short time he had in this new existence, would compel him to research something so frantically. I made a mental note to myself to figure out what books he was looking at. I pretended to be looking for something in the stack of art books as I tried to come up with my exit plan. I got my Athen fix, and he was alone, which made me feel a million times better. That's all I needed for now.

As I did my best to pretend to be interested in the stack of books, I accidentally knocked the top book off the pile. As it was about to crash to the floor, I caught it but not before causing enough of a commotion to get a group of guys to look over at me from the table across from Athen. One of them winked at me, which made me cringe. In normal circumstances, he was probably good looking. However, nobody compared to Athen. Other guys were on the verge of being repulsive.

Before I knew what was happening, I felt a singeing pain coming from behind me. I quickly spun around to see Athen staring right at me. Our eyes locked. I opened my mouth to speak, nothing would come out. It was like the first time I saw him at the Pub in Whistler.

Concern washed over his face. His body became rigid, and his eyes were distant. I couldn't understand why. Was I seeing recognition or fear in his eyes? He quickly grabbed his coat and notebook, giving me one last look and darted out before I could say anything, leaving a pile of books in his wake.

I knew what I did was wrong. I never should have come to get a glimpse of Athen. I had to be reminded of his presence. I couldn't stay away. The wait had been excruciating, and I wanted to make sure he was okay. Thanks to my clumsiness, I wasn't sure if he was now. I found my way quickly over to the table where he was sitting to see what he was researching. As I got closer to the table, my hands began to shake. I wasn't sure what I was expecting, maybe historical or technical books or how about comics? There were seven books laid out all over the table, some open and others in tidy piles. My gut became snarled as I approached the first book he left open. I recognized it instantly.

The book was a dictionary on Angels and Demons. The same one we had in our collection back in Whistler.

Chills began at the base of my spine running quickly through the rest of my body. Why would he be interested in this topic? I began quickly shuffling through all the books. Every one of them was on either one or the other subject. I had no idea what this meant. I also recognized that the only people who would know what this signifies would be infuriated that I was even at the library - let alone making eye contact with him, but I needed to tell them everything. The industrial, dull metal clock on the wall was ticking away my fate as my insides twisted with fear at the prospect of having to come clean with Arie and Cyril. A sigh escaped as I headed out the way I came in. Only this time, there wasn't excitement building - just fear and disappointment.

I hoped I hadn't screwed everything up. What if I now had to wait decades because I was foolish and let my emotions take over? I shivered at the thought of being alone without Athen's comfort all because of a single clumsy mistake I made. I suddenly realized I was beginning to fall into Athen's footsteps. This was how he lost me for all those years. He let his emotions take over, something I swore I'd never do. I reached the double metal doors leading out to the parking lot, swinging them open only to notice a guy pulling out of the parking lot on a Ducati Diavel. The very bike Athen had been talking about getting before he was taken away from us. The familiar pull began again. It was Athen riding away, completely drenched in black riding gear. His worlds were juxtaposing. I was pretty certain this wasn't typical. I had to figure out why.

***

I heard Arie and Cyril talking in the kitchen and followed the scent of fresh-baked cookies. I knew what I was about to tell them would destroy the pleasant night that Arie had been hoping to create before our big day of training. With every step closer to the kitchen, I gained the courage I needed to fill them in on my afternoon's activities. I knew I'd disappoint them greatly with what I was about to tell them. However, I was pretty sure they couldn't make me feel any worse than I already did. I might have destroyed my one chance to get Athen back in a decent amount of time, and I needed their help in figuring out what to do to fix my mess. I was the one who would have to live with the anguish every second of every day if this didn't go right.

"Hey," I hollered from the hallway. "I've got some news."

I tried my best to sound normal, which was impossible around my kind if the intentions weren't pure. We always knew.

"What's going on? What's wrong?" Arie came running to me, grabbing my hand.

My heart sunk knowing what I was about to tell them could change our fate.

"I saw Athen - on purpose." I looked at Arie, watching her face fall as the words sunk in. Watching her eyes search the room for Cyril to support her told me what I already knew. They looked at each other. Arie dropped my hand.

"Why would you do that? We had everything planned out. Tomorrow was the day to start training. I don't understand why you would go seek him out knowing what happened when Athen interfered too early with you." Arie began walking aimlessly to the sitting room with Cyril following quickly behind her.

I could feel the tears beginning to overflow down my cheek when I heard Arie's muffled cries into Cyril's shoulder. I felt absolutely sick for what I had done. It was so selfish of me. I wasn't the only one who cared for Athen, and my actions could affect us all. I dropped my bag in the hall before moving into the sitting room.

"I'm so sorry. I honestly never thought I'd be in this situation. I had prided myself on my strength, the lessons learned from Athen's mistakes, but something came over me that I never expected. I went out for a walk, and then, it was like his force was pulling me. I thought if I caught a glimpse, it would satisfy my craving for him. It did...until I made a commotion, and he glanced at me. I honestly never thought this would happen. I never intended for him to see me."

Arie looked up at me, her face streaked in tears. She shook her head as if to tell me she understood, but I knew no one could understand unless they were in this situation.

Cyril began, "So tell me, what went on, every step. Maybe, we can still salvage this."

I nodded, taking a deep breath in, hoping to regain my composure. I sat back on the couch, grabbing one of the velvet pillows in hopes that it would provide me with comfort. It did nothing of the sort. Cyril reached over to the lamp next to him and switched it on. I was mentally prepared for my interrogation. It was my fault, after all.

"He was at the library. I could sense him. I had been walking around, trying to get a feel for Victoria. Then I felt this sense of loneliness and overwhelming concern wash over me. Images of Athen wouldn't stop rushing through me. I got so scared that the serpent woman was with him, or that something was happening that would screw up my chances. Before I knew it, I was following a path to the library."

"Did you know, at that point, you were going to go in and try to find him?" Arie asked, trying to gauge when my emotional side began overruling common sense.

"No, I had no intention of the sort. I sat outside the library trying to get clear images of what was going through him and sense what he was feeling. That's when I first started feeling the ultimate depths of despair wash over me. I knew they were coming from him along with a trace of confusion. For the life of me, I couldn't figure out why he would be feeling that, especially in a library. I never experienced feelings that drastic when I was in his shoes. I had occasional lonely fits but nothing this extreme. I don't know. I began feeling this intense pull like I had that first night in the pub. I couldn't resist. I don't know what came over me. I'm more sorry than you know for any damage it could have caused. All it did was leave me wanting more."

"I know, sweetie. It just took me by surprise. You had been so in control up until now." Arie took a deep sigh and patted Cyril's hand. "So what now?"

Cyril shook his head.

"Well, there's more." I looked at them for a sign that now was the time to continue.

They both nodded.

"After sitting outside several minutes, I realized I couldn't shake the feelings. So I thought I should go in and do a quick check on him and then dart out. I could sense him immediately once I was inside. I went to the large area where mostly students were located, and even though he should have blended in, he didn't. That's where I saw him sitting at a table all by himself. On a side note, I do admit I was thankful for that... him being alone and all. There were tons of books spread out all over the table. He was taking notes frantically. I was intrigued to find out what would have struck a chord with him so quickly since he phased into this new false life. I made my way closer to see if I could catch a glimpse. That's when I caused the issue that screwed up everything. My clumsiness resurfaced a bit."

Arie rolled her eyes, making me cringe.

"So did he notice you up to that point?" Cyril asked.

"No," I sighed. "I managed to get quite close to him. I had played as if I was searching for something. He didn't seem to notice me at all until I knocked a book off the shelf. I was able to catch it, but I caused enough of a stir that a group of students looked at me and, in turn, so did Athen." I was becoming angrier with myself by the moment as I was reliving these events.

"Then as I was placing the book back on the shelf, a searing pain began, which I recognized immediately. I knew he was staring at me. I turned quickly to glance in his direction, and I saw him staring directly at me. I looked away quickly, but it was too late. Our eyes met – locked rather. The odd part was that I couldn't tell if I saw recognition in his eyes or fear. Regardless, it made him run. Something that struck me, however, was that I noticed his eyes flit over to the prismatic colors on the wall that I was projecting. I don't know if that was coincidence, or if he actually recognized the luminescence. Then he grabbed his coat and the notebook he was writing in and took off."

I was crushing my body against the cushions, hoping I'd dissolve into the fabric and not face the ridiculing I was halfway expecting from Arie and Cyril. The tension in my body kept mounting.

"So, this is the part that has been concerning me. I can tell you in my previous existence, I had no clue about anything until you showed up that night. I'm not sure Athen is as oblivious. That has me worried."

Arie sat forward, suddenly even more concerned, which I didn't think was possible.

"What do you mean, Ana?" she asked.

There was a long pause as I tried to figure out the best way to come out with it. I decided to be blunt. Get it over with.

"All the books on the table were on Angels and Demons." I looked at them for some sign.

"...And he rode away on a Ducati Diaveli."

"The bike he was going to get... Wow. It's like his worlds are somehow colliding. He isn't sure which is which. Truthfully, I'm not sure I know either," Cyril finally spoke.

"Have you ever heard of this? I didn't think it was possible," I asked them both.

"No. This isn't anything I even thought possible. You know, maybe there's a reason this happened. Maybe we were taking the wrong approach. If he thinks something is going on, he might be more receptive than he would be otherwise. Our chances might be better this way."

"Are you only saying that to make me feel better?" I asked Arie.

"No, I wouldn't do that. I'm serious. I think we're going to use this to our advantage. Tomorrow is still going to happen. The training needs to begin," she said, winking at me.

"Huh. This isn't how I pictured this conversation going. I must admit I'm relieved," I said, trying my best at a smile.

"Well, let's hope we're right. Now's the time to put our little saying to the test, all things happen for a reason. Let's start dinner so we can get to bed early," she said, slapping Cyril on the knee and bounding up, almost back to her old self.

I was so thankful for Arie's positive attitude. I, once again, felt a multitude of emotions ranging from despair to great anticipation in a matter of hours. I needed someone like her to give me hope. I was exhausted and seeing Athen today made the agony even worse. I missed him beyond anything I thought possible.

"Thanks for not making me feel even worse than I already do by the way," I told them both, as we headed for the kitchen.

I could feel Cyril patting my shoulder, and I turned to him and hugged him.

"I'm truly so sorry."

"Don't be. I'm sure you're beating up yourself far more than anyone should ever do. I know Athen did."

Hearing those words made me want to shrink into myself and hide. That's exactly what I dreaded - a comparison between our two situations.

"You're right on that one, Cyril."

Even by going to bed early, sleep would not come. I tossed and turned. Every little noise shot me right up. Athen was on the tip of every thought that was floating through my brain. After seeing him earlier, all I could think of was how to rectify what I had done, and I was confused as to why I would so easily fall into the same pattern that he had decades earlier when trying to get me back. The thought of being without him for decades made me shiver under my covers. It also gave me an entirely new set of circumstances to worry about.

Arie had told me that one of the factors with my rephasing was that Athen interrupted the process too early, playing a role in me being away from the family for so many decades. I hoped I didn't fall into the same pattern, but it felt like it may have already begun to happen. I had no idea what came over me. Now that I was away from him, I could think straight again – kind of. I could recognize that I should not ever have risked it, but the pull I felt was something that I couldn't resist.

My mind kept wandering back to his eyes. They were lacking the green that I was so accustomed to, but he was still amazingly beautiful. The entire set of circumstances seemed surreal. It was like I could feel him next to me right now. I wanted him so badly to be near me tonight, to feel a kiss against my lips, or his fingers against my neck. My mind, finally letting itself believe in the possibility of being with him again, allowed sleep to enter into my body at long last.

Chapter Seven

We were strolling the grounds of Butchart Gardens, taking in all the beauty that nature and horticulturists had to offer, winding from one magnificent garden area to the next. All the paths led from one awesome spectacle of nature to the next. Everything was so tidily groomed. Even though we were on the edge of winter, leading into spring, the gardens were absolutely beautiful. The deciduous trees arched their limbs, directing you to view the tiered perfection of pruned conifers. Tiny grape hyacinths were beginning to make their appearance under the dark green ferns. The Sunken Garden overlook was breathtaking. I could only imagine how incredible it would be when everything was in full bloom, and someone I loved was standing beside me, holding me.

Cyril and Arie had walked down the path, heading towards the Bog Garden, and I decided to lag behind a little bit. I did my best to keep my emotions at bay and scolded myself for the little snags of jealousy that entered my brain as Cyril and Arie held each other so closely walking the path to my first training ground. That wasn't a side of myself that I wanted to explore, but it kept reappearing.

I took a deep breath in, feeling the cold, fresh air permeate my insides, reminding me that I really was alive, even though I felt as dull and alone as one could probably get. Every breath was a heavy effort, betraying my own senses. Looking down on the beauty of everything made me want Athen next to me so badly it hurt. The wind began picking up a little, signaling for me to follow Cyril and Arie to our destination. I wasn't sure why they picked the bogs but assumed there must be a good reason. Realizing the wind wasn't calming down, I zipped my jacket up and pulled the hood over my head. Doing my best to snap out of my woe-is-me attitude, I jogged to catch up to Arie and Cyril, praying that the training would get me out of my element.

"Hey! Wait up!" I was close to catching up to them, but they were gracious and slowed down, so I didn't wear myself out before the training even started.

The clouds started parting a little but not enough to make up for the fact that the trees were larger, and the gardens more towering to block the light. I followed them as they briskly moved off the path to exactly where we weren't supposed to be. My heart began to quicken a little at the thought of getting caught as we traipsed further into the bog, but really that should be the least of my worries.

When we were far enough out of view, Arie and Cyril stopped and spun around.

"Well, are ya ready?" Cyril asked.

"Sure." I had barely stopped walking when he grabbed me and swung me behind him, climbing up the lichen drenched tree. Within seconds, we were at the tiptop of the tree staring down at Arie.

"You've got to be kidding," I uttered.

"Ah, that's nothing. Wait until you don't need a tree," Cyril said, his smile as wide as I had seen it in a long time.

I rolled my eyes as he let go of the tree, descending quicker than I thought possible and making my stomach arrive to greet my throat, before he quickly slowed us down to gently land on the marshy grounds.

"Wow. I don't know how much of that I can handle at once." Still trying to catch my breath from the fear and excitement of the Cyril-made thrill ride.

"Your turn!" Arie announced emphatically.

"Right. That's a real possibility. Why didn't I think of that sooner?" I blew out my cheeks, pretending I was reaching for the sky with my arms extending.

Arie obviously not impressed, grabbed my waist and sprouted from tree limb to tree limb barely touching any of them, creating a slosh of movement in my gut. Upon reaching the top, she, too, let go, leaving me to do nothing but close my eyes until we reached the safety of the bog. Knowing that this was going to continue until I tried to figure out what they were doing, I decided to try my hand at it.

I squished my way over to the tree that they both had been using for the elevator rides, now understanding why they chose a bog. It was Mother Nature's own mattress, patiently waiting for me to fall on my butt.

"Good one, guys." I closed my eyes and reached my arms up to the sky like they had done – only nothing happened. I didn't move at all, not even a hop. I opened one eye to see Cyril and Arie chuckling.

"Laughing with me, not at me. Right, guys?"

"Oh, most definitely. It's a shame Athen's missing out, truly," Cyril laughed. It felt like a knife was inserted into my spine hearing those words.

"True." Was all that I could mumble aloud.

"Nice one, Cy. Now go help her." Arie pushed him towards me as his boot got sucked back down into the marsh, creating a swallowing sound with a squirt.

"Ewww! You're forgiven after that." I knew he hadn't meant anything, and he was right. I wished Athen was here to see it too – but he wasn't.

"Alright, so what you want to do is feel it in your spine. Your whole being, really. Feel the tree, know where you want to go and imagine it as you take your first step. Don't think about the process to get there – just imagine yourself already there. Picture your foot on that branch already leaving for the next one."

Not realizing how scrunched up my eyebrows must have been, Arie stepped in and tried explaining it instead.

"So, you know that feeling right before you're about to jump? You get that little feeling of excitement and exhilaration building up. Capture it and spring with all of your might. Go towards your target like you can't miss."

Ziplining in Whistler with Athen popped into my head. That feeling of floating, gliding down the mountain – but more importantly - that feeling right before you step your foot off the ledge was what began making an entrance to my extremities- getting the jitters started. Having the built up energy and tingling that started in the base of my toes traveling like the speed of light to match my mind's anticipation, I allowed myself to experience something beyond myself. I nodded at them both and remembered that this was for Athen. Everything I did was for Athen. My hand found its way to the tree trunk, feeling the wetness that was releasing from the verdigris sponge wrapping itself around the tree. I knew where I wanted to be, where I wanted to go, and felt my body's movement as the power began to build up in my calves, quickly moving towards my spine as I hurled myself towards my target.

Excitement began replacing fear as my body darted from one tree limb to the next without missing a step. The freedom was beginning to overtake my soul as the heaviness of the moment made itself known. I was no longer an observer. I was a participant in this fight. I reached the top of the tree and suddenly realized that I had no idea what to do next. I looked down to see Cyril and Arie waving me down. I knew what they wanted me to do and hoped with everything that now was the time to trust them.

I let go of the tree, feeling my body glide down from the sky, sailing against the wind as my hand grasped onto nothingness. This was only the beginning, but I was ready for more – much more. I felt my feet touch the soggy earth as my knees buckled with the unexpected weight of gravity. This life was sensational.

Chapter Eight

The morning was a beautiful one in Victoria. The grey sky had rolled back its grasp on the city leaving brilliant blue skies, and I only hoped that was a sign for the day to come. My dreams were so vivid I almost thought I was awake and with Athen. The woman we saw in the Starbucks was with Athen in my dreams, but what made it a dream instead of a nightmare was that he looked deep into her eyes and asked her to leave him alone. The setting was a sterile one; I'm guessing the hospital. I only hoped it wasn't a dream but reality. I had a new stirring within me at the thought of him rejecting the woman who had suddenly made me fault my self-image in comparison. The thought of her evil eyes interpreting his discarding of her made me almost giddy with delight.

I decided to go let Arie and Cyril in on my dream. I was hoping they wouldn't talk me out of my theory. The slight gnawing feeling that this could be my hopefulness outweighing my visions was something I discarded quickly.

They were both already at the table eating a bagel they had split between them and slurping down coffee. Obviously, the pep in my step couldn't be missed.

"Well?" Arie pulled the chair back for me. "What's got you in such a great mood? Was it the training?" she asked amused. This new positive energy certainly wasn't something that was exuding from me as of late.

"I had a wonderful dream that I'm hoping isn't a dream at all." I grabbed an orange out of the fruit bowl and began hastily peeling it. The fact that my hunger had resurfaced certainly was a sign of things changing – good things.

"Fill us in!" Cyril exclaimed, pushing back his chair to go refill his coffee cup. I quickly scanned the kitchen and was thankful that it was so bright and cheery to fit my mood of the moment.

"Okay! You know that thing woman, whatever, I keep seeing in my visions with Athen?" I didn't want to give her any human qualities any longer.

"Yeah, what about her?" Arie asked, eyes curious.

"Last night in my dream, he rejected her. FINALLY! Do you think it is wishful thinking or a possibility?"

"Judging by your mood, I would trust your gut. This could be a really good thing." Cyril was scouring the fridge, obviously the half a bagel didn't cut it.

"Are you just saying that?" Not wanting to hear the answer.

"Nope." Cyril found his next morning snack of hard boiled eggs. "This kind of opens up the possibility of getting things started sooner. For some reason, he seems more receptive than I ever thought possible. I'm dying to know why, though."

"Leave it to my brother," Arie said, her grin showing through her last bite of bagel. "I think he knew more than we thought when he was taken from us. It's almost like he set up clues for himself or something. I don't know – maybe that's just bits of crazy talk. The memsors haven't ever actually worked for anyone that I know of."

"What the heck are memsors?" I was totally puzzled.

"Supposedly, we have the ability to leave memories in this world before we go to the next. Meaning, if we somehow know harm is coming our way, we can make it so when we wake up in the next life, our 'pretend life', there are clues that can trigger the memories of who we truly are. It doesn't usually work though - or hasn't in the past."

"That would make sense with his research habits, wouldn't it? Why didn't you guys mention it before?" I asked.

Cyril was standing behind Arie rubbing her neck, and a little twinge of jealousy entered my body for which I felt complete shame.

"I really didn't let myself consider it as a valid possibility until enough incidents started stacking up. We didn't want to get your hopes up for no reason, but I guess, at this point, it doesn't matter. We can all be excited or devastated as a unit depending on which way this thing turns out," Cyril said, only half joking.

"Huh, well, I'm going to take this as a positive sign and let myself float through the day in a happy mood, for once, until I do some other stupid move to knock me off my feet."

"Sounds good to me, sweetie." Arie was getting up from the kitchen table, reaching for the plate that the bagel once made home, and Cyril reached over her arm and grabbed it first. He treated her like such a queen, like Athen treated me. My heart ached as I commanded myself to listen to my earlier advice.

Chapter Nine

I was driving along Highway 14 on my way to Botanical Beach to escape from everything. My thoughts, my worries, my family, my inability to get Athen back – everything was overwhelming, and the house felt confining – this was my escape. I needed some time by myself, and this drive was providing just that.

The music was blaring as loud as my ears could handle with my favorite playlist of indie and alternative music that I always found comfort in. Doing my best to sing along with most songs, I began to feel free again. The weight of the last few weeks beginning to slowly drift away as I internalized the lyrics, flipping from one song to another. Imagining Athen and I together listioning to these songs, messing around to these songs and doing absolutely nothing but enjoying our time together, with music serenading us in the background, made me enthralled at what I was about to attempt by myself. It was going to be my own form of therapy.

With the pavement wet from the morning's last rainfall, I was extra cautious as I turned sharp corner after corner, zigzagging back and forth following the shiny, grey surface leading to my own training ground. The views of the Strait of Juan De Fuca were lovely as glimpse after glimpse was offered up through the breaks in the large trees that were shadowing the highway. The sea was beautiful and was beckoning me to continue on my journey. Every mile closer to the park brought me reassurance that I was making the right choice. I needed time away from everything and everyone to practice what I had learned at the bog.

Something was on the horizon, and I needed to be prepared. I didn't know what exactly, but I wanted to be ready. The itch of a fight was spreading through my visions, and the tingle of fear was beginning to seed itself exactly as it had happened before Athen was taken away from us, from me. The only difference was that this time I was ready, and I was expecting it. I would no longer be ignoring my visions. That's why I needed the practice and the time alone.

Looking at Google earlier, this park seemed like the perfect place to practice what I wanted, especially on a gloomy, rain-drenched day when most mortals wouldn't dare be staring at tide pools, perching themselves on slimy, cold rocks. They were smarter than that. This portion of the beach was just tricky enough that in weather like this, it could be very dangerous.

That danger was another reason that led me to this spot for my training. There had been some disturbances around this area dealing with humans, and my gut was telling me the demons were involved.

I didn't think I'd actually be running into any. I only wanted to survey the area – get a feel for it and the possibilities that may lay ahead.

The cliffs were edging closer to the highway's edge cueing me to the fact that I was getting nearer to my destination. As I turned into the public parking area, my suspicions were confirmed. The lot was completely vacant except for one vehicle, an older, white Mazda sedan. The crunch of my wheels hitting the gravel fighting with the loudness of my music, began to build a little anxiety that I wasn't expecting to feel. Turning into a parking spot at the far end of the lot, I flipped off my music and took a deep breath in, scanning the area. I wasn't sure for exactly what, but I had already had to promise my soul to Cyril and Arie that I'd be extra vigilant on my little trip. They weren't thrilled at the idea of me going out on my own, but I think they understood. I needed to practice my training, and I needed clarity.

I was following the path down towards the beach and finally made it to the tide pools. The water was crystal clear exposing all sorts of wonderful sea life from the beautiful purple starfish sprawled on the side of a rock to the sea anemone's tentacles waving to match the rhythm of the water's ripples. I could see why this was such a popular place for visitors to come. I, also, understood what an easy way it would be to get prey here, for the dark demons. There's nowhere for the humans to run. Looking back along the beach, the jagged, black cliffs were rising from the ground exposing beautiful quartz etching throughout, with old tree roots wrapping themselves along the boulders and cliff perches.

The harshness of the Northwest beaches were at their most brilliant here. Even much of the vegetation was rugged and beaten to death, barely hanging on to the cliff's edge. The rawness of everything I was witnessing made me realize the gravity of the situation even more. There was no room for error around this landscape, and there was no room for error when fighting our enemies. Hopefully, if I can learn to negotiate my way around this rugged terrain, I'll be that much more prepared to face the Legions.

Taking the far most hiking trail, I followed it for what felt like forever as I was constantly walking uphill along the side of the cliff, heading towards the large towering trees. This was the perfect place for me to bounce from limb to limb and, maybe, even try it without the trees, like Cyril mentioned.

The corner of forest with the Douglas firs clumped together that I picked was perfect. There was no way anyone would be able to see what I was up to, but if on the off chance there were any visitors, I'd be able to spot them before they saw me. Piling my backpack and jacket on one of the almost dry rocks, I prepared myself as best I could for my practice session. I threw some downed branches over my stuff, just in case.

Stepping back to take a look at how tall the tree I chose was, I found myself sucking in the air and not wanting to let any of it out. Somehow it worked back at the bog, I only hoped it would continue to work here. Closing my eyes, I pictured myself at the top of the fir tree. I felt where I wanted to be, the wind blowing my hair, the tiny fear in the pit of my stomach as I would look down. I envisioned myself already up top looking at the meadows and cliffs.

I reached up towards the sky and felt my legs spring off the ground as the air began hitting my face as I shot up towards the first set of limbs. Grateful the method I learned was still working, my body kept darting towards the top of the tree. My feet were barely touching the limb before moving onto the next one. The needles were smacking my legs and poking through my jeans as I bounced from one limb to the next. My goal was to get faster, think less, and begin to see how I could apply this to other things I needed to learn. The tree limbs were bouncing and snapping so quickly as I leapt from one to another, I realized that my speed must have increased tenfold compared to the bog. The exhilaration was building in my fingertips as I saw the sky through the treetops. I was almost to the top of my first tree.

Letting out a scream that I had been holding in for months, I knew this was what I needed. I looked around the landscape, enjoying the freedom and the quiet that was surrounding me. Now was my true time to mourn Athen's loss. My lungs hollered Athen's name over and over, and with every tearful scream, my heart began to feel a little more whole. When my voice had become hoarse, and no more tears were able to come, I sat quietly at the top of the world, silent. I knew going forward my mission was to stay strong and learn as much as I could as fast as I could.

Letting go of the tree, my body went sailing down to the forest floor. I sprung onto the next tree and shot up the limbs faster than the last time and, again, let myself fall back down to the ground. Ziplining with Athen back in Whistler entered my mind. The way he held me as we went flying down the mountain harnessed together. Him wanting to tell me so badly what I was, and what I was capable of but unable to.

If he could see me now, he would be so proud. I was sure of it.

I was balancing on the tip of my latest treetop, when I grabbed my iPhone to look at the time. I had no idea how long I had been practicing. What I saw shocked me. I had been scaling these firs for hours, and I hadn't even completed the one task I was willing myself to do my entire drive up here. I wanted to be able to hop from tree to tree before I left. Shoving my phone into my back pocket, I took a deep breath and pictured myself landing perfectly on the top of the tree next to me. Looking over at the tree next to me, noticing how spindly the treetop looked, I began to get jittery, but I forced myself to go for it, and I did.

Landing it perfectly, the giddiness was impossible to hide. I had no one to share it with, but I was thrilled regardless. My smile was impossibly wide, and the chill from the rain that was coming down in buckets now didn't even phase me. Seeing the next tree in front of me, I hopped onto it as well. Nothing was interfering with my balance. If I could ever feel like a being with wings, this was the time.

While arguing with myself as to whether this would be the last jump or not, I spotted a group of people walking towards one of the trails. I did my best to not move one muscle for fear that I'd cause attention. It's not everyday someone was seventy feet in the air wrapped around the top of a Douglas fir. As I rested my head against the bark, doing my best not to get poked by the needles, my mind began to drift to what I was planning on doing with my newfound talents. Daydreaming about saving Athen from the serpent-eyed woman gave me hope and helped to make the time pass when I realized the group of people wasn't leaving. I snapped to and began trying to figure out what they were up to. Something didn't seem right. It was as if they were surveying something down there. They were looking up at trees, pointing at rocks, arguing, and then it hit me. These weren't naturalists.

I kept deathly still and tried staring as hard as I could and listened to try to pick up what they were doing. Watching them deliberate over an unknown, continued to raise the red flags. To my horror, they started their way over towards where I was. They didn't seem to know I was up in the tree, and I was able to see them better. Unfortunately, with the close proximity, I could now sense them as well. They were what I expected.

The closer they got, the quieter I breathed, the slower I blinked my eyes, the harder I prayed they wouldn't see me. When they were only about one hundred feet away, they stopped. My heart began beating so fast that I was worried I was going to give myself away.

They were spreading out and, before I knew it, fighting began amongst them. The females and males were going at it irrespective of gender. One of the demons somersaulted and missed the intended target, landing on his back. Another one of the demons came over to help him up. One of the females attempted to jump on the shoulders of another, missing as well, landing with a thud on her side. I couldn't believe what I was witnessing. These demons were horrible. There was no way they could be this bad. Unless it was a trap, and they knew I was here, luring me down thinking I could take them, and then they could finish me off.

I didn't get that feeling, however. I think they were truly this bad. They must be minions or newly-formed - not sure which one. Either way, it was fascinating. I couldn't believe my good luck or bad luck, depending on how I'd want to look at it considering I was stuck up a tree like a cat. The fighting actually seemed to be getting worse by the minute, and I was worried that I might not be able to stifle my laugh. I hoped I wasn't going to be that poor in my battles.

The confidence began growing lightning-quick inside of me, and that's when I decided to do it. These were about as unskilled as I could get, and I took it as a sign. I think it was time to practice. Cyril and Arie would be furious, but that thought only popped in after I had already let go of the tree, flying down to the soil awaiting my arrival.

Landing with one knee on the ground, and the other ready to lunge, I looked up at the group of demons. A smile appeared across my lips, as a laughter I didn't recognize began coming from deep within. A sound, I didn't know was possible, began charging out of my soul. Pointing at my first victim and curling my finger to welcome her, I imagined she was the serpent woman luring Athen. She didn't have a chance. I snapped her in half without thinking. Her body's black smoke already lifting towards the clouds, I was thrilled to welcome my next victim.

The larger demon, who was dressed completely in black and a ridiculous-looking cowboy hat, charged towards me with a barreling effort. My body jumped up into the tree just as he was about to collide into me. I was almost embarrassed about even trying to fight these creatures. I already knew I was horrible but seeing that I could outwit and outfight them was even more puzzling. He began scaling the tree at such a slow pace that I let my body fall to the ground to begin my next fight. The other demon girl ran towards me but stopped right in front of me. Her fist landed right in my side as I stepped backwards, dulling the ache of the potential force that could have been. I grabbed her neck with my right hand and swiped her knees with a left kick, pushing her onto the ground. The cowboy hat guy dropped behind me with a thud, and I spun around with a quickness that surprised me. I jumped back into the tree. Breaking off one of the branches, I threw the limb down into him, watching the point penetrate his flesh. He never saw it coming, and it was just enough to have the other two run off back towards the trail.

I jumped out of the tree, as the demon fell onto his knees and flat on his face. It was ridiculous. The black mist slowly began releasing into the air. Feeling more confident than I had in a long time, I grabbed my things and went back down towards the beach and parking lot. It was time to get home and explain what happened to Cyril and Arie, because I honestly didn't know.

Chapter Ten

We were all in the kitchen playing with our food rather than eating it, knowing the choice that we were making carried a heavy burden. It carried consequences I wasn't sure I could handle but had to do my best to try. The quiet tapping of Arie's spoon hitting the ceramic bowl began to get on my nerves. I did my best to squash the annoyance. It wasn't her fault.

The Legions were making themselves known to as many of us as they could. Arie was getting endless texts and emails with updates on family members who had either been recently returned from the Awakening and reintroduction processes, or who had just been taken away. We were all being scattered around trying to find our loved ones or were helping others who were searching, leaving us to possibly fall right into the demons' trap. Yet, there was nothing we could do about it. That's how we were wired, unlike them. We had emotions. We were easily distracted, compared to them. We had to find our loved ones.

Even though, I'd been on a high from the day before, the heaviness of the situation wiped the slate clean again. It was hard to revel in the tiny successes when hearing about new people experiencing the heartache that I had now been feeling for months.

It seemed the demons that I'd run into the day before were newly turned, easily destroyed. Even with hearing that though, my happiness couldn't be swayed. It felt pretty good to kick butt like that. It, also, showed just how weak these new demons truly were. If they were building the Legions with lots of new members, it could really be a benefit for our side.

Because of the run-in at the library, we decided to do something pretty unprecedented and move things along a little quicker than the normal process. We were going to force contact. The thought that he may have seen the waves of prismatic colors from my soul bounce off the library walls gave us enough hope to pounce on things.

A battle was looming, and the sooner we could get Athen back, the better for us all. Or we needed to come to the realization that it might be a lot longer than we thought to get him back and prepare for the battle without him.

"Well, we've got some good news and some bad news," Cyril offered up, grabbing his glass of ice water.

"Yep! I think we're on the right track," Arie agreed, nodding her head.

"Okay, want to share it with me?" I was completely puzzled. We hadn't really been surrounded by much good news lately, so I wasn't sure what it could possibly cover.

"Athen and that serpent woman, you keep seeing in your dreams, do seem to be together. To what degree, we don't know yet... But tomorrow they are likely going to be together at that Starbucks we've been avoiding for so long. I think it's time to meet up with them both."

"So what's the good news?" I looked at Cyril while waiting for his answer, but he was just stirring his soup in circles.

"That was the good news."

***

Looking over all my notes from my recent dreams made it pretty hard to stay focused on just one idea. I never wanted to miss something that I should have told my family when it came to my dreams and premonitions, so I made it my mission to take notes. Placing my journal back in the drawer, I looked at my wonderfully inviting bed, pushing away the sadness knowing I'd be climbing into it alone yet again.

It was pretty hard to imagine life as a typical nineteen year old any longer. I had given that notion up. Even when I thought I was one, I knew I wasn't deep inside. I was plugging away up in Whistler and everything, but even then, things didn't fit. Everyone would go out wanting to party, and I just wanted to curl up with a good book and Matilda snoozing by my side. The drinking age being what it was compared to the states made most of the under twenty-one crowd go crazy, and it just didn't do it for me.

Always thinking I bored the heck out of whoever I was around, I tended to do things I enjoyed, by myself. I knew I wanted someone to love but didn't think that was possible, especially at my age. Little did I know I wasn't really that age, in the normal fashion. It was like the best present in the entire world to find out that this life was waiting for me and had always been mine for the taking. To have Athen show up, offering me a world that was beyond perfection and allowing myself to believe, truly believe in what was being offered, only to have him taken away so quickly, made me question everything. The worst question of all that I kept fighting became was it even worth it? In my previous existence, I didn't even know our love existed. I got through all the days just fine. Knowing what I was missing was the most excruciating experience ever.

I fell asleep as soon as my head hit the pillow. We didn't come up with much of a plan for the next day, but I hoped sleep would bring one to me. Only time would tell.

My body jerked up with a sudden start as something awoke me. Realizing that my cheek carried the sensation that someone was running their finger along it, began my heart pumping wildly with the knowledge that someone had to be in my room. Scanning my room, the darkness provided the uncomfortable stillness that managed to make me dreadfully aware that I wasn't alone, only I couldn't see my visitor. I started panicking as I looked all around. I saw no one.

I reached up and retraced the tracks of the strange feeling on my flesh, not understanding what I actually felt. I tried to calm myself down, but the sound of my heart beating so quickly made it impossible – that and the surge of the adrenaline that was running thought my veins. I slowly moved my body from the side position to flat on my back thinking I had a better shot of protecting myself if I could see the entire room at once, darkness or not. I did my best to move slowly, fearing that I might frighten whoever was in my room to act in haste and possibly hurt me.

I managed to slide both hands under my sheet as if that layer of cotton could somehow provide the level of protection I felt I needed. With only my head sticking out of the covers, my eyes darted from one breezy motion to the next. There was definitely someone in my room.

"I know you're in here. Whoever you are," I whispered, wishing I had chosen to play dead instead.

Athen's voice entered my head at the same time creating a calming force as I remembered back to our time in Seattle right before Thanksgiving. I was able to take a deep breath in as opposed to the shallow ones I had been taking since I woke up. I didn't understand the significance of Athen's words at this very moment, but all the fear inside me began diminishing. I'd be okay.

I turned on my bedside lamp to see absolutely nothing, and I didn't care any longer. In fact, I was almost certain it was in my head - all of it. I was probably just in that half-dream, half-reality state that can make me so foggy sometimes. Doing a fabulous job of convincing myself of that, I flipped the light back off and slipped under the covers. Tomorrow was important and playing mind games all night wasn't going to be helpful. Feeling my body drift into the brilliant haze of someplace in between here and there, the figure continued to look on. I wasn't alone.

Chapter Eleven

The comforter embraced me with a warmth that surrounded me entirely, as the sunlight radiated into my bedroom. I knew any more sleep was pointless. So I got out of bed and began my morning full of anticipation, sprinkled with a little bit of fear. Our plan was to meet up with Athen at the Starbucks he seemed to frequent every afternoon. I hoped the sight of me wouldn't make him spring into action again and flee out the door without his latte or me. Arie and Cyril told me I'd be able to recognize the signs that he was ready, and I hoped they came in full force because being around Athen often made me unable to recognize that I was about to walk into a wall, let alone look for a sign that I don't even know exists yet. I pulled out the red wool sweater with the white piping that I was wearing on the day he was taken, in part, hoping that would spur some recognition on his end.

The sunlight sparkled into the bathroom where I was taking my bath. I knew today was possibly the day that I'd get to see Athen again, but I couldn't help but be nervous, in addition to the excitement that was building. We'll be able to find out more concretely what the state of everything was in the next few meetings. It was such a peculiar experience. I almost felt as if I was stalking my prey, but I knew this was what they had to do time and time again for me, until that fateful night in Whistler. I simply hoped that this would be the only occurrence we would need, unlike their many failed attempts over the years.

I leaned back in the tub and tried to gain a bit of serenity before my nerves took over at the prospect of seeing Athen again. I listened intently to Bach's *Air on a G String* as the soap bubbles began to dissipate in the tub, reminding me I needed to start my day and, hopefully, become that much closer to getting Athen back. He seemed receptive, and now that may be lost.

***

We were on our way to the one and only Starbucks in town that I hadn't yet frequented because it was Athen's turf. This was the Starbucks that I wasn't allowed into because Athen had been there so many times before, and apparently, he was often not alone. She had been in there with him many times. Unfortunately, I was able to sense that from the moment I stepped foot on this island. One of my so-called wonderful abilities, which is to be able to sense another's presence, to feel their energy really, lately only seemed to lead me into trouble. Now, it felt like a curse.

I'd rather have driven off of the ferry and right by this Starbucks not knowing he was in there and especially not in there with the serpent. It told me what I didn't want to ever think possible. Athen wasn't mine any longer. He wasn't truly hers either, but only time would tell. The serpent, with her raven colored hair and her smile made of stone, seemed to have gotten to Athen immediately. Having her connect with him so quickly after his demise created a bit of conundrum for our family.

I wondered what all had taken place between them. The images of her fingers wrapping though his and whispering into his ear were, hopefully, the worst of the things that occurred. I was so creeped out at the thought, I made myself dismiss the images from my nightmares immediately. I didn't know if it was my jealousy disrupting my ability to foresee certain events or if these things were actually happening.

My stomach was in knots at the prospect of seeing Athen again, and possibly assessing the damage I may have caused by my previous mishap of running into him at the library. I did my best to focus on my abilities and dismiss the negativity that I was sure the dark demons kept planting inside of me. I was strong and was getting stronger by the day, but they still had the ability to grab hold of my weaknesses.

"So is everyone ready for their latte today? I think I'm having the Cinnamon Dulce latte." I tried to sound perky and get my mind off the impending encounter that was imminent. "I don't know why they take away their holiday drinks so fast. I really like Pumpkin Spice and Gingerbread, and I bet they would sell well at least through February."

"You could start a letter writing campaign in your spare time," Arie suggested.

"In between getting my soul mate back and fighting off demons of the world? Yeah, I guess I could stick it in somewhere," I said laughing.

"For a girl who didn't even celebrate the holidays, it's nice to see such an attachment to even the most commercial of traditions," Cyril said purely amused.

"Love does crazy things, I guess." I realized just the thought of getting Athen back had put me into my old spirits, and I was so relieved about that. I was beginning to think I'd lost my ability to care or be happy.

We were about a block away from the Starbucks that Athen visited every afternoon like clockwork, when I saw a line of cars in front of us. The traffic was completely stopped.

"What's going on? Can you see anything?" I asked, trying to stretch my neck as far to the right as I could.

"I can't see a thing," Cyril muttered. "Maybe we should park on the street over here and walk to the Starbucks."

Glancing quickly at the tree lined streets, my happiness was interrupted by the sirens that began coming up directly behind us, and I immediately got concerned. I hoped that everything was okay.

"You know Athen will be there tomorrow. I don't want to get in the way of anything that involves sirens," I told Cyril and Arie, genuinely concerned.

My heart began to beat uncontrollably, and then my hands got clammy as they did in the library. I tried my hardest to concentrate on what I was feeling inside when I realized it was my worst fear.

"It's Athen. Something is wrong with Athen," I screamed, letting myself out of the car and running towards the scene over a block away.

I heard Arie getting out of the car, hollering for me to stop, and she was right. I *knew* she was right, but I kept running. I didn't listen to her. The scene was like a magnet pulling only me over. I had to see what was going on. I ran as fast as I possibly could without bringing attention to myself. As I got closer, I saw the ambulance that was on the scene already leaving, and a police car arriving near an intersection. From what I could tell by the people congregating, something happened in the vicinity of the crosswalk. I tried to push myself through the crowds, worrying more with every step that Athen was the one hit, wounded in the crosswalk.

"Miss, we need you to stay back." I heard the officer telling me.

"I was supposed to meet someone at the Starbucks, and they aren't there. Can you tell me what's going on?"

"There was some guy, who was trying to save a little girl from getting hit in the crosswalk, but instead he got nailed. None of the witnesses really can figure out how or why the little girl was out there, or how he got there so quickly to push her aside. Her parents are over there. Undeniably shaken," the officer said, pointing to a family who looked like they now understood that every day was truly a gift.

The color was draining from my face. My eyelids were becoming so heavy. My arms felt as if they were pinned to my sides. The flashing lights bringing on a headache like no other, challenging me to stay focused. I knew it was Athen. He was trying to save a little girl's life. I tried to get the words out, but my lips could barely move, and no sound was coming out. They knew we were coming and planted that poor girl out there. The demons knew he still had good in him. His natural instinct would be to save her.

"I'm sorry, Miss, what? Are you okay?" he asked, as he was guiding traffic around the blocked lane.

"No, yeah, I'm fine. It sounds horrible. Is the guy okay?"

"Well, that's the really odd part. He hasn't a scratch on him, but they're going to take him over to Victoria General, just in case."

"Really?" Was all I was able to get out before the wave of nausea came flooding over me.

Arie came bounding up behind me.

"Is that the friend you were looking for?" I heard the officer asking me as he summed up Arie, which was always a hard thing not to do with her effortless beauty.

"Uh, yeah. That's her alright," I said, relieved for the timing of everything.

"Thanks for the info, Officer. Sorry to bother you."

Arie and I headed over to the Starbucks to regroup with Cyril. It seemed that our plans were not necessarily in sync with someone else's around here. It was now our goal to figure out who that could be.

"So that throws a wrench in things doesn't it?" I stated, as I claimed chairs for us all. Cyril went to stand in line and order for us since it seemed like we would be here for a while trying to figure things out.

Arie grabbed the green plush chair by the window, and I grabbed the one next to her. I moved the little table close to me knowing I wouldn't do a good job of balancing things right now without a flat surface to help. My nerves were toast.

"Do you think he's okay?" I finally uttered the words that I'd been wanting to ask since standing next to the officer.

"Yeah, he's fine. If he wasn't, you wouldn't be able to wander around and speak to me. It would render you about as useless as the day he was first taken away."

"Well, I guess I should find some comfort in that one. Not to get overly cocky, but it's kind of matching my dream, huh?" I offered.

Cyril was ordering our drinks and pastries when I felt another presence, one of us – but on the wrong side. Arie caught my gaze as I searched the coffeehouse for the answer. I saw a couple in the corner looking at real estate ads, and a group of students snacking and doing homework. Nothing out of the ordinary until the door opened.

A woman with raven colored hair walked in with as much confidence as I'd expect from one of them. Her dark eyes and pale skin were such a startling contrast that I found myself taking a deep breath just to concentrate. She was the woman from my dreams. Everyone behind the counter waved at her as if she was a regular. With a sharp and sudden movement the creature turned her head to look over at us. She was beautiful, obviously a great façade. The demon was dressed in a dark grey wool coat and black faded jeans. She had an emerald colored scarf tied simply around her neck, and she looked very polished. When I looked in her eyes, I knew she recognized us immediately, and as if not to miss a beat, she nodded at us and turned her attention to the workers behind the counter. There was a dark shadow following her. There was no rest with these beings around. I wanted to tear her apart. I wanted her to suffer like I was.

"Is Athen all right?" they all asked at once.

My heart plummeted to my toes, and I felt as if no air would go out or come in from my lungs. I thought someone literally punched me in the stomach. I braced the chair for support, but it gave me none. How could Athen be involved with someone like her. How could they get to him so quickly? Was this part of the plan or just a coincidence? I was beginning to believe there were no coincidences however. Arie reached over and grabbed my knee.

"Yeah, surprisingly so. Typical Athen, he wanted me to meet him over at the hospital with a Caramel Macchiato as if he didn't just get hit by a car. Told me it was a tap at most." Her drawl floated through the air alongside her laughter.

My skin crawled at the thought of her mentioning his name. How dare she speak about Athen as if she actually knew him or loved him. I felt the anger brewing inside of me far more than I had before. I knew if I just looked in her eyes one more time, I'd not be able to resist the temptation building inside of me. Cyril and Arie saw what was happening and quickly acted. Cyril grabbed my coffee, and Arie pulled me out of the chair so we could get to the car before I made a scene that would jeopardize everything.

We made it to the car without incident, but I was shaking intensely and was so nauseous that I needed to lay down in the backseat. The coolness of the leather helped calm my nerves immediately. It shocked me back into reality, which at this point I wasn't really sure what that meant.

"Let me guess, this hasn't happened before," I blurted out.

"Not that I know of," Arie began, situating my hair so she could slide in next to me.

"I think we need to do this sooner than later. Actually, I don't think, I know," I began, letting the anger build into its normal productivity.

My mind was zipping all over, playing as many scenarios as possible, weighing the different outcomes, and constantly pushing out the jealousy that was attempting to cast itself into all my thoughts.

"What if they..." My voice trailed off. There was no way I could utter the words.

"They haven't."

"We don't know that."

"Yeah, we do. Don't think like that. Athen never lost hope in you."

"Well, was there a demon always trying to get with me?"

"That one time."

"Uh, yeah, but I was already with you guys, and you knew to expect it. This is completely different. Thanks for trying to make me feel better though." I rolled my eyes.

"We can tell it helped," Cyril quipped.

"Come on let's go home and figure out a plan B."

***

None of us had appetites, but Arie took care of us and made sure we at least downed some soup while we devised our plan of attack. There was no longer the leisure of waiting until we were sure he was ready. The situation was now such that we had to get to him before they did, regardless of whether he recognized me or not. We had to ensure that he was on our side, and when it happened it happened. We had to protect him. This plan was going to make it excruciatingly painful for me. Everything about it was constantly playing with my emotions. It was as if I had to be alongside of him, and he knew nothing about me, could care less really. I had to hope for the best, which was that he would recognize me soon, and we could reunite. But after seeing her today, I wasn't so sure of myself or the situation.

"So this thing... You think she's part of the bigger picture? I'm guessing, yes," I asked, as I picked at my bread.

"Without a doubt. Now, in addition to getting Athen back, we have to figure out a plan to communicate to everyone the latest snafu. I'm sure we won't be the only ones this is going to happen to. I'm really curious to know what he has been feeling from her to make him research what he was at the library. Seeing her at the Starbucks might be the sole answer, but why he would be able to pick up on anything so soon is odd." Arie was rinsing the soup pot as she spoke.

"Do you know who she might be? Is she a major player?" Watching Cyril and Arie look at each other as they both began to fidget told me everything I needed to know.

"Her name is Lilith. She's truly the epitome of evil." Arie took a deep breath in. "Her type's been around longer than any of us. She's part of the Lamiai. They have the ability to seduce men by luring them with their beauty. She knows what she's got, and she knows how to use it, both with mankind and in the underworld. As you saw, she can encompass beauty in the blink of an eye. Her true form, though, leaves her with a serpent tail and fiery red hair. Unfortunately, when she's in some of her other forms, no one can see her."

"I could feel it. That's gotta count for something. Obviously, Athen can feel it too, judging by his recent reading selection. So, what's her goal?" I inquired. It seemed odd that all she would care about is seducing mankind and the underworld.

"Her goal is to wreak havoc – create distractions. Throw her into the mix of any situation, and you've just added an unpleasant element. But you don't need to be told that. You've seen it firsthand."

That last shot was like a nail gun aimed directly at my soul.

"It seems so peculiar that someone with her clout would be involved in something to do with us."

"Well, our lineage is such that..." Arie stopped herself. Her green eyes looking as if they lost some of the usual glow I was used to seeing.

"What? It takes one to know one? Or are we so super powerful it takes someone like her? Come on. I can't take much more of this. Why don't you just tell me everything all at once." I was full of contention and spite. My eyes wouldn't stop darting around the room, and I was about to explode. I was tired of knowing half-truths. It seemed the last three months had been full of almosts and not quites, and I was tired of it. I needed to know what I was facing. What we were facing. What or who Athen was involved with. The last thought truly making me nauseous.

"Actually, yes," Cyril snarled.

My heart started to pound - missing a beat between every three. I had never seen this side of Cyril. He was usually so laid back, and now he looked like he was about to come apart at the seams, possibly at me.

"Our family is partly descended of Remiel, which makes us pretty damn important. How does that sound for pompous?" Cyril's voice was getting louder by the second.

"This isn't just about you getting your dear Athen back, Ana. It never has been. Plainly, without us all as a unit we can't defeat the demons, and we need to defeat them. They are preparing for something that the world isn't ready for. We aren't ready for. The last century has been them gearing up to defeat all things good- including us. The longer they keep us distracted, the better their odds. Do you get it, Ana? The world would change forever. We would be destroyed. They would control it, and all humanity. It would be hell on earth." Cyril had calmed down now, realizing I'd have no way of knowing these things on my own.

I understood his frustration. Athen and I had been causing quite a distraction for over half a century, if unwittingly, and we appear to be the least of the problems. Yet, we seemed to certainly be defining the course of how it could possibly end.

I looked at them both with nothing to say. I was so sad, I couldn't cry. I was so angry, I couldn't yell. I grabbed my iPhone and vowed to myself that I'd do whatever it took to make things right. No more senseless emotions getting in the way - even if that meant forgetting what he meant to me - what Athen was to me. On my way back to my room, I grabbed all the photos in the hall off the wall. I didn't need any more constant reminders of what I was missing, especially if I was expected to figure out a method to control myself in Athen's presence. He could no longer be the one to provide me with the love I yearned for. I couldn't allow myself to be distracted by him. I'd find another. Athen was just a *he* and a *him* to me - no more personal identity and nothing special. We had to be finished for the sake of mankind. The lump in the back of my throat felt as if it could explode and possibly close off my windpipe. I could barely breath. I didn't care.

I threw all the framed photographs onto the floor of the linen closet with a crash, vowing to get my towels out of another closet. Life was much simpler working as a waitress up in Whistler. I think I actually missed it. Less complication, no heartsick nights, and no world to save that didn't know it needed saving.

I fell onto my bed, staring at the ceiling, looking at all the little endless grooves and trails, trying to match up a path for the quickest way to an end. Anything to get my mind off the decision I had just made. The pit of my stomach was churning nonstop, and I doubted I could do anything about it.

I started looking up some items on my iPhone. The least I could do was figure this out on my own, without feeling like a complete burden to Arie and Cyril. As I typed in the letters R-E-M-I-E-L, I prayed for an answer that would need no explanation, just the plain text the web had to offer. Unfortunately, that was exactly what I got. It wasn't them who was related to Remiel. It was me. I was his daughter. I had to stop this. I was the only one who could stop this, stop her.

Chapter Twelve

The sun hadn't even made an introduction to this part of the world yet, and I was fully dressed and ready to execute my plan from the night before. It came to me in one of my dreams. I had thought about it long and hard, granted with very little sleep, but I knew it was solid. This was the only answer that I could come up with.

If I had to give *him* up, then I wouldn't let anyone else have *him* either, especially her. The evilness that permeated the air around that woman, or more pointedly, demon, made my skin crawl and only made the world that much worse to live in. I knew I could dispose of her, even if it was only to have her wake-up on the other side of the world. At least, she wouldn't be in my world any longer or *his*. I was no longer on the sidelines.

I should have the protection of my father. That's what I told myself. What's the point of lineage, if it doesn't come into play at some point? There is no way Remiel wouldn't give me the strength that I might be missing to defeat Lilith, even if he was stuck in the otherworld as punishment.

I grabbed my jacket and snuck down the hall, grabbing the keys on the way out. I quietly closed the front door and headed to the hospital. *He* was still there, but I didn't care about that. I didn't care about him. I was only going there to destroy her. He was long gone out of my world. He had to be. I only hoped I wasn't fooling myself.

The streets were dark, and the city still sound asleep. Puddles from a recent rainfall glistened from the streetlights' reflections. The old-fashioned streetlamps provided an especially haunting element to my journey. There wasn't a sound to be had on the paved streets. I was thankful for that, until I turned up the street leading me to the hospital. The towering concrete building looked as if it was waiting for me – as if the structure itself was possessed. Part of me hoped that she wasn't there, but I knew she was. She was smart enough not to leave her prey. Little did she know, it wasn't the prey I was after - it was her. If he got damaged in the scuffle, that wasn't my issue. I had to remove her so she wouldn't continue to interfere in our pilgrimage for what was right.

I slid my car into the parking stall that was closest to the street. I looked up at the hospital and saw a soft glow coming from most of the windows. Just enough light on in the hospital rooms so the medical staff could perform their procedures without waking up their patients. At least, that was the goal. Nine times out of ten, I'm sure the patient was jolted out of whatever low-grade sleep they were in as they got poked and prodded. I scanned each floor, window by window until I landed on the one that they were in. My heart sunk as I envisioned her by his side, holding his hand. Her ability to run on little sleep giving her the appearance of a saint, rather than the true beastly self that she was.

I proceeded up to the lobby as the sliding doors opened to greet me like a monster welcoming its latest victim. I quietly coasted past the daytime reception desk turned nighttime guard desk that was completely vacant. Maybe, luck was on my side tonight. I took a deep breath in, shocking my senses that, indeed, I was in a hospital as I turned to step on the already open elevator.

The button for floor three was already glowing a fiery orange, and the metal doors closed swiftly. I never pushed the button. She knew I was coming. I wasn't prepared for this.

My heart ached as I tried to fool myself into believing that I magically turned the switch off on my heart for Athen. When, truthfully, I couldn't even bear to utter his name without possibly breaking down. I needed Athen. The elevator ride only going three stories felt like an eternity. As the doors opened, I knew now that I was the prey.

I instinctively moved closer to his hospital room, passing by only empty nurse stations on the way to my destination. I could feel the chill of defeat slowly creeping up along my spine. How could she have made everyone vanish? What reality was I in? It was as if time stopped, and we were in another universe. I didn't know that was even possible, but it obviously was judging by the look of things.

I was now only two rooms away, I peeked into the room next to his and saw an elderly man with slight breaths, eyes closed. Guess she didn't feel he would notice. I hoped my next actions wouldn't end him prematurely. My world turned dark. There was no stopping the chain of events that I had started by pulling into the hospital parking lot. I looked at the elderly man one last time and hoped his next breath wouldn't be inhaling the spirit of Lilith, turning him to the darkness of the underworld. I said a little prayer for his soul and continued on. Now wasn't the moment to get distracted. It was now or never.

The door was open into Athen's room, but the light grey-blue curtain was pulled closed for privacy. My veins spasming with grief in every part of my body as the blood was rushing throughout made it almost impossible to walk. Why would they need privacy? I saw her black boots right next to his bed. Just like I pictured, she must be nestled up to his hospital bed sitting in an uncomfortable sterile chair. The thought almost made me sick. I heard his voice, quietly speaking to her as any other couple would in this type of setting. I tried to push the pangs of remorse aside. My decision was set. This wasn't about him any longer.

"Oh, Athen." Her drawl hit me like a ton of bricks. I stopped dead in my tracks.

"My sister is here now. What a sweetheart. I thought for sure she would go to the hotel first." I saw her black boots get up quickly and swiftly move towards the curtain. I was frozen.

"Wow, she didn't have to come. I'm getting out later today. You know that. I shouldn't even have been here today. There is nothing wrong with me. I told you, she didn't have to fly in to greet me this way." His voice floated through the thick air, swirling around my body like a straight jacket. She knew I was coming and told him I was her sister to prepare him? I was completely at her mercy.

The curtain was thrown open with the metal beads sliding and clanking with the force of her toss and before me was Athen staring directly at me from the hospital bed that was inclined only slightly. The television hung in front of his bed and was casting a light blue hue onto the room, from what looked like a news channel, reflecting off of his white terry cloth looking blanket that was the only thing covering him.

"Hi, sis!" the demon of all demons exclaimed, as she was hugging me with her claws. She was good.

"Hey!" I exclaimed, as she squeezed me just tight enough to let me feel her strength.

"I thought you would go to the hotel first. You never cease to amaze me." Her eyes sparkling as if there actually might be a hint of life to them - too bad only I knew the truth in this room.

I felt the pull beginning despite my best efforts to ignore Athen. I had to use his name again. I had to acknowledge his presence in order to maintain mine. He was my destiny.

"So, is this the guy I'm hearing endlessly about?" I tried my best to not reach out and crush her neck. Instead, I moved over to Athen's bed as gracefully as I could, which doesn't ever count for much, even in this new form. I reached the side of his bed and was thankful for its sturdy sides to keep me balanced.

His smile was radiant, and I didn't know if it was because I said she was speaking endlessly about him, or if it was because he was looking at me. I tried to push the first thought away, even though I knew the answer. I did the unthinkable and placed my hand on his shoulder.

"It's so nice to meet you in person. You're pretty outstanding if you can look this great after being hit by a car." I gave him a wink and felt the all too familiar electricity begin to run between us. I did nothing to remove my hand. I needed to be reminded of him. I looked down at him and saw the same look of recognition and confusion that I saw in the library. I just might be able to pull this off.

"You know, you look really familiar to me." His voice was soothing as ever, but very conflicted. "Do you come to the island much?"

"I think we've connected before. I was thinking the same thing."

He nodded his head and laid back on the pillow. I patted his shoulder and turned to Lilith. Realizing now that he never mentioned our encounter at the library, she had no way to know what this interaction could represent. I couldn't stop the smile from spreading.

"I should get going. Just wanted stop by for a quick hello... Want me to buy you something scrumptious from the vending machine?" I did my best to look over at her as innocently as possible.

"Yeah, that would be great. I'll be right back, Athen." She turned to Athen and patted his knee, but his leg jerked away from her.

I wasn't sure what was happening, but I hoped it had to do with my touch.

"Uh, yeah, Athen. I'll see you too." I locked eyes with him for longer than I should have, and he felt it. Horror began to fill his eyes, for what reason I wasn't sure of, but then they became quickly replaced with another emotion. One I didn't recognize. I only hoped it would help me in my next endeavor in the visitors' lounge.

As Lilith and I walked out of the room together, she wrapped her arm around my waist doing her best to squeeze the last breath I had in me into oblivion. I swung around to take one last look at Athen, and his eyes were glued to me, so I mouthed to him the words that only seemed appropriate.

"I LOVE YOU."

Lilith and I reached the lounge in a flash, and before I knew it, my instincts kicked in. I was in the familiar crouch position that I saw Athen, Cyril, and Arie exhibit many times before protecting one of us or all of us, - never completely sure how it worked. A hissing deep from within began to roll out of my mouth as I leaned deeper into my stance. My arms were away from my body as if to steady myself. I felt my mere existence hovering above the ground as if I had done this a million times before. I was no longer in need of the ground to keep me steady. To the lame eye, it might even look as if I was on the floor, but that was definitely not the case.

To feel the level of emotion running through my veins, that I witnessed so many times before as my family protected me, energized me beyond belief. I began to see Lilith's form change. Her raven hair began its flaming transformation to a violent red that was unlike any red I had seen before. It was dirty. Her legs dissolved and spiraled themselves into a serpent like appendage. I wasn't sure if this development was about to hurt or help me. I chose the latter. Two legs were better than one.

She glided along the floor and up the wall in a blink of an eye. I felt a roar build up inside me that surely would unleash the fury that I'd been keeping quiet for so long. Her black and scaly tail whipped around to grab me. The movement was nothing I saw. It was what I felt, and within a heartbeat's time, I felt my legs rise up into the air missing the swipe of the tail as it landed onto the floor, shaking the tables that were so carefully placed. My heart was racing, but the adrenaline that was pumping through my veins was only helping me fine-tune my ability to see things before they happen. A skill I took for granted, but one apparently, my father Remiel had passed on. Hopefully his attributes would help me through this.

I felt her next move and saw her slither down the other wall next to the exit sign. I spun around with my right leg jetted out, and my arm extended to reach for her hair. My world had become a slow motion version of instantaneous events as I grabbed her hair to bring me quickly to her side. Now side by side with this creature, I used my other hand to grab the knife out of my pocket, which I jabbed into her side, leaving a huge gash, oozing out nothing but a mist of poison into the air. I took my knife out of her and then penetrated the tip deep into her chest as the screech of wickedness entered the room. I knew the fight had only begun.

I flipped the knife back into my pocket while she slithered down to the floor, towing me alongside her with her free hand as she nursed her two fresh wounds with the other. I looked into her ugliness and was no longer threatened by her fraudulent beauty. She was pulling me along with her as she quickly slithered from one corner of the room to the other, not realizing she was creating an opportunity for me to break free.

I grabbed the metal chair closest to me and ripped off the legs creating stakes that I thrust immediately into her. I took the opportunity and grabbed her neck as I squeezed with an enormous amount of hatred that had built up since getting off the ferry. Her neck began turning to a silvery sheen. Before I could congratulate myself, her hand reached around, and I was thrown to the floor with such a crashing force that I wasn't sure I'd be able to move again. It felt like every bone in my body was shattered - until the images of Athen flashed into my mind. Pushing her away, my legs filled with fury, I was ready for round two.

"Is that all you've got?" I hissed at her, as my body began to spring to life again, spiraling into action. Feeling the same energy as in the bog, my legs began to strengthen and prickle, readying myself for my next move. I spun around on the ground before lifting myself to the ceiling, grabbing one of the stakes out of her chest as I went. My body was hanging from the ceiling like a spider, but my hand was outreached and ready to attack. She rushed towards me with her arms flailing as I fell back down to the ground, ramming the other homemade stake into her tail, letting another wave of shrill screams echo through the building. My arm began to feel as if it were on fire, and before I could stop the pain from spreading, I realized it was her digging one of the chair stakes into my arm that she removed from her chest. I saw bone - my bone revealing its ivory self. I fell to the ground. Instantly wishing I had told Cyril and Arie what my plan was. I needed their help.

"You didn't think I'd let you win that easily, did you?" she wailed to the world more than to me. Her laughter was reverberating against the man-made walls.

I took in the spectacle that was before me. Her chest was seething with every breath. The gashes were continually oozing black mist into the air, but it didn't seem to accomplish as much as I'd hoped. Her strength wasn't weakening that I could tell. I inhaled as deeply as possible to gather my strength as the pain in my arm began to subside.

"I saved my best for last," I uttered, not knowing where the strength came from, but welcoming it with every ounce of my being. I surged into the air landing directly in front of her. Her tail lifted from the floor, and I knew to watch for it. She grabbed my arm and twisted it behind my back. I noticed she had the same ugly nails that I had seen time and time again on these beasts.

My revulsion turned to deep seated anger, and I spun myself around escaping her embrace, while jumping on her back squeezing her as tightly as possible, attempting to crush her neck like I had seen Athen and Cyril do so many times before. I was out of her tail's way as long as I kept in this position. Her energy began to escape. The black mist rushed more aggressively out of her wounds. I could possibly win this. The excitement began welling inside of me. But then her face spun completely around, mouth wide open, exposing several rows of teeth ready to engulf me in my wildest fear. I slumped to the ground, afraid to move as the cavernous opening came to swallow me.

I sensed movement from the other side of the door and glanced over to see the familiar shoes of Arie and Cyril running in. Relief flooded my body. More hissing circulated through the air from all of us, and I knew that in order to defeat this monster, I was needed as well. I instinctively returned to my fighting stance and began to follow Cyril and Arie's moves. Arie had jumped to the ceiling and was hanging in wait, while Cyril jetted through the air grabbing Lilith's neck. Arie fell from the ceiling to face Lilith so she couldn't apparently do what she attempted on me. I grabbed my knife and jumped on her tail slicing it away from her body. The shrill shrieks of pain rang through the air as her gangly body began to swirl away into oblivion. Cyril was crushing her neck with more force than I ever could have attempted. Lilith turned to nothing, the mist escaped. I could breathe. My family saved me, again.

Suddenly, I heard the metal from the door handle scrape and felt Athen's eyes taking in the unbelievable scene that was before him. I refused to look at him, and before I knew it the door slammed shut, and Athen was gone, long gone. The others did nothing to stop him either.

Chapter Thirteen

We quietly rode back to the house. The pain in my arm was beginning to throb more and more as the adrenaline wore off. I wasn't sure whether to fill them in on my earlier encounter before the fight just yet or not. I was leaning to the side of divulging everything but was afraid of their reaction. Cyril drove our Jeep into the driveway, and I decided to broach the idea.

"Thanks again for coming to my rescue. I don't think I'd have lasted much longer." I was rather blunt in my delivery.

"Don't be hard on yourself. I'm actually quite impressed. The fact that you held your own with her for as long as you did was pretty amazing." Cyril's tone was completely recovered from the day before, and I couldn't detect any hostility from my latest escapades either.

"You never know. You might have been able to finish her off yourself. You just got a silly little scratch." Arie's always optimistic spin made me feel instantly better.

"Let's not get ahead of ourselves. I think we need to continue training with her ASAP since she insists on doing things her own way," Cyril spoke every syllable very slowly, as if that was my punishment in itself.

"Thanks for that, Arie... and yes, Cyril, I couldn't agree more with you. Training is a must!" I won. Finally, they were going to let me in on some of these secrets.

Looking down at the exposed bone on my arm reinforced how badly I needed combat training. I would finally learn how to fight. Because they gave me a little, I felt I should give them something too, honesty. "I saw Athen."

"We all did." Arie turned around to stare at me.

"No, I mean before that." My voice trailed off.

"How so?"

"First of all, last night I actually fooled myself into believing I could forget about Athen and valiantly save the world. In my panic, anger, whatever it was, I made myself believe I needed to detach from Athen – start fresh, et cetera. Well, I got to the hospital thinking I'd get her away from him - make my attack, but to my dismay, she was expecting me. The elevator was even set to his floor. It felt like the entire place was frozen in time. None of the workers were around. She knew when I was outside of his room, and she pretended I was her sister once I entered. I went right in, and before I knew it I had my hand on his shoulder, and I felt the electricity between us. It was incredible. Something I know I shouldn't have done, but it was absolutely worth it. Not only that, when she touched him, he recoiled from her."

"Really?" Arie seemed genuinely excited about this news. Rather than scold me for this, she was more interested in hearing about Athen's reaction to the demon. Thank God. But, I definitely decided to leave out the part of me telling him that I loved him. "It seems like he's far more receptive than I'd have thought. Luck could be on our side."

"Except for the fact that he stumbled upon the scene and darted," I mumbled.

"Well, yeah. That's a definite complication. But, honestly, nothing is going as it has in the past. So I don't think we should think the worst. I mean, he has already felt that something was other than it seemed. There was something clueing him into the idea of Angels and Demons at the library. My guess is right now he's trying to come to grips with everything he has felt and most recently saw. I think, oddly enough, he's intrigued, not scared."

"Intrigued? I'd guess suicidal. If I had stumbled onto something like that while I was working up in Whistler, I'd have locked myself away on behalf of society."

"Yeah, well you weren't even thinking that we existed. I doubt your coffee table books dealt with Fallen Angels either. So things are definitely a bit more complex with good old Athen."

"I just hope he didn't split," I was wrestling with getting the key into the door, as I spoke, "for good."

My arm was throbbing intensely.

"I'd be willing to bet he's at his place right now, trying to figure out what his next steps should be and Googling every possible notion that he's coming up with."

"You think Lilith's gone from here?"

"For now, yes. I don't think we should waste time, though, to get him back. I know she'll show up again." Arie took the keys away from me and let us all in to our house, since I couldn't apparently function.

We all piled our stuff on the living room couch and wandered into the kitchen. Cyril grabbed some Rockstar energy drinks out of the fridge and snapped them open for us all, shoving them at us. I didn't realize how thirsty or tired I was until I started gulping from the can. He grabbed some medical supplies and began working his magic on my arm.

Arie had wandered off to her MacBook and seemed to be intrigued by whatever it was that was sitting in her inbox. I was trying to fight the fatigue that was reaching every part of my body. I was hoping the drink would hit soon before I wound up crawling into bed.

"Ok, guys. Movement is pretty intense out there. Another family member was taken in Montana. They're getting ready to track them. It happened while their loved one was alone. We've got to take this more seriously, you two. That means you too, Ana. No more sneaking off to handle business. We are stronger as a team." I could feel her eyes penetrating through me etching her seriousness into my soul. I knew they had been too kind to me with everything that I kept doing. She's been doing a great job of keeping it quiet.

"I know, and you're right. I'm really trying to keep everything in check. I even thought I could detach myself from Athen, but that action didn't even last twenty-four hours. I'm not in control like I think I am. I apologize, guys, for putting you in harm's way. I really do."

"Ana, you really need to start sharing more with us. No matter how big or small, honestly. The feelings that keep coming over you are normal, and we would understand. In fact, we've been through it with Athen and could probably help guide the choices you're making a little better. You can't keep everything bottled up. It's not healthy, and it keeps leading you in the wrong direction. There is no way you can undo your relationship with Athen. We saw you took down the pictures in the hallway, but that doesn't do it. You've got to be more willing to talk to us, Ana. It may not seem like it, but we can help." Cyril was crushing his can and tossing it into the recycle bin as he spoke his last sentence. "Athen wouldn't want you to go through this alone. He didn't."

Arie spun around in her chair quickly with her legs tucked in under her and had the typical Arie smile encompassing her lips.

"Ok, I just fired off an update to everyone. I think we need to get some things done around the house, possibly rest, and definitely put the pictures back up. Most importantly, though, we need to discuss our next moves. Let's get some great takeout for dinner and plan on a regrouping."

I was relieved at those words as I realized that the energy drink didn't quite do everything I needed, no fault of the drink. Cyril pressed some sort of odd smelling compress on my arm, slowly taking away the pain. Thing were starting to look up.

"Is that starting to feel better?" Cyril snuck a smile as he headed to the fridge for another Rockstar.

"Yes. It really is. I like the idea of no pain," I paused. "So now, how about that training? I'm not going to let you guys off the hook," I said grinning, the buzz of the energy drink beginning to overtake my body at long last, and the pain in my arm slowly diminishing.

Chapter Fourteen

We had found a secluded area to continue my training. The goal was to go through some of the fundamentals of fighting. Fighting in the underworld was a heck of a lot different than a few fist-fights and slaps. I think once Cyril and Arie walked in on me while I was giving my best effort against Lilith at the hospital, it became pitifully obvious that the best thing for me was to expose me to as much as possible. Demon fighting being one of the topics they wanted to explore - along with a glimpse into shapeshifting. Not knowing what other trouble I could possibly get myself into, I wholeheartedly agreed.

We had walked about four miles up from Anderson Cove in the Sooke Basin. It was drizzling, making it perfect for the activities we had planned. We hadn't run into any hikers on the entire trail, and I was pretty sure none would show up since the day's weather was expected to only get worse. Privacy was best for this type of thing.

The views were absolutely breathtaking, overlooking the Strait of Juan de Fuca and the Olympic Peninsula, it made me a little homesick for our Kingston home. Seeing the edge of the Olympic Peninsula, remembering everything wonderful that took place there, I wanted Athen to magically appear by my side and tell me it was all another bad dream. Taking in the lush rain forests from this vantage point gave me an entirely new respect for the forests that could someday help or hinder us in our fight against the demons. The jagged cliffs were a severe reminder of the danger presented both by human nature and the apparent otherworld that existed in between.

"Alright, daydreamer," Cyril shouted, competing against the howling wind and crashing waves from below. "It's time!"

Before I knew it, he jumped through the wind and disappeared. My heart started pounding because I had never seen any of them do that before. I was pretty sure it was possible, but I had never seen it. I whipped my head in all directions and couldn't find him. He literally vanished before my eyes. I hollered for Arie and craned my neck to where she was last standing, but all that was left was her backpack.

"Ok, guys, not cool. Where are you?" I was backing up away from the cliff trying to stay somewhat centered. I was staring intently into the air, and nothing was surfacing – nobody was around. All I heard was the wind and possibly laughter.

The laughter was getting louder and louder, but I still saw nothing. I kept backing up until I was on the edge of the dark forest, not a place I wanted to enter at the moment. Before I knew what happened, I felt my entire body being pulled with a hurricane force. I was no longer on the ground. I saw Arie swirling around in front of me. I felt for what was holding me up and finally found Cyril's hand around my waist. I reached up behind me, and he was holding onto me. How he was able to grab me so quickly was one of the many tricks I'd soon be learning. I looked around and realized we were above the forests. I wasn't just a foot or two off the ground - I was above the Douglas firs and Hemlocks. We weren't flying. We were floating. I scanned below and saw the crashing waves at the bottom of the granite ledge I had only left moments before. The feeling of freedom was beginning to spread throughout my entire body. This was a real possibility for me. At the moment, yes, I was being held up, but I knew soon I'd be able to do this myself.

"Watch this, Ana," Arie shouted, as she dove back down to the ground in a swooping motion almost more graceful than the bald eagles we spied on our hike up to this locale. I was in total awe. In the next moment, she shot back into the sky with such energy she turned into a blur. However, she was coming right at us, blur or not. I squeezed onto Cyril's arm as the threat of her crashing into us became very real.

"Don't you worry about us, Ana," Cyril spoke, attempting to calm my nerves and doing nothing of the sort. She shot right past us and disappeared into thin air, leaving nothing in her trace.

"Where are you guys going when you do that? I don't get it," I asked Cyril.

"We are still here, but we are so fast, we can't be seen. It takes some getting used to," he replied.

"Well then, how can we trace each other when we are in battle? It seems like it could be a real disadvantage if we can't see one another." I felt our bodies slowly begin to descend back down to stable ground. It felt like the most bizarre elevator ride I had ever encountered. I just prayed Cyril didn't let go.

"You'll learn to be able to track energy. See," Cyril said, pointing to a boulder resting on the far edge of the cliff. "Arie is over there."

I followed his finger and saw nothing but a moss-covered boulder.

"Really?" I said, a little perturbed.

"Yeah, I promise. Think of it this way, what do you feel most when you think of Arie? What pops into your head about her?"

"I'd have to say her positive energy. She gets excited over everything, doesn't seem to matter what it is. She's really a bundle of positive energy."

"Alright, well, close your eyes and really *feel* that. Think about Arie, and what she means to us and to the world. Concentrate on what she leaves behind wherever she goes. Feel the vibe she gives off to people around her and her surroundings."

My eyes were closed tightly, and I was thinking hard about the infectious way Arie had about her. She was the life of the party and always cheered me up for sure by mere proximity. I thought of her bouncing around in excitement when we were all at the Christmas tree farm when Athen was with us. My heart immediately began warming with these thoughts of her and Athen. I did my best to push him out of my mind for this exercise.

"Now, open your eyes, and look where I pointed last."

I opened my eyes, holding onto the feelings that I had imagined when thinking of Arie. I looked at the boulder and didn't see anything. Then I looked up above the boulder towards the cloud-covered sky and saw her gracefully making her way down to the boulder, but she was going warp speed.

"I can see her!" I squealed. I couldn't believe it. Her hair was blowing behind her swirling around indicating she was going pretty fast.

"I knew you could do it, Ana. This is the kind of thing we need. You can see why this is pretty important, huh?" Cyril said, smiling as we started walking over to meet Arie.

"So why don't we use that all the time?" I asked, kind of wondering why we took the slow way around places.

"It drains quite a bit of energy. We can do it in quick spurts, but it isn't something that we want to always do because if we need it, we could be out of luck. That and shapeshifting can leave us pretty drained. In certain circumstances, it's a must. We don't want to use it as a crutch though. The real things we need to focus on with you right now are your fighting abilities and your strength.

"So is that speed thing something you think I'll be able to do pretty soon or is that a sneak preview that I'll have to wait years for?" I asked, unsure that I could ever master that kind of power.

"Geez, Ana. As fast as you seem to be catching onto things I'd say, with practice, a month or so... Not that far off really," Arie said, hugging Cyril. "Better get started with the serious stuff now, Cy." She swatted him on his butt.

100

"Gotcha.   Ana, stand over by the trees.   First thing we want to work on is your running attacks."

I walked back over to the trees that were dripping with moss, creating the rich rain forest green the Northwest was so known for. I spun around ready to absorb everything Cyril and Arie were ready to divulge. This time it looked like it was Cyril's turn to show off. He was positioned in a crouch, not unlike the ones I had seen him in during the attacks when Athen was with us all. He was low to the ground, hunching over with his arm in front of him like he was ready to win a track event.

He jetted towards me with a speed that rivaled Arie's acrobatics in the air. I wasn't sure if he was on the ground or possibly just grazing it as he moved towards me. In a flash, he was behind me pushing down the towering Douglas fir with momentum from his movements, nothing more. The ground began to shake as the roots were flinging up, releasing themselves through the soil like a bucket full of snakes being thrown into the wind. Arie pulled me into the air with her before I was engulfed by the havoc that was being created in mere seconds by Cyril. The loud snapping of the limbs as they brushed against the other trees on their way down was nothing compared to the thunderous crash the trunk of the fir tree made once it contacted the ground. I couldn't believe that kind of destruction could be done with Cyril only running 30 feet. It also made me wonder with such power, how could Athen have lost against the demons? How much more powerful are they than us? Arie set me back down on the ground where a mini crater was now staring back at us from Cyril's act of destruction.

"Good thing a wind storm is scheduled for tonight," Cyril said, his cockiness not to be missed.

"Now, I want you to emulate what you saw, Ana," Cyril said, as if that were a real possibility.

"Um, right, okay. I'll just start running towards that boulder over there and hope for the best. By the way, should I stop once I get to it or just keep going?" I joked.

"With that attitude, I'd suggest stopping beforehand," Cyril said, not amused with my humor. This wasn't a side of Cyril I had really seen before. "Come on, Ana. Think about what you learned when you saw Arie when you thought you couldn't."

"What... I'm supposed to become one with the rock? Honestly, I'm sorry. I don't see the correlation between a living person and a piece of stone."

"It's not about living or not living, Ana. It's about energy. Projecting your energy on an item, and receiving energy from an item. Tell yourself what you want to do, and let the energy begin to consume you and the item of interest. You'll be surprised."

Interestingly enough, I was kind of starting to get what they were talking about. If I can see it, and if I can believe it, then I can achieve it - self help 101. Great!

I shook my head at Cyril and Arie and stood in place. I took a deep breath in, letting the moist air penetrate my lungs as I thought about what it was I wanted from that boulder. I wanted it to move. I wanted to move the piece of earth. I felt my knuckles begin to feel as if I needed to pound them against something. Anger was beginning to build - excitement was next. I envisioned myself taking control of a completely inanimate object and controlling it. I let the air escape my lungs as I felt an uncontrollable energy build. I found myself crouching in the position I had seen my family do so many times before. I was in another element. I let my eyes slowly open to view the large boulder in front of me. I took in one more breath and shot myself towards the insurmountable piece of rock. I felt like I was on fire as I sped directly for my target. I closed my eyes picturing the boulder being displaced while my speed continued to burn my flesh. My voice screamed out for Athen with all my might as I shoved the boulder off of the cliff, with my body following directly behind the mass as we tumbled towards the ocean.

Chapter Fifteen

After the cliff incident, I began to understand my strength a little better. Shockingly, as I fell over the cliff, there was no fear – only desperation. There was the desperation to get Athen back, and the desperation for my training to be over with, and the desperation to just be done with everything - have a bit of normalcy. I was thankful that Cyril and Arie were able to save me before I crashed into the waves - don't get me wrong. But the weight of the world was resting on my shoulders, and there was a milli-second or two where crashing towards the ocean didn't seem like the worst thing. Cyril's words interrupted my thoughts, probably for the better.

"I've been thinking about it...With him fleeing the hospital like that, our plan could really be delayed. Not that I blame him with what he saw. He very well may want to throw himself off a cliff after that one.

Walking in on a girl you thought you knew, looking like a serpent, fighting who he thinks is her sister? Pair that up with whatever hunch he has been having about Angels and Demons, and he probably thought he went off the deep end." Cyril almost seemed amused.

"Glad you can find the humor in this, Cy, but I'm not. I feel like I'm doomed to make this Awakening and reintroduction process fail. I can't seem to control my actions. I find myself in a fight with that demon woman, only steps away from Athen where he can and does walk into it? Come on! I should be the one committed! You know, it's amazing you guys were able to get me so quickly from the fall. I still can't quite get over that."

"Well, our odds might have improved to get Athen back if we had let you fall into the ocean," Cyril said, trying to add some levity to the seriousness of my mistakes.

"The truth is, Ana, that if somehow he lets himself understand or believe what is going on, and he taps into some of those powers, he could stay away for a very long time. He has the ability to stay away, stay hidden. We all do. Usually, it never comes into play because once the Awakening has begun, the person has no clue what's going on, and it's the family that can reintroduce everything in a somewhat safe environment. They would have no reason to run because they don't think anything is going on. Unfortunately, I think it's safe to say that might not be the case any longer with Athen."

My head began throbbing, right behind my eyes. I squeezed my eyes shut attempting to not let any light reach my soul. The pain was overwhelming, or maybe, it was the desperation that was welling up inside. Maybe, it was one creating the other. I had no idea, and I didn't care. Now thinking that Athen could be fleeing not only the demon woman but us as well, created a sickness well beyond anything I had control over.

"So we can stay gone? Forever? I thought we could always track our loved ones. Remember the homing beacon and all?" In addition to the intense throbbing, I was certain things were beginning to spin. "I don't understand. I really don't understand."

"This doesn't normally happen. But being that he doesn't really remember us, I'm guessing, the nonsensical scene that he witnessed created a real glitch in the process. It seems like he was onto this world or the idea of Demons and Angels and somehow still connected to his past just enough to make some of these things seem tangible. I think there was a good chance he was on the verge of getting some memories back, maybe not the ones we needed. So when he saw what he saw at the hospital, he might have realized he was onto something a little too frightening. Things may have come back, leading him to the conclusion to stay away. Since we weren't there to place the memories, there is no certainty what he does or does not remember. He could be escaping everything, including us." Arie was shifting uncomfortably on the couch.

"Like a nomad? I thought that was only for the dark demons? I didn't think the white demons went through that." I needed to lie down. This wasn't even an option that I knew was possible. But, if he can disappear maybe I could too.

"They are usually the only ones that use it because the families never want to separate. This situation is creating circumstances I never accounted for, Ana. My guess is that he wants to stay hidden, and he will until he's ready. *If* he is ready."

Feeling numb, I stood up and waved to them both to stop talking. I needed to lie down. I felt as if I was mourning Athen all over again. Was that the last time I saw him? In the hospital? The thought of him not wanting to be found, especially not be found by me, brought my world crashing down around me.

I crawled under my covers wishing that I could take back so many things. The library, Starbucks, the hospital - all encounters that could have been harmless, but I interfered, forcing myself onto him in ways that seemed so innocuous. Not realizing that my jealousy was raging created a platform for destruction far worse than whether or not Lilith might win him over. Here for months, I was filled with worry beyond anything that I would lose him to her. Instead, it wasn't Lilith that I lost him to. It was me chasing him away as fast as I could, probably leaving him to want to hide from the world.

I began calculating how long I should give myself before I offer my soul up to the other side, become a dark one. It was the only way I could imagine leaving the memories behind, avoid the Awakening from my family, become just a listless ghoul roaming from place to place. I wouldn't have to suffer feeling this pain any longer. I could just disappear as Athen did. If I won't ever get him back, it seems like the only solution. Never mind becoming the very creature I loathe. At least, the pain would go away. Should I give it a week, a month? I wondered how to get a more definite timeline out of Arie and Cyril without raising suspicion. The disappointment and disgust I would leave them with was indescribable, that I was sure. Maybe, they would understand; maybe, they wouldn't. I doubt they have ever thought that they might be faced with never seeing each other again. Never again getting to feel the love that flows between them.

The gravity and disgust of the situation, I was debating, made the pain in my head searing. I grappled with the idea of leaving everything and everyone I loved behind. I wondered if there was a way to actually achieve this. I felt myself moving closer to the edge - the edge of insanity, the edge of darkness, and worse of all, the edge of not caring.

I looked around my room through different lenses. I could actually feel the change beginning to take place. The coldness was infiltrating every thought. The walls were beginning to build around my heart. I hated to think about this, but I couldn't fight it. The potential of not being with Athen was creating a monster inside of me.

***

Certain that I again had a visitor in the night, I decided to let Cyril and Arie know. If the visitor wanted to cause harm, wouldn't that have happened already? My mind drifted to a possibility that I knew wasn't feasible, but there was a tiny glimmer of hope that I couldn't squash.

It seemed like when I needed faith and hope the most, that's when it would appear. A lingering message meant only for me but from whom? Last night I was certain, I recognized his touch. My hair lightly blew against my neck before feeling his hand caress my face. Not wanting it to end, I kept my eyes shut. As I felt the touch of his skin against mine, I did my best to promise myself I wasn't dreaming. But I couldn't be sure because when I finally did open my eyes there was no one in sight, yet again.

I didn't want to approach it with Cyril and Arie as if I was thinking it was Athen. There was no way that they would believe it. I had to present it as a stranger in my room, which, truthfully, was far more plausible than the other option. Even I knew this deep inside.

Waking up without Matilda was killing me. She would have provided clarity on my sanity, that I was sure of. But, I wasn't the lucky one to have her right now. The silence of my bedroom was deafening as I got ready for the day. No snorts, snores, or grunts from Matilda preparing me for the day's adventures. I really did hope that she was providing the same level of comfort for Athen as she had for me for so many years.

Hearing Arie in the kitchen, I decided to bring it up with her first. My goal was to make these strange occurrences sound more casual than they felt. That was my first mission. My second was to do my best to muffle the desperation that I was feeling deep within my soul. I had to take these appearances as a sign – a sign not to give up. I had to do my best to rid myself of these awful feelings that kept trying to drift through my world. The level of conflict, I was feeling constantly, was exhausting.

Pouring myself a glass of orange juice, I looked over at Arie.

"Can I talk to you for a sec?"

"Of course, sweetie. What's up?" she asked, spinning around from the sink where she was washing berries.

"I've been having something happening to me at night. It's kind of weird, and maybe I'm dreaming is all..." Uttering the words out loud made me more nervous than I realized.

"Okaaay?" She was staring at me like I had horns growing out of my head.

"Someone has been in my room. It has happened twice. I can't see them, but I know they're there."

Completely alarmed now, Arie put the dish of berries down searching for the right words.

"If you can't see them or it, how do you know there is someone there, Ana?"

"A touch." Was all I could get out before I turned quickly to the fridge to play like I needed more orange juice. The tears were starting their way into my life again, and I didn't want anyone to see them. To me, they meant something different than what they would represent to anyone else. Blinking as fast as I could to make them dissolve back to where they came from, I did my best to seem normal and sat down at the table where Arie was already sitting.

Looking intently at me, she asked the question I wished she didn't.

"Who do you think it was?"

"I don't know." I knew she knew I was lying but bringing up something that I was told was impossible was useless anyhow.

"And you're sure it wasn't like those other times like at Thanksgiving where the demon was appearing before you?"

"Oh, most definitely not that type of thing," I said, doing my best to divulge as little as possible. I didn't need that last little tweak implying I was crazy on top of everything else. I was fighting that feeling enough, privately.

Silence was how our conversation ended, making me wonder what I really did by divulging it all.

Chapter Sixteen

We pulled up to our home in Kingston, searching for what I wasn't actually sure. We had all made some lame excuse about needing certain things from this particular house. Arie announced that she needed another jacket and rain boots. Cyril said he wanted some of his tools for working on the house in Victoria. I only claimed that I wanted to sleep in our bed once more since he seemed to be slipping away from me bit by bit. I know our stay up there was longer than we thought it would be. Truth be told, none of us needed anything except a break. We needed to regroup and regain some sort of normalcy.

Attacks were becoming more frequent. Athen was still AWOL, and I had absolutely no energy left to participate in life whatsoever. We needed a vacation from our daily lives. I had been searching for some sign of Athen for so long now and was coming up empty-handed beyond what was possibly a figment of my imagination. I needed to come back to a place where we shared some very special memories. I was pretty certain that my non-talk with Arie had something to do with our unexpected trip back down to Kingston as well. Honestly, I didn't care what the reason was. I was simply happy to be back. I was tired of fighting the evil thoughts that kept infiltrating me to my core.

Being able to crawl under the covers that Athen and I last inhabited was all I craved. I hoped that by being back at the Kingston home, I'd find a little bit of solitude and let go of the monstrous thoughts that kept creeping in. I knew Whistler certainly wouldn't provide that especially with the off-chance of running into some of my acquaintances. The only people who understood even a glimpse of what I was going through were right here in this car.

The garage door opened welcoming us back to a calmer life - minus one person and a very affectionate bulldog. I was relieved to see Athen's Lotus parked in the garage. It made me feel like he was possibly upstairs waiting for us to return from a day of shopping or some such errand. I was willing to let myself play the fantasy if it gave me even a few seconds of relief. Cyril put the brake on, and we all climbed out of the car. As Arie unlocked the door leading into the house, I found myself holding my breath.

The door swung open, and something seemed off immediately. I looked at Arie and Cyril to gauge their reaction. They didn't seem to be taken aback at all. I lugged in my overnight bag, flipping on the lights as I went from the mudroom to the kitchen to the stairs. I felt that someone had been in this house since we last were. I spun around dropping my bag on the floor.

"Aren't you guys going to say anything? I know it isn't just me feeling that?" I was looking straight at Arie waiting for some sort of affirmation.

"I honestly don't feel anything. What do you mean?" Arie set her purse down and looked at Cyril, shaking her head in confusion. "Do you feel anything?"

"Ana, what are we supposed to be feeling?" Cyril seemed genuinely puzzled.

"Ugh, forget it you two!" I grabbed my bag and stomped upstairs.

I made my way down the hall, passing by the guest room that had played host to me for a little while when I was here with Athen my first time. I felt my legs going a little quicker. I wasn't sure what I thought I was going to see when I got to our room. Did I truly believe I was going to swing open the door to have Athen staring back at me? I was angry at myself for being so pathetic. I finally reached the door to our bedroom, which wasn't closed all the way, and I slowly opened it up with my bag, walking onto our shag rug placed in front of the door. I immediately inhaled the largest amount of air I could. I wanted to get the last little bit of essence of Athen before I contaminated it. I threw my bag down and did what I came for. I crawled under the covers, thankful that we didn't change the sheets before we left.

I laid on my back stretching, imagining Athen holding me and whispering to me some silly joke. The thrill of hearing his voice, even though it was only in my mind, brought an automatic smile to my face. A movement my lips hadn't felt for a very long time.

Coming back to our Kingston home was a really good idea. I let these feelings of relief and happiness wash over me. I could somehow feel him again. I knew it was silly, and maybe, it was only because this was where we had last joined our bodies together, but I felt him here, and I needed that. Not knowing how long I could be facing without him made me appreciate every little reminder that I could scoop up around me.

I heard Arie and Cyril going down the stairs probably to watch television or something. I was relieved. I needed sleep. I was happy that they have both been with me during this time, but I needed my own time too. I needed to be able to grieve in peace.

The morning sun shot through my bedroom window, greeting me with a freshness I hadn't felt for some time. I had no idea how long I had been out. I didn't even wake up for dinner last night. I fell asleep dreaming about Athen and woke up thinking about him. For once, it was all positive. My thoughts were overflowing with images of him and I together up in Whistler or picking out our first Christmas tree since my own reintroduction.

I knew these were the images that would keep me strong, strong enough to wait fifty years if I had to. He was worth waiting for. He was worth fighting for. I wasn't going to slip to the other side. I had the strength within me. I needed to tap into it and avoid the demons' traps.

I grabbed my bag that I had dumped on the floor the night before without emptying it out and began placing my clothes in the drawers. I opened up the bottom drawer to see what was actually filling it up since I never actually paid attention before. There were some of Athen's nice sweaters folded, and underneath those, I saw what looked like a leather journal of some sort. I was tempted to grab it and devour it. But there was the other side of me that didn't want to violate Athen's trust. Right now, that side was winning. I moved the sweaters gently to cover up the edge of the leather journal and closed the drawer back up.

The house seemed empty so I decided to venture downstairs and see if my instincts were right. Things were very quiet, the air still. I was pretty sure that I was alone. They had probably decided to grab some items at the store for us. I slipped from the family room to the dining room to the kitchen looking at everything again as if I hadn't seen it before. My hands moving over the granite countertops, the shock of the ice cold stone awakening my senses more than I was used to recently.

I grabbed a mug out of the cabinet and filled it up with some water from the hot water tap to prepare some tea. I found the remote for the stereo turning it on through the house as I tried my best to warm up from the chill in the air. The house was still warming up from nobody occupying it for awhile. Walking over to the window to watch the ferries, I grabbed a pillow to sit on and threw it down as I tried to make myself comfy. I rested my back against the ottoman taking in the beautiful water gently moving in the distance. My eyes quickly fell to the beach access down the path from where I was taking in the scene of the ferries. I did my best to ignore the urge to go down to the beach.

My eyes began to fill with tears, and I placed my cup of tea on the ground doing my best to wipe away the wetness before it was released down my cheeks. I got up onto my knees looking through the window towards the beach. Placing my hands on the cold glass, I saw the boulder where we had made love for the first time. I was almost feeling the same jolt of cold running through me as the memories were pumping through my body. It was like the boulder was speaking to me, confirming that Athen and I really did exist, like our love was truly possible. The only thing stopping me from running down there and collapsing onto the grounds where we were so close was my outfit, flannel pjs and house slippers. I didn't need to cause any more concern for my family as boaters and ferry passengers saw some crazy woman in her pajamas crying hysterically, pounding a boulder.

***

Night had fallen, and we had just finished watching a movie, gorging on popcorn and trying to escape a little. It was a good choice considering we had to impose laughter on ourselves somehow. Cyril and Arie were doing their best at giving me space but, also, keeping me busy enough so I didn't put myself in an early grave by jumping off a cliff again or something. Not that an act like that seemed to do much to us, but it was the thought that counts.

"Hey, guys. That was fun, but I think I'm gonna hit the sack now," I said.

Arie was curled up on Cyril, and she looked like she had barely been able to keep her eyes open the last few minutes.

"Sure thing," Cyril said, scooping up Arie, who was now almost completely asleep. "I'll see you in the morning."

"Yeah, you too. I'll lock everything up... and thanks, Cyril. I appreciate everything you guys have been doing." I really did. I don't know that I could have made it this far without them.

"That's what family is for. Ana, we'll get him back. Don't give up on him."

I nodded, and he carried Arie up the stairs. I did my best to keep my tears at bay until he reached the top, and as if on cue, the tear that started the flood rolled down my cheek. I used my sleeve to wipe away the excess misery from my face. I checked the garage door and French doors, and both were locked.

I turned to go up the stairs and felt a spark. My hair began to softly blow against my neck as if a light wind had crossed my path, but no windows were open. I looked around quickly and saw nothing. I felt it again. Only this time, it seemed to almost grab me and then let me go. The same feeling when we first entered the house began to present itself. I wasn't alone. I darted up the stairs knowing whatever I might be faced with was something I'd have to deal with by myself. Whether it was internal fear, or one of the demons attempting to make me crack, I needed to decipher its meaning alone. I needed to learn to count on myself not Arie and Cyril. It was the only way I'd get stronger.

I made it to my bedroom without hyperventilating, quietly and quickly closing the door behind me. I charged over to my window not sure what I was expecting to see. At first, the only thing in view was darkness, but as my eyes adjusted to the gentle cast of light the moon was throwing down, I saw very subtle movements. Fear welled up inside of me. I wasn't sure what I was seeing. I quickly arranged myself so I'd hopefully not be seen as I saw what I was sure was a human figure. It was so dark outside. I couldn't see any distinguishing features. I did my best to move forward a little closer to the window hoping to make something out. I was not feeling contempt or disgust that would often accompany my encounters with the demons, so I was guessing it might be a human who was just wandering our property. At least, that was what I was hoping.

I watched intently as I saw the figure move from the trail over to the beach. Whatever his plan, it seemed rather harmless, especially since he was moving away from the house, but the fear would not subside. Seeing any sort of person or thing wandering around in pitch black does nothing to calm even the bravest of souls.

I slowly backed up from the window, grabbing a bathrobe to wrap around me since the cold air from the window was chilling me more than I thought. The terry cloth collar gently wrapped around my neck when I realized I had grabbed Athen's robe. The smell of his cologne encircled my senses. I suddenly felt so near him. I felt his presence close to me; his arms wrapping around me. I looked back down at the ground and the person strolling around, only to see him stop. And then the person looked up at me. Even though the distance was great between myself and the figure staring back at me, I was frightened and confused.

I braced myself against the wall as I stared back, focusing as best I could, disappointed in my inability to see who was out there. I knew it would be foolish to go out there with everything that had been going on, but there was a part of me that wondered if it could be Athen. That part of me was so small because the logic part won out for once, not my heart. Rather than make matters worse, I closed the curtains disconnecting my gaze from the stranger's.

I felt pretty confident it wasn't a dark demon. They had never been much for hiding their evilness. I had been exposed enough to know the feelings that would have come over me.

I slowly got into bed refusing to remove Athen's robe and the comfort that it brought me. The gentle ache in my heart began to spread through my body as I worried that it very well might be Athen outside, and I shut him out. I knew it was impossible. There was no reason for him to remember this place yet. But, I also knew the feelings I felt when we arrived here weren't right either. What else were we hoping for when we came here? We all needed to somehow connect with Athen on some level. Maybe this was it, and all I could do was crawl under the covers. I would know if it was him, and it wasn't. It wasn't him.

The wonderful calmness of my dream world began to invite me in as I slowly drifted off to sleep hearing a gentle bark off in the distance. My two worlds were once again colliding as Matilda welcomed me back to happiness. I was grateful for her loyal spirit as I heard Athen call her off in the distance.

Chapter Seventeen

I woke up from a wonderful peace, beating the sun's presence. I dreamed of being with Matilda and Athen again. We were all on the beach together playing Frisbee. Laughing as Matilda attempted to jump in the air to retrieve the flying saucer. Part of me wanted to force myself back to my dream state so that I could be there in their presence, even if for only a few more minutes, but I, also, wanted to get down to the beach before Cyril and Arie were up.

I had to investigate what I swore I saw last night. Promising myself it wasn't a dream, the swirl of emotions began to run wild in my body. My inability to sense who or what that was last night really unnerved me. Knowing that this being had the ability to reach me inside my home and did so without filling me with complete terror, puzzled me. The actions fit none of the creatures I had encountered so far. I had been in this very home only months before, approached by demons. It was a horrible experience. One that I could never forget, and one that I could never mistake. That's why I knew this was different.

I quickly got dressed and got my shoes on, sneaking quietly down the stairs attempting to make no noise whatsoever. This was something I wanted to do privately. I had been avoiding this area of our yard since we arrived back here. I decided now was as a good of a time as any to go check it out. I gently closed the French doors that led down the path where I saw the figure traipsing around. I took a deep breath hoping for a sense of tranquility as I traveled the very same path to the beach where Athen and I had last gone. A smile returned to my lips as I remembered us attempting to make s'mores on the beach and enjoying each other's company in every way possible.

I was thankful that it hadn't rained recently which lessened my chances of slipping all the way down the path. As I proceeded, I looked for any kind of clue that I thought would tell me who this person or creature was. I was pretty sure what I hoped for versus what was actually possible were two conflicting things. I got closer to the beach and noticed that I didn't see one footprint the entire length of the trail. I was leaving a print with every step I took; so I found that unnerving. When I reached the beach, the feelings came crashing down on me. The memories were flooding my mind of Athen and I becoming one on this beach. I was unable to concentrate on anything but his images. The way he held me and spoke to me during our most intimate moments. The sound of the fire crackling from that night was echoing through me. I swore I could smell the burnt logs. I remembered how we left the chocolate that was supposed to be for our s'mores too close to the fire, but we got too carried away with each other to care. The emotions traveling though me were almost more than I could handle.

The wind gently tore my hair away from my headband creating a chill as the strands of hair ran across my cheek. I looked up at the trees and realized there was no breeze. It was the same sensation as the night before. I quickly glanced around, thankful the sun had begun to make its appearance. Frightened for what I might find, I saw nothing that should have caused a sensation like this to appear. I kept on moving towards the boulder. I needed to touch it, be near it. So much had happened there. I needed that closeness we experienced here. The waves of the ocean were lapping against the rocks quietly guiding me closer to my destination. I saw off in the distance what was probably the first ferry of the morning, chugging away. Hoping that I didn't attract the attention of any of the ferry passengers, I made my movements more slow and deliberate, reaching my hand out to finally come into contact with the boulder. Feeling a charge, I knew I had made it. I looked down for a place to stick my foot to steady myself on the pebbles when I saw it. There before me was a long-stemmed, white rose laying on the only section of sand that existed in this tiny stretch of beach. I was no longer in my body. My head was fuzzy; my world was no longer my own.

My head began spinning as I did my best to prop myself up against the boulder. I didn't understand what was going on. But I knew that Athen had to have been part of it. I slowly bent down to pick up the rose, careful not to make any sudden movements for fear that I might collapse at the enormity of the situation.

I was certain this rose had to be from Athen. But why? How? Did he know what he was doing or why? If he truly knew, why would he not come to the door?

A pebble began skipping across the water, and I quickly turned my head in the direction it was coming from, only to see nothing staring right back at me. My mind was beginning to feel very fragile again, like someone was playing games with me. I was positive if it was a demon trying to trick me or send me a message that I'd be able to sense it. I could recognize their evil. I had been able to recognize the close proximity of those evil creatures time and time again. I knew in my heart, if it was one of them, I'd have caught it. It left only one answer for me to slowly embrace. I scanned the brush, mostly tangled blackberries, trying to ascertain what I could be missing. Where he could be hiding. All I could see was my hopes diminishing with every second that passed.

"I'm all yours, Athen. I'll wait for you for as long as it takes. They can take you away, but they can't take you out of my thoughts or out of my memories."

I held onto the single white rose that was placed for me with such care, unable to understand what was possibly the significance of any of it.

Chapter Eighteen

A week had gone by, and the white rose was still as upright as the morning I had picked it up off of the beach. We had made our way back up to Victoria, and I made sure that the rose made it across the border with me. It was a sign. I was certain of it. Cyril and Arie thought I was reading too much into it. I knew I wasn't. It gave me the hope I needed. So many distractions had started to spring up in the last several days that I needed what solace I could find by staring at the purity of the petals.

We had been so busy Athen hunting that we had put some of our other important duties on hold. We were contacted by some of our friends in Whistler to let us know the severity of meddling by the Legions had increased. Arie had reached out to several other families, and they had all warned of the same thing. Besides the demons' interfering more with the humans, they were beginning to pick off family members that much more aggressively amongst our network.

I went into the kitchen where Arie was baking cookies. Cyril was already in the family room making lists of things he wanted to investigate. He felt there was a pattern that we were overlooking. I kind of thought that maybe we were over thinking things. Demons are bad, and they are going to do bad things. Maybe, we need to start confronting them more head on and play the game they wanted us to play. I knew, regardless, it was time that we started to channel some of our energy into these events again. Otherwise, it wouldn't much matter if Athen returned or not. If our worst fear was realized, there might not be much to come back too.

I grabbed the newspaper off our porch. I was thankful the newspaper carrier put it in the plastic baggie. The rain was coming down in buckets, and even though the paperboy threw the paper under the eaves, the Northwest's version of rain had a tendency to be able to get anything and everything wet. Maybe that was why everyone's skin had such a beautiful, dewy glow - not enough sun to ever dry a person out and create the dreaded leather effect.

I went over to the dining room table where my orange juice and toasted bagel with cream cheese was waiting for me. The window was still open from the night before, allowing the dampness to creep inside our home. I had to admit I kind of liked it. It wasn't the same feeling as crisp snow-filled air but it definitely provided a comforting feeling.

As I slipped the rubber band off and unfolded the paper, I noticed the front-page headline reading "THIRD COUGAR ATTACK IN 2 MONTHS" blazed across the page in the black, looming font with a picture of a man underneath.

The hair on the back of my neck began to rise. Something didn't seem right about this. Granted, Vancouver Island had its fair share of wildlife, but I didn't like the feel of this. I scanned the page looking for something to confirm my suspicion. Nothing was there. There had to be something to this. I grabbed my bagel and orange juice, heading to my bedroom where I could look up these other alleged cougar attacks in private. I hoped I was wrong, but I was pretty sure I wasn't.

I curled my legs underneath me as I scanned the articles I read on the other victims who were attacked by cougars. From what it looked like, none of them had seen the cougar. All the attacks had been from behind and close to dusk - two on the beach and one on a local trail. The morning's paper had been a bit misleading. Technically, you could call it three attacks in two months, but there had been four victims, not three. The first cougar attack occurred with a couple who was on their honeymoon. Neither of them saw the cougar. Yet they were both attacked. He was on the beach, and she was found on the trail leading back to the parking lot, which was very contradictory to a normal cougar attack. The first victim should have been plenty to satisfy the cougar's needs. Thankfully, the attack occurred near a popular park so help was called almost instantly. Yet, nobody was able to identify a cougar, and the hounds that were brought in were unable to trace any sort of scent. The couple was interviewed while still in the hospital recovering from their wounds. Neither saw a cougar attack the other. It didn't make sense. I was pretty sure this wasn't a cougar. I knew

I had to bring it up to Cyril and Arie immediately. I may not be having any premonitions surrounding this, but I certainly wasn't going to discount good old-fashioned instinct.

Scanning the newspaper, my heart began beating faster and faster as I knew the very thing that I was looking for was waiting for me to find it, right in there among the mix of useless facts. The attack was about ten miles from my practice ground. I knew it. This was no coincidence. The Legions were announcing their presence to us all. It was our turn to announce our stance. We hadn't been doing a very good job of that lately.

I wish I had Athen here to discuss my hypothesis. My heart ached as I looked at the white rose. I knew he was getting closer. I needed to be patient.

***

It turned out that humans being attacked by wild animals wasn't unique to Vancouver Island. Every family we contacted throughout this country and the next, confirmed that wild animal attacks were on the rise. Whether it was an alleged bear attack in Yellowstone or Russia, the details were always the same. Nobody saw the animals, and the attacks were gruesome. It was definitely the Legions beginning their formations, making their intentions known, and now they were heavily involving humans. I did my best to push the thought of Athen away and tried to concentrate on the tasks at hand, but it would be so much easier to bounce my ideas off of him. Cyril and Arie were great to talk with. They really were supportive, and I felt like I could tell them most things, but the emptiness that I felt was sometimes overwhelming. Seeing them together made it worse at times too.

We decided to go to some of the areas where the attacks were taking place to scope out the surroundings and see if we could find anything. I doubted we would find all that much. They were very good at being noticed when they wanted to be and hiding when they didn't want to be. Cyril and Arie had gone to the library to grab some topographic information we couldn't get online. They promised to be back by noon. I had about thirty more minutes before they would be home, so I decided to go for a walk.

I had started seeing Athen in my dreams again, and I was pretty sure it was the real thing. I think he was getting closer to finding his way home to us, and all I could do was wait. I had scared him off enough already, first at the library and again at the hospital where the poor guy was supposed to be recuperating. I'm lucky he was on the same continent let alone in the same area, or at least, I hoped he was in the same area. It was still pretty hard to track him down. Cyril and Arie led me to believe that he was around, but for all I knew, that was to keep me from going hysterical. I already felt on the verge more often than not. I wanted to be held by him or have his familiar laugh bounce off the walls. I now understood what he meant about it being harder on him than me because he knew what he was missing, and I had no recollection. I never thought I'd be the one with the memories, and he wouldn't. It was pretty hard to fathom in such a short time that so many things had reversed. Not only that, I missed my little Matilda too. I worried about her a lot as well since we couldn't completely sense her, I didn't know what that meant either. I was trying my best to trust, but it was hard.

I had wandered down into town and was walking towards the sandwich shop when I felt the same presence as on the beach. I stopped in my tracks and scanned the sidewalk. I did my best to look as normal as possible, even though my excitement level was building tenfold. My hands began to get clammy, and I felt like my vision was going in and out. It was like I was having a massive head rush, but I hadn't moved. There was an empty bench that was covered in leftover rain droplets, and I didn't care. I sat down immediately feeling the wetness penetrate through my jeans doing nothing to bring me out of my fog. I continued to scan the streets and sidewalk looking for someone who I knew was impossible to find. The electricity began zipping through my veins. I knew he was close. I didn't know where. There were city workers placing hanging baskets on the light posts and street signs, a supposedly welcoming sign of spring. All that did for me was remind me that Athen still wasn't with me, and the winter season has almost already exited.

My cell phone began to vibrate. It was Arie. I couldn't answer it. I didn't want to lose this trace to Athen. As distant as it might be, I didn't want to lose it. A couple minutes passed by, and I received a text from Arie. She was wondering where I went. Apparently my idea of only being gone 15 minutes turned into 45, and they had made it home already.

I didn't want them to worry needlessly so I texted back where I was. I knew they were going to come get me. I wasn't ready to leave. I had no choice though. I had to, also, stay focused on figuring out the Legion's modus operandi. Their master plan was to have us all distracted, and it certainly had worked better than I'd like to admit.

It was off to the first beach where the latest attack had occurred. I'd be on my best behavior and give my full attention to the task at hand. And on that, Cyril and Arie pulled up to the sidewalk waiting for our day's adventures. I climbed into the back of the Jeep and shut the door as I head Matilda's bark chasing after us. I was sure of it. Turning my head to peer out the back window, I saw nothing of familiarity. There was no dog in sight.

"Let's get going. I want to show you the place where I was practicing. I think there is a definite connection," I said, trying my best to get back into the reality of my life rather than the wishful imagery I kept tricking myself into believing as a possibility.

We were about to our destination, and I felt my nerves come to the surface a little. I wasn't exactly sure why since I was arriving this time with Cyril and Arie, and before, I managed to fight and win against the demons I ran into last by myself.

The day was fabulous for a drive. We had finally had some sun for a few hours so lots of things had started to dry out, which was kind of nice, especially for our little hike. I've done it in the rain but not slipping and sliding along the trails will certainly make a quicker trip for us all, and I really liked the idea of getting in and out of the area. The events were far too creepy.

The parking lot was far more filled than when I had been there by myself. Good weather brings out the people in droves, especially in the Northwest.

The very beginnings of the wildflower season was starting to make its introduction, and it was a beautiful sight to be able to see the delicate, white flowers peaking out from under the logs, and the pink florets guiding us along the trails.

We began making our way down to the beach, and I truly did feel safer in the company of my family. The sea air was full of the salty dampness that I'd come to expect being so near the ocean. Feeling the moist air coat my lungs made me appreciate the moment that much more. Laughter from the families, who were already searching out the greatest finds in the tide pools, brought me such happiness. Not having Athen by my side, as we made this trek, made my heart quiver, but knowing that we might be able to figure out the demons' next move or prevent an attack on any innocent victim made my day feel a lot more important.

The scene was beautiful with the rays of the sun dancing off the ocean, creating a clarity in the tide pools as the sea life did its best to make the tourists happy. I did my best to stay away from the slippery rocks, and I think Cyril and Arie were appreciative since they didn't feel like doing any rescues on their inept in-law.

We climbed up the trail that was now a lot less rough than when I was there last time after a rain. The long sea grass bowed, leading the way as we climbed further and further up the hill, leaving the families to play down by the ocean. As I began scanning our destination as a predator, I realized this would be an ideal spot for the next so-called cougar attack. When we reached the top near the forest that I last practiced at, I studied the landscape understanding completely now why the demons would have chosen this for their possible next stomping grounds or attack grounds.

"Wow, guys. I don't know why I didn't think about it sooner. This place gets just enough foot traffic to ensure a victim, but it's far enough from the beach and main groups to get away with it."

"I think we may have found the next attack site. What about you, Arie? Think we stumbled upon it?" Cyril asked, squeezing her neck muscles.

"Yeah, I'd say so. I'm getting a really horrible feeling to match the geography."

"I agree. It's like the longer we stand here, the worse it gets. I don't know how I didn't pick up on it before," I said, shaking my head.

"They may not have decided on this place yet. It may have been a recent development," Cyril said, walking over to where I jumped from tree limb to tree limb during my private practice session.

"Is this where you took those guys out?" he asked, kneeling down touching his fingers to the dirt.

"Yep, that's the spot. Why?" I wondered how he could find the exact spot out of the entire field we were standing in.

"One of my special talents, I guess we could say."

"Really? You can scope out battle places?" I asked laughing.

"Kinda," Cyril said, unable to resist, "I can figure out when battles have occurred, if recent enough, and I can see how they ended."

"That's an odd skill," I said genuinely perplexed, unable to see how useful that could be.

"You're one to talk." He shook his head, throwing a pebble at my feet.

"I'm sure I'll figure out the significance of that."

A noise grabbed our attention coming from the direction of the woods, and Cyril slowly backed up towards where Arie and I were standing.

"Guess we aren't alone," Arie whispered.

Feeling the same sensation wash over me like many times before, I realized we were in the presence of the dark demons. We very well may have stumbled upon something once more.

The figures began to emerge from the dark wooded area and sure enough they were demons. Two of them were from my last encounter. The two I took care of were obviously easily replaced. They'd been up to something suspicious for sure. Their eyes meeting ours, I looked them over realizing they didn't actually seem to have any plan to try to attack us, which seemed odd.

Before I knew it, I'd walked past Cyril to confront the strangers.

"What's your intent here?" I asked staring at the male, whose eyes were just as dead as the others, but his teeth looked less threatening.

"I'm sure you read the newspaper," he replied wryly.

"Why don't you tell Azazel, that this is child's play. If it's us he wants, why not come after us. Why target such easy human prey?" I was searching them for answers. Foolishly thinking that they would actually be able to reveal some sort of nuance that I'd catch, as if they were close to us or a mortal in their gestures.

"In fact, I'd love the chance to tell him that myself." I was beginning to wish that I'd kept my mouth shut, fear beginning to invade my thoughts.

Cyril took a step forward, standing next to me.

"Do you honestly think that we'll continue to allow this?" he asked, nudging himself closer to the group of demons. Arie stood next to me as well, her body stiffening in place as Cyril provoked the demons.

"You haven't done anything yet," replied one of the demons.

"That time has changed." Cyril's body now slightly hovering over the ground.

I started laughing from deep within.

"My suggestion is that one of you run off to Azazel and invite him to a discussion with me. I'd love to be able to hash some things out," I said, grinning widely, excited by my confidence. "In the meantime, whoever wants to stay around for a match that I can assure you'll not win, feel free."

My body shot towards the demon closest to Cyril. A young minion like that was my best shot for victory. My leg was stuck straight out as I stretched my entire body in an attempt to knock the minion to the ground. Cyril began to take out the one that appeared to be the leader, the one who escaped last time. The ball of my foot landed directly in the chest of my target.

"Make sure you leave one capable of telling Azazel of our message," Arie said giggling.

We were obviously making our threat viable enough as two of the demons fled back into the woods. My only hope was that my message really would reach Azazel. He was the key. It was time to escalate the situation, get the ball rolling. Looking over at Cyril and Arie, I wasn't sure they agreed.

Chapter Nineteen

It was dead silent. I wasn't really sure where I'd wandered off to in this city. The sun had set, leaving only the shadows of trees and lamp posts to frighten me enough to think about turning around and going back home. Doing my best to hop over the puddles that the latest rainfall had brought, my mind wandered to Athen. Things felt so pointless without him. My mind, body, and soul ached for him. I wanted to be touched by him, or glance at his smirk, or stare into his eyes - anything to remind myself that he truly existed. Something to assure me that the last few months were not a dream turned nightmare. It was foolish to think that my wandering would lead me to him somehow, but it was the closest thing I had to hope. Doing every move wrong in the book, from running into him at the library, to going out of my way to see him at the hospital, put me in this position.

When he was first taken away from us, I swore to myself that I wouldn't fall into the traps that Athen fell into. I was going to follow the rules. I was going to get him back quickly and without issue. That was the plan, and I truly believed it. The pull I felt to him, however, was indescribable. It was like a drug. A little was good at first, but then I needed a little more...and after that, a little more. My first little Athen fix at the library satisfied me for a while but not long enough. It was if the thought of losing him forever couldn't override the immediate need to be in his presence. It was uncontrollable. I now fully understood how he messed up enough to keep me away for fifty some years. Because at this rate, it seemed like I was on track to do the same.

The one emotion that has taken me completely by surprise, however, was the anger - the madness that crept in when I least expected it. Anger at Athen for not being able to fight the demons off, anger at myself for not warning Athen, anger at Cyril and Arie for not controlling me better. For instance, why am I trekking the streets of Victoria hoping to run into him? Maybe, they gave up on me playing by the rules.

The clapping of footsteps began getting louder behind me. It was an urgent pace and that of a woman's. My pace began to quicken unexpectedly, not wanting to see who might actually be behind me. The level of fear that was always brewing right at the surface made me lengthen my stride even more. There was a coffee shop at the end of the street that looked pretty busy, right where I needed to be. I jetted up the sidewalk towards the safe haven, only to look behind me and see Lilith, the serpent. She nodded at me, with her large grin, and kept walking right past the coffee shop. I felt the breath that I had been holding in slowly escape as I climbed up the stairs to the Starbucks. Feeling the defeat of not finding Athen but running directly into her made my stomach turn to knots. I couldn't believe she was back so quickly. I thought our victory against her would have bought us more time before she began interfering again. Fighting her in the hospital had given me a little too much confidence and seeing that she was alive and well, still roaming the streets of Victoria, only made the urgency that much more to find Athen again, before she did.

The wooden door swung open with a woman dressed in khakis and a thin, red sweater draping her shoulders, holding her pot of gold, with a man following right behind her. They were both laughing as if there wasn't a care in the world, their world.

"Thanks." I was able to utter to the couple as he held the door open for me. I went up to the counter, ordering an Island Oat bar and a Cinnamon Dulce latte. Not wanting to admit defeat and call Cyril and Arie for a ride back to the house, I thought about all my options. My drink was called, which I grabbed quickly and stepped back from the counter, only to have déjà vu flood over me. I scanned the entire coffee shop, realizing that everyone was in their place, exactly like my dream. The only two missing were Lilith and Athen.

My head started spinning, and I was lightheaded. I did my best to steady myself using one of the overstuffed, velvet chairs they had near the fireplace. The tiny sweat droplets began to form at my hairline. I was a mess. I never expected for this dream to become a reality, especially after my hospital encounter. Sure that I had disrupted destiny enough, I never let myself see otherwise. Lilith's defeat should have sent her far away. Yet, she was back quicker than I ever imagined.

With every swing of the front door bringing in more customers, my gut twisted into a tighter knot making me cringe with pain. Seeing Lilith outside on the sidewalk now made sense. We had scared her off but not enough. She was back but was she back with Athen or was she ever truly with Athen? I grabbed my phone out of my coat and texted Arie. I needed them now. As my dream played out directly in front of me, I went on the other side of the chair where I could position myself for the door to swing open and reveal the greatest disappointment of my life. I was placing my coffee on the table when I felt the blast of air ripple through me. It was him.

Seeing Athen, gorgeous as ever made my heart begin to swell. The pain, from not being able to run over to him and jump in his arms, made the tears begin to form, and I didn't know what else to do besides stare. Then it hit me, Lilith was nowhere to be found. In my dream she was waiting for him at the counter, and he only had eyes for her, ignored me completely. She wasn't in here, but this was my dream. Maybe the hospital disrupted things enough. The theme park ride of emotions that were inching their way through my body made me so nervous, I knocked over my latte.

The laughter bounced off the walls like I had heard so many times before. Athen's beautiful voice reached every part of my body as I prayed for us to magically reunite in this very moment. Nothing prepared me for being this close to him. His smile was beyond welcoming, and I knew it was directed at me. The baristas came running over with towels to sop up the beige-colored liquid as best they could. But I felt like I wasn't even in the scene that was playing out. All I could do was watch Athen hoping for some sort of recognition. He ordered his drink and came to stand near me while he waited. Why he wasn't running out the door after seeing me, I didn't know. I'm sure he would have had to recognize me from the hospital. These two realities were playing a cruel joke on me, and I was willing to surrender anything to be with him again. I was completely stuck. I didn't know whether to play into the old act, or ignore him, or what. My entire body began getting so warm, I didn't know if I'd be able to act even a little civilized being so close to him.

"Hey, miss. What was your order? This one's on the house."

"Um, the barista's talking to you." Athen's lips were moving. He was talking directly to me.

"Huh? Oh, sorry. You don't have to do that. I'm so sorry."

"Well, we will just look at your cup if you don't tell us." The barista was such a friendly guy.

"Cinnamon Dulce then," I said, trying to play as if I was somewhat human.

"That's totally embarrassing," I said under my breath, more to me than anyone.

"I've a feeling there's been worse moments for ya," Athen said, winking at me as he grabbed his drink on the counter. It was like before with him. My heart knew the familiarity before my mind did. I only hoped that he recognized that we were tethered to one another somehow, if not tonight - soon.

"Quite possibly," I said, trying to keep up the charade.

"You know," he said. "Have I seen you around before?"

Totally puzzled now, I didn't know what to say or do. I wanted to touch him, maybe only a little, like an accident - possibly trip into him or place my hand on his back - anything, to quench the urge that was literally growing stronger by the second.

I grabbed my bag quickly before I did something I'd regret. Darting to the counter to get my newly refreshed drink, I forced myself to barely look at him. The pull was too great. I had to escape.

"It's a small town," I said, flashing a smile, doing my best to make it outside to wait for Arie.

I didn't care that it was dark outside or that Lilith was now roaming the streets. I had to stay away from him before I did something stupid, again. The stirring was almost more than I could handle. The lightheadedness was wrapping around my consciousness, making everything so fuzzy. All I could think of was my fingers caressing his face, bringing him towards me, his lips softly meeting mine. I was so involved in my own thoughts, I didn't even realize that he had snuck up behind me.

"Not sure what I said to make you hurry out the door to wait outside in the cold and dark night for, apparently, nobody." His smirk was more than I could handle, as he looked around the empty street. It was like the old Athen was standing in front of me, my Athen, only he didn't know it yet. He didn't know we belonged together. He didn't know me or did he? His confidence overflowed, exactly like I remembered.

"I'll let you be," he said grinning and nodding at me, spinning in the other direction, but not before raising his arm and patting me on the shoulder. My world was spinning. I needed him to pick me up and carry me to wherever he was going. We needed to be together, and all I could do was watch him walk away to somewhere I couldn't find. I wanted to scream at the top of my lungs to not leave me, but I knew it would do no good. It wasn't time.

As he turned down the block where I couldn't see him any longer, I saw Arie and Cyril pull up. I ran to the car, almost unable to utter anything that made any sense.

"My dream. It was my dream, only different. But it was my dream. Guys, we were able to change my dream. She wasn't there. He didn't ignore me. He saw me. He touched me!" I exclaimed, slamming the door.

"Whoa! What are you talking about?" Arie was completely confused, but not nearly as much as I was.

"Remember the dream I had where Lilith, my nemesis the serpent-eyed woman, blah-blah, was waiting for him at a Starbucks, and I was there – only when he came in he completely ignored me and went straight for her? Well, that just happened! Except she wasn't there! Everyone else was, but she wasn't there! I ran into her outside, but that doesn't count. Anyway, he saw me – partially because I spilled my drink all over the place, but then he initiated a conversation. I freaked and ran outside, only to have him right behind me, joking with me. It was like he didn't remember me from the hospital fight, which I can't imagine, or I don't even know what." I ran out of air and took a deep breath in ready for round two.

"Which way did he go?" Cyril asked, looking at me in the rearview.

"Down the block, to the left. Why?"

Cyril put the blinker on as we turned left towards Athen's direction scanning the sidewalks.

"He probably rode his Ducati here. I'm sure he's long gone." My disappointment was felt with every syllable.

"Yeah, probably. Thought I'd give it a shot though."

Unable to do much but think about his fingers touching my shoulder and the electricity I felt merely by being in his presence, I knew the evening was shot. I wanted nothing more than to go home and crawl under the covers and sleep all this away until Athen reappeared.

"I think he knows. I think he knows enough, at least, to not be scared, Ana. This doesn't make sense otherwise. I think it is out of our hands for now."

"Well, as long as it doesn't fall back into Lilith's hands, I think I'll be okay." Saying the words more to myself than to anyone else, my jaw clenching in agony as I thought about the months alone with her he had possibly had.

***

Cyril had dropped Arie and I off back at the house and decided to take a drive. I didn't blame him. My curiosity was killing me, but I felt that anything I interfered with only screwed things up. Besides, the encounter with him had made me exhausted or maybe depressed – not sure which. The familiarity surrounding his every move, whether it was his sense of humor that came out with the baristas, or the curl of his lips, or the clench of his fists while he laughed, created a stir of desire deep within me that if I couldn't quench it soon, I didn't think I could go on much longer. The idea of complete ignorance seemed almost blissful at this point.

Arie was up and around in the kitchen, and I was hiding out in my bedroom. Cyril wanted to case some of the streets down the direction that Athen went in, looking for his bike. I wasn't sure if I wanted to know or not. At this point, I felt like I'd go knock on his door and mess everything up.

Looking up at the white rose that I had now hung upside down on my wall to dry reminded me why I shouldn't give up. Why I needed to stay in this reality and not exit into the otherworld. He was getting close.

Grabbing the iPad off my dresser, I flipped open the case and began checking our email. The destruction was undeniable in many locations, and the battles were going to begin soon. Whistler was becoming a hotbed of activity again. I wasn't sure if we would wind up going up there soon or not. I hoped not until we got Athen back.

As I was stretching out on my bed, a single light was reflecting off my window. I couldn't tell exactly where it was coming from, but it seemed larger than a flashlight. Regardless, my pulse began quickening as I thought about someone lurking outside staring at me- especially with Lilith already back in town, possibly ready to pounce.

"Hey, Arie!" My voice was a cross between a whisper and a hoarse yell. Unsure if she heard, I tried again. This time footsteps came running down the hall.

I slowly got up and went to the window to track down the light I was seeing. The darkness of the night, mixed with the streetlight from above, made it difficult to distinguish what I was looking at. As my hand rested on the glass, the coldness shocked me into believing that the light was something it couldn't sensibly be, but my exhaustion began to be replaced by excitement.

"What's up?" Arie whispered.

"There's a light out here. Not a flashlight, but something is odd for sure. I can't make it out."

Arie peered out the window, her body freezing in place.

"Oh my God. I don't think Cyril will find his bike after all. Go to the living room window. I'm sure you'll see him from that view."

The color drained from my face.

"What does this mean? Are you serious?" I was running to the living room window as fast as I could make it.

When I got there, I was only left with watching the guy on the bike drive away. Athen was driving away. We were so close. He was so close. It was like he was waiting for some sort of revelation, and I wasn't sure if it was going to come in time. Watching the brake light reflect red as he stopped at the intersection before taking off made my heart ache as he took off again to that unknown place.

***

The warmth from the fireplace was barely reaching me. Not because I wasn't sitting close enough. That certainly wasn't the reason. I was practically propped on top of the hearth. It was because nothing in this world could take the chill out of my bones. The longer Athen was out my reach the sicker I got, physically and mentally. That I recognized. Seeing him intermittently wasn't helping the situation, rather it made the longing worse.

Arie and Cyril had gotten used to me being useless, and they attempted to get back to some sort of routine. I imagined they were getting pretty sick of the situation and pretty sick of me. I wrapped the blanket around my shoulders trying to dismiss the overwhelming bite in the air.

"Guys?" I tried my best to sound cheerful. "Are you around?"

Nothing. In all my wallowing, I was embarrassed to admit, I didn't even know if they were home. If they left, I'm sure they told me. I obviously didn't retain it. I wracked my brain trying to figure out where they might have gone. Not much came to me. I honestly don't remember them telling me anything.

I sluggishly moved to the back of the house to take a quick look out back in case they were out there, doubtful being as cold as it was. But maybe being outside was more hospitable than what I was dumping into the atmosphere. I quickly scanned the backyard seeing nothing but the empty bench and overflowing cement birdbath. I tromped back into the living room, looking outside through the big picture window. Seeing nothing, I decided to slump down where I was, good a place as any. I reached for one of the photo albums that I had gone through a thousand times before in the time that I had been at this house, our old house. Athen's house, my house – so strange to think we lived here by ourselves at some point without Cyril and Arie. I can't even imagine not having them as appendages. I couldn't handle this alone. Who am I kidding? I can't handle this regardless of anyone being around or not around.

I laid down on my stomach wrapping the blanket over my body a little better as I dove into the first page of Athen and I hugging each other in a frozen memory. I'd take any frozen memory over no memory at this point. The tears began to form in the corner of my eyes. The coldness began trickling down my cheek. I did my best to flush them away but they would not vanish. Without understanding what I was doing, my finger kept tracing his image in the photograph over and over again. As if touching his lips with my fingertip could lead me to him. Before I could stop it, a tear bounced down onto the image staring back at me. I quickly grabbed the corner of the blanket to wipe away the wetness. I wasn't sure I was brave enough to turn the page so I closed my eyes, laying my head on my arms. I'm sure Cyril and Arie would be gone for a bit. I had time to compose myself a little.

The vibrations slowly began to creep up through my body. I sat upright quickly, and the tiny pulses vanished as quickly as they came. I strained to hear something, anything! But the streets were deathly silent. I quickly laid back down on the floor, not sure what I was expecting or hoping for, and then there it was - again. A rumbling, a trembling was coming through the floor timbers. I was certain of it. I could feel him. He was on his way here. How could that be?

I was sprawled on the floor, letting every extremity feel the vibrations that were getting stronger and stronger with every second that passed. My ear pressed to the cold wood floor waiting to hear something more definite, more real. I wanted more than a hum. Although, I was willing to let that be a sign. I wanted it to be him more than anything. As the seconds ticked by, the shaking was becoming impossible not to detect.

I slowly let myself sit up not wanting to miss a shake or shudder as I saw the lampshade move slightly. My blood started to pump in the same rhythm as the walls around me. I was afraid a fire truck was about to drive by, shattering my hopes. The energy was building all around me. Afraid for what I might see or, more plainly, not see, I very slowly moved to the living room window, not knowing what it might have in store for me. Very gingerly, I began moving aside the silk curtains hoping for something that wasn't possible, and then the rumbling stopped. I was crushed. My imagination had gotten the better of me again. I whipped the curtains open, fully prepared to see nothing but glistening leaves from the day's latest rainfall plastered against the cement. Instead, what I saw left me breathless. I reached for the windowsill to steady myself. The wait was over.

Athen was removing his matte black helmet as he stood straddling his Ducati. Shaking his head to get the hair out of his eyes, he began peeling off his black gloves and jacket carefully. It seemed so natural. Like he had been here a million times before, doing the exact same thing. I didn't know what to do. I had nobody to ask. It was so surreal. Did they know this was going to happen? Was that why they weren't here? Does Athen really know where he's at? I don't even know where to begin. I've screwed this up so many times before. I was paralyzed.

Watching him swing his leg over the bike so smoothly sparked an excitement like all the other times I had seen him, only it felt tangible this time. He looked so gorgeous. I needed him so badly. I wanted to connect with him in the worst way. I waited for him to see me in the window, but he wouldn't look up. I was staring at him as hard as I could, hoping I'd somehow get him to look up. He wouldn't. He turned away and began opening the box on his bike. I was guessing to put his helmet and gloves away. The distance between us was almost unbearable. The chill that I was so accustomed to began to be replaced with a heat running though my body. I was on fire - if I could only see his eyes, his smile, anything to connect with him again. His hand grabbed the top of the box and slammed it shut.

Athen spun around so quickly, his eyes finally meeting mine. His lips curled in the half smirk as our eyes locked, this time for eternity. We would not be kept apart. As he walked to the sidewalk leading to our home, I saw that he was carrying a beautiful bouquet of red roses, with a lone white rose in the middle. My heart began to sing. The wetness from my tears began puddling at the base of my neck. There was no holding back.

I ran to the front door, swinging it open, crushing the flowers as I jumped onto him, not letting go for anything. I felt his arms wrap around me as the rose petals began their journey to the floor. His kisses violently grabbing every part of my skin, before moving onto the next while my tears would not cease. My legs completely wrapped themselves around his waist, and my head was buried into his neck. It felt like a dream.

"My baby's back." Were the only words that left my lips.

"I was never gone. Just a little lost, my angel."

Hearing those words made me slip away into the madness that was our world. The world between us two, built for only us to share. The worries of before slipping away with every kiss creating our fortress that no one could penetrate.

Chapter Twenty

What do you say we take off before Arie and Cyril get here?" Athen's eyes were full of mischief. He knew their names. He knew me. I had no idea what was taking place, and I didn't care. He was here. He was back.

"Are you serious?"

"Yeah, I'm serious." He picked me up off the couch before I had a chance to say anything. He already knew my answer. He carried me to the front door and plopped me down outside, closing the door and locking it behind us.

"Shall we?" he asked, winking at me.

The thought of being alone with him was almost more than I could handle. I really didn't understand what was going on but knew that Athen had somehow figured this thing out on his own or at least parts of it. He wasn't scared off. His worlds were colliding, and none of us had expected this. I wasn't even sure that this was possible.

I got on the bike behind him securing the pink helmet that he had apparently picked out for me. I was in complete disbelief. I was the one who was supposed to be showing him things, not the other way around. His eyes didn't even have the familiar green glow that I was used to. Yet, he was accepting our world – his world. The sound of the bike's roaring engine tripped up my thoughts. Grabbing his waist tighter as we took off, I soaked up everything that was happening.

He wouldn't tell me where we were going, and we had been on the bike for what seemed like an eternity, mainly because of the rain. But I wouldn't trade it for the world. Resting my head on his back to resist the continuous pelts of rain was stirring up the desire I had for him even more. The firmness of his muscles, my arms wrapped around his waist, I felt like I was in the middle of a magical dream.

We started down this long driveway, and I began to tense up a bit. This could be a trap. Maybe Lilith did get to him, and he was only following orders. My body temperature began to rise as I played out all sorts of scenarios of my impending doom, with the wicked woman hovering over the entire scene. I was disgusted with this woman continually entering my thoughts and planting seeds of paranoia and jealousy.

He pulled into the sparse garage, and my nerves didn't lessen any.

"What's up? Why are you so tense?" he asked, helping me get my helmet off. His fingers were gently undoing the straps on my helmet as I was looking up into his eyes. They may have been missing the beautiful green glow, but they were not evil. They were as kind as ever. His fingertips gracefully touched my chin, bringing my lips so close to his. He was absolutely incredible. His hair was tousled, the way I loved. I was in awe. I grabbed his shoulders, running my fingers down his arm, trying to find some fault or giveaway this wasn't really happening. It was as if I was looking at my old Athen. The kindness was radiating out from his soul, his eyes searching mine for acceptance. He was here for me.

We walked up the two tiny stairs leading into the house, he pushed open the door, only to have Matilda standing there trying her best to wag her little stub tail. Tears instantly began streaming down my face. I had missed her so much.

"Surprise!" he said faintly, nodding at me to move through the door.

Grabbing Matilda, I spun around with her up high, hugging and kissing all forty pounds of her. She recognized me instantly and began panting as soon I put her back on the ground. Athen grabbed my waist and spun me around to look at him. Matilda started barking in excitement, but her warbles became more faint every second that Athen held me. I didn't want to let go. It was as if nothing had taken him away, except that his eyes were still not changed. My head was resting on his chest. Hearing his heartbeat, created a comfort I couldn't explain. Feeling the warmth from every breath he exhaled was a gift like no other. My Athen had returned. I felt foolish for thinking that he could cause harm. There were so many unanswered questions, but those all had to wait. Right now, all I cared about was being in his embrace.

"I love you so much," he murmured into my hair, sending chills up my spine.

"I love you too, and I'm so sorry." My eyes began filling with tears, knowing how lucky I was to have him back.

"Don't cry, my angel." Athen scooped me up and began heading towards the back of the house. There was barely anything in the home. Obviously, he didn't make himself too comfortable here. Everything was ultra modern, and nothing was out of place, not that there was much to be out of place. My heart began pumping quickly with every step he took, not knowing his intentions. He carried me through the living room and down the hallway to the bedrooms with the strength and confidence that I remembered.

"I knew I'd find my way back to you," he whispered into my ear, "You were never far from my thoughts. I just didn't know it."

I ran my fingers through his hair, pulling myself back from him to be able to take in his whole being. His spirit couldn't be missed. It felt like this day would never come. His kind, caring eyes were a gentle reminder that this wasn't a dream. Athen had returned. I didn't have to wait decades.

"I love you so much, Athen. A piece of me died every second waiting for your return. I began to worry that I'd run out of pieces to give. Every minute you were gone felt like an eternity. In the morning I'd wake up feeling a weight on my chest knowing you weren't there to hold me or make me smile. It felt like breathing was even an effort. I couldn't bear the thought of going through the turmoil I felt for decades as you had done. I don't know how you did it." I felt the tears begin to well up, and my throat begin to constrict. I looked into his eyes and felt as if I was able to see deep into his soul.

I closed my eyes to take in a deep breath and regain my composure, and before I knew it, I felt the gentleness of his lips glide against mine. I knew whatever plans we had for the afternoon would be put on hold. Athen's fingertips began running along the length of my arm. It had only been months since I was last held in his embrace, but his touch felt so new and exciting. I felt his lips on my neck gracing every inch as he worked his way down. I began grabbing his shirt as he made his next move.

"At least, I'm not making you wait," I whispered coyly.

His lips immediately stopped gliding over my skin as he looked up at me. My heart plummeted down ten stories wondering what I did wrong.

"Unlike you, I wouldn't have accepted no as an answer," he said, with his all too familiar half grin, half smirk, "You did."

"I had a choice?" Was all that slipped out as I sunk into the embrace of the comforter.

"It was worth it, wasn't it?" His eyes penetrated through to my core. They were so mesmerizing. I felt his fingers lightly grazing my collarbone and my entire body began to tremble with an eagerness that surprised me. He brought his lips down to mine, and I felt his breath hovering on my skin. It smelled so sweet. I released myself fully to him. There was no room for playful arguing. I needed him now. As his breath hovered on every crevice of my body, the chill began to invigorate me as our bodies became one, as if we had never been separated.

Chapter Twenty-One

We were all in our living room spread out, taking in the moment of having Athen back. Athen and I never wanted to leave each other's embrace from earlier in the afternoon, but we knew we had to get back to Cyril and Arie.

"Alright, so you've got to fill us in. Arie wasn't able to locate Matilda. She couldn't find you guys. Ana couldn't see any images. After the incident at the hospital, it was like you were gone into the mist. I searched the place you were staying, finding nothing. Where did you go? I don't understand, man. You've got to tell us what the heck has been going on?"

My head spun to glare at Cyril.

"What do you mean you searched the place he was staying? I didn't think you guys knew exactly where he was staying."

Cyril began to shift uncomfortably in his chair, and I felt Athen's arms wrap around me to calm me a tad.

"I took off. I couldn't deal with it. I think I knew what was up from the beginning, but none of it made sense. It was becoming clear, bit by bit, and yet, I didn't want to see it or believe it," Athen answered Cyril's question before giving me a chance to go off.

"I had placed clues for myself about our life, but I can tell you they seem really absurd when you find them in a mortal state, or what you think is a mortal state."

"So you really did try the memsors? I didn't think that was even possible," Arie said, shaking her head in disbelief.

"Where all did you place these clues?" I asked, letting Cyril off the hook for now. I didn't want to dampen the excitement of Athen being back in my arms by chewing out Cyril. It could wait.

"The first place was underneath Matilda's collar. Another one pointed me to a leather journal back at the Kingston home. I had written a lot of stuff in that journal." Athen seemed rather impressed with himself on that one.

"Whoa, I picked that up just a week ago! I almost opened it too."

"It was probably best you didn't," he said, winking at me and hugging me.

"We are still going to have to do the reintroduction process, you know," Cyril stated, in a very serious tone.

"I totally agree." Athen nodded his head. "Tonight we should get it done. Lilith is still around. I don't want any complications."

Hearing him now actually utter her name made the anger begin to burn in my soul. I never imagined those syllables would roll off his tongue, and here they made an entrance.

"Well, we might as well. Nothing else has followed protocol."

Cyril and Arie got up from the couch.

"We should all get some rest." Arie patted her brother's knee on her way out the living room.

Leaving us to stare at each other was the best gift. There was so much I wanted to say, and so much I never wanted to hear.

"Can I ask you something? It's kind of odd, I'm sure." I looked into Athen's eyes hoping for a positive response.

"Sure. Why wouldn't you be able to?" he chided, lightly touching my hand.

"When you were in the library researching Angels and Demons, did you notice me? And why were you researching those subjects? How did you know or what did you know?" His gaze moved quickly from mine, and I noticed he looked down.

"Well, the first part of the question is yes. I certainly did notice you, but I was afraid you were like the others. And that leads into the next answer. There was someone pursuing me pretty intensely. Yet, I knew something was off. There was a beauty to her but a lack of kindness. She was like stone, even her laughter. I felt she was something other than what she represented. I couldn't put my finger on it. Her eyes were so dark, almost lifeless. The rest of her didn't seem to match that persona. It was very confusing."

I curled my legs up, sinking into the couch and deeper into his gaze.

"I had an evil feeling follow me every time she was around. But, I kept being pulled to her, so I thought I should check it out. Not being privy to the information that I am now, I had no idea the enormity of everything. I, also, always noticed a black marking near her, either reflected on the floor or the wall. I thought I was going crazy. Then when I saw you and your otherworldly, completely wholesome beauty gazing back at me with your wondrous green eyes, I thought I was really losing it. Especially when I saw the beautiful light bouncing off the library wall. It was like the exact opposite of the woman pursuing me. I couldn't fathom if that was what I was really seeing or if it was somehow related to the dark markings. It was beautiful, but I didn't see any crystals or glass that could be causing the prism effect, and I realized that on some level you and the other woman had something in common. Somehow, you had to be connected. I didn't know what was going on, and I decided to take off immediately and barricade myself in my rental house for awhile. Only she wouldn't leave me alone, and she had the ability to be charming," he said somewhat laughing.

"Yes, serpents are known for their charming abilities." I rolled my eyes and smacked his leg.

"When I realized she was part of the equation, I almost quit. Then finding out that my mistakes could have turned you away from us, I just..."

"Quit on what?" Athen asked so quietly, I almost couldn't hear him.

I couldn't bring myself to say it. It felt like the ultimate betrayal. Here Athen lasted for decades, and I almost gave up in a matter of months. I could feel the tears beginning to well up. I vowed I wasn't going to tell him these things, and here they were pouring out.

"What was it, Ana? What did you almost quit on?" Anger was edging into his voice now.

"I just... It was only for a few hours. I didn't think it was good for us or the situation if I kept thinking of you. I know I couldn't have stuck to it, but I thought I was making so many mistakes that either involved you or were because of you that I had to detach myself from you." Tears were streaming down my cheeks.

"I know I couldn't have done it. I think it was my coping mechanism or something. I was so worried that I'd lose you to her. I was messing up left and right, putting us all in jeopardy and the process in limbo. It makes me sick to think about it."

There was a long pause, and I wasn't sure what his reaction was going to be. Fear started to creep into my mind as I began thinking about how selfish I sounded.

"Sweetie, it's okay. I understand. I'm so thankful you stayed strong, but you can't ever give up on us. There is always a way. Granted, I never had to deal with a situation quite like this with you. I can only imagine what you went through. Please don't let it eat you up."

My tears had no intention of stopping, and I felt the warmth of his arms wrap around me and wondered how I was so lucky to have him. I wasn't sure I wanted to hear anything else, but there was a part of me that longed to hear every detail, no matter how horrible.

***

The moment had finally arrived. Our family was going to become complete once again. I looked into Athen's eyes, and even though, they were still beautiful in this state, I couldn't wait for the familiar green to return to them.

The intense feeling of fire began spreading through my body, and I knew it would reach Athen's soon. I held on to his hand as much as I could considering the amount of pain that was darting through every inch of my body. I quickly thought back to when I was reintroduced. I had no idea that he was in agony as well. He never once mentioned it. He only appeared strong and concerned for my well-being. I hoped that I could someday be as strong as Athen was.

"I love you, baby." I heard his soothing voice hover in the air, and then he grabbed my hand with such a grasp, I knew the process had begun.

Arie and Cyril were in the corner of the room waiting helplessly as we both transferred as much energy as we could. The memories that were missing were being placed through his psyche. This time was so different than with me. He knew and remembered so much, I wasn't certain exactly what this process had in store for him.

Athen's eyes closed as the ache was no doubt becoming impossible to control. His body stiffening as the images continued to run through him. I placed my hand on his cheek, caressing it as best I could.

His voice quiet, but resolute as he uttered. "Never let me go."

"I never will, my love," I whispered into his ear, as I held him tightly as the pain ran through both of our bodies.

Not realizing that I would be seeing images from his time away from us, I was shocked beyond belief. I wanted to shield myself from the images that I was seeing, especially when Lilith would appear. The blazing pain was etching a semi-permanent mark on my heart. I wanted this to be over. I wanted the images to stop. The pain I could handle, but the images of Lilith and him over the last few months made a storm of emotions swell inside of me.

Seeing the agony on Athen's face as the pain ran through his body, I forced myself to get out of my own insecurities and be strong for him. He was here with me now, and that was what I needed to concentrate on. She was no longer part of our future. Not wanting to disrupt or impede the reintroduction process, I took a deep breath in, closing my eyes and began to allow the images to wash over me.

Not all images included Lilith, but the ones that did were like a knife right into my heart. They were together walking along the beach, and chatting at Starbucks together, going out to dinner and hanging out at someone's home. So far no pictures of her at the place he was staying emerged. I was secretly thankful for that.

Seeing Athen alone brought me the most solace. Invading his most private thoughts during this process was not something I expected. Following him on his journey to discover what he thought was going on was fascinating, but the images were so jumbled with the quickness that these thoughts were running between us, making it confusing.

Athen began to become restless. Opening my eyes and touching him with my other hand, I noticed the beads of sweat that were now canvassing his forehead. The process had only begun, but I knew we had a long journey ahead of us. I only hoped I could be as strong as he was for me, just a few short months ago.

***

Athen was sleeping quietly in our room. I snuck out to chat with Cyril and Arie for a little bit and get a refresher on some tea. After the reintroduction process, Athen was knocked out like I had been after mine only a few months before. However, he has been coming to earlier than I.

"So how's he doing?" Arie asked me, as I was steeping my loose tea.

"Like ten times better than I ever was. Somehow the memsors really seemed to have worked for him. Instead of him being flooded with memories like I was, it's like his mind is only having to sort them out. Hopefully it lasts, for his sake. Since I am still trying to figure things out from before, it would be wonderful if he could at least regain most of his memories pretty quickly."

"That would be nice. Wouldn't it?" Cyril asked. "Especially in light of everything."

Athen's voice came booming down the hall.

"In light of what?" Athen's words reached us all.

"What is he doing out of bed already?" I was shocked.

I ran down the hall to greet him as he made his way towards us all in the kitchen, hugging him as hard as I could.

"How are you up?" I asked him, holding on and not letting go. It took me days to get through the reintroduction process.

"I honestly couldn't do it anymore. There was no more sleep to be had. Besides, I think I remember just about everything or, at least, the important stuff," he said, gently touching my cheek softly.

I became completely flustered knowing exactly what he was thinking about and felt the heat wrap itself around my body in embarrassment as Cyril and Arie most certainly heard.

"Well, that's comforting," I whispered to him with a giggle.

We made our way into the kitchen where Cyril and Arie were both smiling widely. Arie had left the pot of stew on the stove on simmer to come and hug Athen. It was like heaven having him back in our lives. Everything was coming back to him so quickly. I can't even imagine how pitifully slow everything must have felt for them all when I was in the process.

"So, back to what Cyril was saying," Athen began. "What's going on that is so horrible? Have things ramped up that much since I was taken?"

He made his way to the table and pulled out a chair to sit, making me feel like maybe the whole process really had taken a toll, regardless of what it initially looked like.

"They are snatching family members left and right and interfering in the mortal world continually." Cyril sat down at the table as well, sipping on his water that Arie had laid out for us for dinner.

"Have you guys figured out why this is going on?" he asked, looking at me only.

I felt like he already knew.

"We've got some ideas but nothing concrete. Truthfully, we weren't giving it the attention it deserved. None of the families probably have, which is all part of the demons' master plan. Distract us enough, and they can continue the destruction with the mortals. We are just running around trying to reunite our families."

Athen grabbed my hand under the table. It was like nothing had happened to him. He was picking up right where he left off.

"Have you filled in Ana on her history? Her lineage?" he asked, staring directly at Cyril and Arie.

"Yes, we've told her who her father was, if that's what you're referring to." Arie nodded.

"What are you getting at?" I asked Athen, feeling my stomach begin to do flip-flops. Not understanding what my father, Remiel, would have to do with any of us. "Why is this suddenly about me again?"

"Well, Lilith didn't realize how astute I actually was so I was able to pay attention to some of her communications without her recognizing it," Athen started.

Again, hearing her name brought an anger within me that I hoped would soon subside.

"Azazel has been forming Legions all around the globe. They are preparing for a battle against us, and they aren't afraid to use humans as pawns. In fact, I think they prefer it. More at stake for us, don't you think? They've got a point to prove, and now, it is up to us to try to figure out what that point is," Cyril said.

"It certainly is Azazel and Asmodeus. Azazel is seeking revenge, and I'm guessing everyone in this room knows why, except for Ana. I think it is time to tell her the truth," Athen announced.

Chapter Twenty-Two

I was laying in bed, listening to the steady breaths of Athen beside me. Even though he had the ability to snap back to things far quicker than anyone thought possible, I knew he was still exhausted. I wanted him to be able to sleep, like I was allowed to only months before.

Learning what I had about my father Remiel, and why I'm now so tied to the events that were continuing to unfold before us, made me feel as if things were completely out of my control. By being in any proximity to me, I felt like I was putting everyone I knew in danger. Knowing that every event that was near, and every move that I'd make was going to possibly affect how the battles were fought was almost impossible to fathom. My family told me to put it out of my head and focus on the here and now. Truthfully, that was all I could do for the time being.

Snuggling slowly into Athen so that I wouldn't wake him up, I thought about everything he told me last night. He had known about my dreams the entire time. He saw what I had seen. I hadn't done a very good job of hiding my dreams from him. He was apparently able to see them all. He knew demons were going to attack him, and he was preparing for it. He felt he had a better shot at coming back quicker than I ever could, so he sacrificed himself for us.

Athen was also aware of something that I wasn't. If he hadn't been attacked and made himself the target, I would have been the victim, and the process would have been far worse to get me back the second time. He went into that battle on the hillside with the full knowledge that they would win – the demons would win, and he would not come out the other end. Athen had, however, began the process of memsors. He put all his energy into the process. Setting out memsors was almost a mythical process. Something everyone apparently knows about, but something seldom ever used since it hadn't always been known to work.

Athen had spent the weeks before practicing different techniques that allowed him to remember just enough to trigger memories. How Athen managed to pull it off was a miracle. He began by sticking a note under Matilda's collar. The tip under Matilda's collar was what seemed to have led to the chain of events that got him researching about everything. Since he knew Matilda would land wherever he was going to end up, he started with placing the initial clue with her. Some of the reminders led him to our home in Kingston and to that leather journal that I almost picked up and read so many times.

Knowing that he chose to get taken away from us to save me was beyond anything I could ever imagine. The bravery and strength it took for him to decide such a fate was the most selfless act I had ever encountered. I hoped one day, I could return the favor to show him that my love was equal to his.

I wondered if he knew about Lilith from my dreams. Maybe, that was why he wouldn't let himself get as close to her as she would have liked. I did my best to push those thoughts aside. I really didn't want to be plagued by anymore Lilith memories or worries.

Matilda was at the foot of our bed with no intention of waking up and between her little snores, and the comforting sounds of Athen breathing, I found my lids getting very tired with the idea of sleep seeming like something I needed.

***

I awoke to Athen holding me. I wasn't sure what had happened, but somehow, he was the one providing me comfort. I felt the heat rolling off of my body and realized I was covered in sweat. My pulse was racing, and my mind wouldn't stop spinning. I tried to get my bearings, but the visions I was trying to sort out were not willing to untangle. Everything was a fog, except for Athen. Athen was real. He was here, right next to me.

"It's okay, hun. You're okay. I'm here. Nothing is going to happen. I'm right here." Athen's words found their way to me just in time.

"What's going on?" I asked him, completely confused.

"You had a nightmare. I'm guessing it is going to begin coming back to you pretty quickly. I think it was a vision and not a good one."

I was doing my best to concentrate and think back to what it could be that caused my body to react like this. Only hours before I was in complete bliss, snuggling next to Athen. Nothing odd had popped into my head. I kept forcing myself to think about what could possibly have caused this.

"How did you know?"

"Your screams alerted us all, sweetie. Whatever it was, it wasn't good. You were hollering for people to run – to run from the fire. I couldn't decipher anything else. I kept hold of you as best I could."

Arie pushed open the door carrying a cup of tea over to me.

"Thanks."

Taking a sip of the burning liquid, shocked me into remembering the horrors from moments before.

I had to stop myself before I uttered something I might regret or wasn't certain of.

***

They were on their way. How many of them I wasn't sure, but I saw swarms of them in my dreams several weeks ago. Everyone had been alerted, but that didn't make waiting for the first round of attacks any easier. I was so thankful that I had Athen back with me now that I was willing to face about anything in order to keep him with me – or near me.

The word of my visions had been spread elsewhere, in case the Legions decided to involve more than only our immediate region. According to my vision, their plan was to begin attacking on the night of the Hunger Moon, and the Hunger Moon was tonight.

It was late afternoon now, and the dark skies began rolling in to welcome the night. We had devised a plan to attack in two stages, hoping to surprise the Legion members by having the second batch of us greet them with a renewed energy. Two rounds would be better than one. That was our hope anyway.

The front door was cracked open a little bit as if the uninvited guest wanted to make his presence known, teasing us some. I took a deep breath in as Athen pushed open the heavy, wood door leading into our home. Once he let go of my hand, I knew he was preparing for whatever fight might be waiting for us on the other side of the door.

What met us, however, was nothing but stale air. Our home was silent. No predators were in our space. I knew this for a fact, and judging by Athen's actions, he did too. They had been here, no doubt, but they were no longer here. Our plan was beginning to unravel piece by piece. Legion members were already supposed to be in our home waiting for us. Arie and Cyril were waiting in town and had planned on spacing their arrival to the home about ten minutes later than us, attempting to surprise the creatures with more of us than the demons' had initially planned.

Realizing now that things weren't going exactly like my premonition had laid them out, we knew we had better contact Arie and Cyril immediately. Athen dialed Cyril's cell only to be greeted by his voicemail. I looked out our living room window and saw a glow off in the distance and couldn't quite place what I was seeing. The orange glow seemed to be getting larger.

"Huh, that's odd." Athen looked at me with his eyebrows raised in a concerned expression. "You would think of all times to want to stay connected, this would be one of them..."

"Look out the window! What is that?"

He dialed Arie's cell and same thing – straight to voicemail.

We moved closer to the window unsure of exactly what we were seeing, not really wanting to believe what might be in front of us, growing by the second.

"Something's not right, hun. I don't have a good feeling," Athen said, leading us to the couch. "Are you doing okay with everything?"

I looked at him in utter disbelief. I should be the one asking him that. He was the one who only recently came back to us. This entire process with him has been screwy from the beginning, so I don't know why I was expecting anything different.

"Yeah, I'm doing fine. It's you I should be worried about. You're handling everything like a pro," I said, placing my head on his chest. We had sat on the couch near the window so we could see anything or anyone coming up to the house. Neither of us wanted to admit what we thought we were seeing off in the distance until we could deny it no longer. Tiny sparks of orange began flying into the skyline, and I was sure of it now. Fires were being set. There had been small peaceful protests earlier in the day over the decision the game department had made to euthanize the cougars that were suspected in the human attacks, rather than removal and relocation. Unfortunately, only the underworld knew it wasn't the cougars attacking at all, and the deaths would be for nothing. Apparently, the protests were peaceful no more.

Athen reached for his phone again and tried Cyril's number on speakerphone.

"Hello?" Cyril was breathing heavily into the phone. It sounded like he was running somewhere. I could hear lots of commotion in the background.

"Hey, what's going on?" Athen asked.

"Nothing good. I can tell you that. How are things at the house?" he asked, as I heard Arie's voice coming over the phone yelling to someone to get down.

"Things are going too good here. Absolutely nothing, actually... Do you need our help?"

I could hear screams coming over the phone, sirens next.

"No, stay where you are. Things are getting hectic over here, and I think we'll do better apart dealing with whatever might be coming our way. Ana was right. The attacks are beginning. Unfortunately, it doesn't look like it was only us who were the target. We'll get a handle on things and come home."

Arie was in the background trying to calm down a child who was looking for her parents. I had no idea what was going on, but it sounded horrible.

"What the heck is going on over there?" Athen asked.

"Well, let's see, in this area of the town we have fires being set, and across town sounds like mobs are beginning to form."

"Alright, well keep us posted." He hung up the phone and slowly placed it in on the couch arm, balancing it carefully as we were taking in information. Sensing my fear, he kissed the top of my head.

"Guess the plans have changed."

I was wracking my brain trying to think of anything that would have foreshadowed this and was coming up with nothing – absolutely nothing. This wasn't part of what I saw in my visions. It seems like the game plan was doing a compete reversal, or it was meant as a distraction. Athen tightened his arm around me, and I was so grateful for his touch again. His strength created a calming force that I needed more than anything right now. I had readied myself all week for this encounter with the demons in our home only to be left with nothing of the sort. Instead, humans were turning against each other and creating havoc in their own town.

A large group of people were making their way down the street, passing right by our home waving things that were on fire, going who knows where. My hands began to get clammy. I didn't understand what was going on. We were set to fight the Legion members, privately in our home - tonight. Instead, it looked like the Legions were set on messing with the humans, persuading them to take to the streets. Seeing the strangers' images reflecting from the faint streetlights holding up their arms chanting, made me almost more frightened of them than the demons themselves.

"Do we really stay inside and do nothing?" I asked Athen. "I don't like the thought of Cyril and Arie out there in this mess. Lord knows what could happen."

"They will be home soon, sweetie. I think they want to check on everything, scope it out so we know what might be next. They won't put themselves in danger. There is only so much we can do."

His words did little to calm me as I waited for Cyril and Arie to return to our home, while watching the mobs of people walking and chanting, with fists full of fire.

Chapter Twenty-Three

"Looks like my vision struck out," I announced, rather deflated, at the breakfast table.

"Doubtful." Arie looked up from her oatmeal. "My guess is the timing was just off. We need to stay vigilant, keep an eye out. I think what you saw, here in the house is still a high possibility. If you saw an attack in the house, I'd count on an attack in the house."

"Not exactly what I wanted to hear."

"Will the city go back to normal?" I was afraid to go into town for what I might see. The destruction that Cyril and Arie described sounded horrible and, in some cases, irreparable. Hearing the screams over the phone and seeing the mobs of flame-carrying people was more than I could understand, especially when thinking about this quaint little area. The worst part was knowing this was all being orchestrated by the demons.

"The Legions know what they're doing. They are definitely stirring it up and keeping us off guard."

"I'd say it was working." I looked directly Athen, hoping he would chime in, and he did.

"You're right. It's working, and it shouldn't be. We've got to stop falling for their traps." His voice was angry. "No more being reactive. We've got to start being proactive, or the battle is already lost," Athen said.

"Yeah, I get it, but we are trying... Right? Here we thought we were going to trick the demons last night that were supposedly waiting for us to fight me in the house. Well, that didn't pan out. We can only play the game when the rules are somewhat consistent. As of now, nothing is off limits, and the rules keep changing. Hard to be proactive with those factors." I was incensed at being accused of not being proactive. Under the circumstances, we were all doing our best.

"We've got to figure out what they really want," Athen chided. "Or maybe admit that we already know," he said, looking at me.

"Well, yeah." Cyril rolled his eyes. "If it were that easy, we wouldn't be talking about it."

"Or are we all gonna keep dancing around things like Ana can't handle the facts. It's her truth for crying out loud." Athen was full-fledged yelling now. Anything to do with me, and his emotions seemed to come unglued. I wasn't sure if it was because of the process he just barely went through or what.

"I thought you guys had told me everything?" My interest level now up tenfold. "What's Athen talking about?" I stood up and went to stand behind Athen's chair glaring at Arie and Cyril.

"What aren't you telling me this time?"

"It's not for sure. That's why we didn't tell you." Arie's voice was almost unintelligible.

"Well, might as well now. Don't you think?" I asked, this time looking directly at Cyril. He looked at Arie and nodded his head.

"It has to do with a relationship of sorts, at least that is our theory."

"My dad? Remiel?"

"Partly, but there's more. It was a complicated relationship and seemed to have far-reaching consequences."

I knew I was going to be in for a long conversation. I only hoped it would provide some answers that I so desperately needed.

"You're actually more like your mother than your father." Athen began.

The weight of what he implied hit me hard. Wondering what my mother had to do with any of this, my head began shaking in confusion. We weren't really ever aware of our mortal parents, and I didn't see the significance of what he was trying to tell me. The mortals were often extinguished right after our births.

"I don't understand what you're getting at. There's not a reason in the world that's relevant." Still shaking my head in confusion, I looked over at Athen hoping to see doubt in his eyes about what he was about to say. There was none.

"What we are facing is something deep-seated in the mythology. We were all hoping it wasn't pointing to it, but there's no way around it."

"Well, I'm not going to live in fear. Why don't you tell me where you're going with this?"

"Your mother was very captivating, to say the least. Just like you," Athen whispered. Catching

Cyril roll his eyes, I couldn't help but chuckle, even though I knew what I was going to be told would change everything.

"Alright, keep truckin'..." My eyebrows seemed to be stuck in a perpetually confused state, and the strain was wearing me out. I needed to hear it; whatever it was.

"Your mother loved only your father. She chose him from many. Their love was like no other. There was one individual who we all have come to find out about recently, who wasn't accepting of that. He felt your mother should have been with him. Your mother never intended for that scenario to even be in the picture. She was quite disgusted by his persistence, and your father stepped in. He had no choice. Your mother's life was in danger."

"Why is that coming back to us now?" I was worried for what was going to come next.

"Because it was Azazel who was in love with your mother. He has never forgiven your father, and apparently, you're the next best thing."

The words Athen finished with shook through my body, carrying with it the weight of the world. Things were beginning to make a lot more sense now and, at the same time, making absolutely no sense at all.

Not wanting to speak the words going through my mind over and over again, I shut my eyes, pretending I was by myself and wouldn't hear the answer. Mind games could always be counted on to cover up for my weaknesses.

My voice left my body. "Can we end it? Do we even have a shot if it's me he's after?"

Athen reached over and pulled me to him.

"We won't give up, if that's what you mean."

That's not what I meant, but the answer would have to do for now.

**

After roaming our home in a zombie-like state, carrying the burden of the knowledge I now had haunting my every move, I decided a change of scenery was definitely in order. Hoping that a trip back to Whistler would bring me the comfort I longed for, remembering all the wonderful times I shared with Athen during the entire reintroduction process I went through, and the amount of love that we had shared made me hopeful that was the exact place to be to get my mind sorted.

I was able to convince everyone that a trip to Whistler was a good idea. It didn't take much effort. We had wanted to check on everything and everyone who was up there. Things had been very rough on us all, but the main excitement it seemed for Cyril and Arie was the thought of more training, flying and shapeshifting. The thought of one, let alone both, freaked me out.

The Sea to Sky highway taking us up to the village was going to be pretty much free and clear of snow. There was still snow on top of Whistler Mountain, and the diehards were up there soaking up every last second of skiing, but down in the village, it would be almost spring-like.

Athen had already gotten what few belongings he had at the other place where he was staying all this time. I wasn't really positive if I wanted to come back to Victoria, but I felt that the away time, even though short, would be good. Maybe, I'd be able to return to the home in Victoria with a fresh slate, Athen by my side. Those words alone were enough to make me float away.

Having him back was my own form of ecstasy. His beautiful green eyes always shining kindly at me, along with his amazing thoughtfulness, would never get old. It was as if we never missed a beat, the last few months were turning into a distant nightmare, or so I told myself.

Athen had taken Matilda out for a walk at the local park, and I was getting the rest of the things packed up. Trying not to let my mind wander to a place I didn't want to go, I found Cyril and Arie in the living room to distract me. They seemed a little disturbed themselves, which struck me as odd, but they had their bags all ready and waiting by the entry.

"Well, you look a little nervous," Arie said, teasing me. Not really being in the mood, I glared at her, shoving away the guilt for doing that to such a nice person.

"Too soon?" she asked grinning.

"Alright, yes, I'm scared to death that Lilith will sink her teeth into him while he's out and about." It felt kind of good to get it out in the open. "Blah, blah, I know I don't need to worry about it, but it's hard not to."

Right on cue, Athen opened the front door with Matilda leading the way. Scanning the room, Athen darted over to me, whipping an entire bunch of white roses out from behind him. My fears instantly melted away, leaving nothing but a dose of foolishness in its trail for letting my paranoia get the better of me. Hoping Cyril and Arie would keep quiet, I did my best at shooting them a stare as Athen grabbed me.

"I thought you needed more than that spindly one you had hanging upside down on the wall." My cheeks immediately filled with the blush that only he could produce.

"Thank you, my love," I whispered.

Matilda was already standing back at the door, obviously waiting for her next adventure. Having missed her for so long, it was fine with me if she got to call the shots as we all proceeded to the door for our trip up north.

***

Whistler greeted us with the warmth that I'd missed so greatly while down south. The familiarity was plastered all over the buildings, statues, and sidewalks creating an excitement for the days to come. But that was knocked down as we turned onto the drive leading us to our home. That's when, unexpectedly, my nerves began to surface a bit. I wasn't sure what exactly was signaling for me to be so cautious, but I began to feel that a lot of things had shifted far more than we realized.

"You feeling that?" I asked.

"Sure am," Cyril answered.

We pulled into our garage, full of uncertainty. Athen grabbed my hand for a quick squeeze before we all got out of the car. Matilda was still sleeping hard so we let her stay behind.

"Let's go check everything out before we grab our bags, okay?" Arie suggested.

"Sounds like a plan." Athen nodded.

As the door swung open, a wave of cold air blasted us all. The demons had been there and recently.

"I thought they didn't come inside our homes much?" I asked, perplexed.

"They tend not to, but I think it's safe to say that they're on a mission and being that it involves us, the rules are changing quickly," Cyril said, as he went through the pantry cautiously.

Cyril and Arie's movements were very calculating and deliberate. They weren't taking this latest violation lightly, which signaled that I shouldn't either. Following their lead, I lightened my footsteps and did my best to become noiseless. Athen was right behind me, quietly closing the door.

As I was making my way to the kitchen, Athen's hand grabbed mine, jerking me to a complete stop. Confused, I turned to look at him, realizing he didn't want me in front of him. I rolled my eyes jokingly and let him move ahead of me. Being that he had only recently come back to us, it was hard to fathom that his skill and strength far exceeded mine. There was a small part of me that was secretly relieved, because I knew, for whatever reason, his fighting level was far better.

Cyril went to the right towards the living room with Arie following behind, and I followed Athen up the stairs to our bedrooms. With every step leading us higher up the stairs, the chill became more and more evident. Once we reached the top, Athen signaled for us to go to our room first. The door was closed, which I knew was different from when we left at the holidays.

Athen grabbed the door handle, turning it slightly, able to open it only a few inches before a crunching sound stopped the movement. Athen jiggled the door a few more times with no success. He shook his head at me, and I reached for the handle myself, moving the door back and forth a few times.

"It's like it's chained from the inside," I whispered. I ran across the hall to check on Cyril and Arie's door, which flew right open. Spinning back around, Cyril and Arie were up the stairs signaling the all-clear for the downstairs of the home.

I shook my head at them and pointed at our door.

"I think it's chained up," I whispered to them.

Completely perplexed, they went over to the door and had the same success as us – none.

"That's weird," Arie muttered.

"Yeah, tell me about it," Athen said. "I think we should bust it down. I don't think anyone's here."

"I agree," seconded Arie.

"I'll let you take that one," I said to Athen. "I don't want to give myself a concussion. Plus, you need the practice." Trying to stifle a nervous laugh, I patted his butt.

Backing up only a foot he rammed into the door, breaking it into thousands of tiny splinters, inviting us all to stare at an extremely disturbing sight. Athen backed up, grabbing me as if to shield me from the images.

Silver chains were dripping from the ceiling, windows, and across all the doors. There were pictures of Athen and Lilith hanging from the links, along with splashes of red spattered on the walls, our bed, and the pictures themselves. I hoped with everything that it wasn't blood canvassing our room but knowing who we were dealing with, only secured that thought.

"Wow, this is pretty creepy." I tried my best to sound unaffected, but it wasn't coming across that way. My voice was barely able to complete a sentence without cracking.

Feeling the tiny twinges of jealousy begin to rise in my abdomen, I knew I was falling right into the hands of the demons. This is what they wanted, and I was determined to be stronger than that. Following Athen into our bedroom, I did my best not to acknowledge the images that were glaring at me from all directions.

Athen's finger ran along the chains, stopping only to rip off the picture dangling directly in front of him. Trying not to let the sadness begin to infiltrate my entire being, I looked away before taking the two figures in completely. What I did see implied a closeness - one that I wasn't willing to accept.

Hearing the chains clank loudly, I looked over at Cyril and Arie who were dismantling the pieces of silver as fast as they could. I began doing the same as quickly as possible and avoided the areas where the photographs hung. The rage was building inside of me, and I knew I needed a place to let it all out.

"So is it animal or human blood?" I asked, not sure why I picked that topic to distract myself with.

"It's not human," was all Cyril said, knowing neither answer he gave would be a good one.

Running down the stairs to get cleaning supplies, I vowed revenge like no other on Lilith. Remembering what my family had told me about the semi-purgatory realm where our kind, good or evil, could be sent, I made it a personal mission to make sure she was going to be sent there. I only had to figure out how.

Chapter Twenty-Four

Not having our quick trip to Whistler begin how we had expected, we decided to spend the rest of our time up here training exclusively. I had managed to avoid my friends back in the village, the last couple of days, to recuperate from being accosted in our home. However, one of the things that Cyril and Arie had wanted us to practice needed someone who I knew or had a past with. Apparently, shapeshifting was easier when your victim was more trusting. I wasn't looking forward to betraying Karen's trust in that way, but no longer had a choice. These things couldn't wait a second more.

Standing in the gondola line, the backpack I was wearing began to feel like a ton of bricks had been placed on my shoulders. Our goal was to hike from the top of the mountain back away so that both Athen and I could work on the things we were most likely to need in the near future. I had learned so many things while he was away, that I was actually excited to finally learn some of these last few items with him present. There was still snow at the top of the mountain so we were all dressed from head to toe in snow gear.

As we made our way to the gondola awaiting our entrance, I tripped over the post that held us all in line, bringing Athen and Cyril to a roar of laughter.

"So predictable," Cyril said, patting my shoulder. "Good thing you're a little more graceful when fighting."

"Don't jinx it," I scolded him.

The doors of the gondola slammed shut with a thud, leading to the jerking motion as the cables started hauling us up the mountain to our training grounds. As our ascent began, the cold slowly began trickling in through the crevices of the metal doors that were holding us in. Leaving the village behind, I began snuggling into Athen as the normally mammoth hotels became smaller and smaller with every minute traveled. So much had happened since the last time we were here together. My role in this life was beginning to become clearer, and my strength was beginning to become stronger and stronger, especially as I held onto Athen.

Still faulting myself for feeling I wasn't as emotionally strong as he had been for all those decades, I hoped that I could somehow make it up to him and begin to forgive myself.

The windows were completely fogged up by the time our thirty minute gondola ride spilled us onto our final destination. I was relieved to be breathing in the cold, fresh air of the mountain rather than the stale air of the gondola.

"Okay, up this way." Cyril pointed towards the side slope where no one seemed to be headed, for good reason. The mountainside was extremely steep and icy.

I was thankful when we arrived at our destination. There was a little plateau where we would be able to practice our attacks and plenty of trees at the far end if we wanted to give a go on our climbing and flying skills.

"Well, this is certainly beautiful," I muttered to Athen, dumping my backpack off. "Are you ready?"

"The question is, are you ready?" he asked, winking at me but not before embracing me in his arms, shooting into the sky. My heart began pounding outside of my chest, realizing how high Athen had me in the air. We were flying. He was flying.

"Oh my God, Athen. I can't believe you remember how to do this. It's beautiful," I said, squeezing onto him as hard as I possibly could. "Are you sure you remember how to land?" I asked him, only somewhat teasing him.

"Do you want to find out now or just keep going?" His eyes were twinkling with the mischief that I'd missed so much over the last few months.

"No, I could get used to this."

"That's good because it's gonna be your turn soon," he said, coyly.

"So did Cy and Arie already know that you could do this?" I asked, in complete awe of my surroundings and the strength that I felt in Athen's arms as we were sailing with the wind.

"Yeah, they knew it. It was a surprise for you. Let's go to that tree over there," he said, and before realizing it, we had already landed at the very top.

Feeling the branches swaying, I knew we shouldn't both be up top.

Letting go of Athen, I made my way from treetop to treetop. My concentration was completely focused on making my landings as graceful as possible. I wanted him to be proud of the progress that I had made while he was gone. Since, apparently, this was truly a train Ana session, not Athen.

Athen was now directly behind me. I spun around seeking his approval and saw far more than that in his eyes.

"Beautiful, my angel. You're amazing to be able to do that already. You should be so proud of yourself." He flew over to the limb I was balancing on, hugging me with the pride I was hoping for during the many times I tried when he wasn't around. Images of me practicing without him at the Bog at Butchart Gardens and up on top of a cliff began filling my mind, thankful that those images were no longer my reality. I had Athen here with me now, and I wasn't going to miss a second of his smile as I did my best to learn.

"Thanks. But after you flying all around with me, I feel like I'm way behind the times."

"Honey, there's a big difference between what I went through and what you went through. You've got to trust us when we tell you that you're doing amazing. I was basically gone for days compared to your decades."

"I love you."

"I love you too, but you aren't getting out of it. You wanna give it a try? Babysteps maybe?" he said laughing.

The anticipation began building deep inside as I thought about all the freedom this could mean. My hope was that the fear that was riding alongside it wouldn't win. Looking into Athen's eyes, I knew I'd be fine. If I were to fall, he would catch me. That I was sure of.

"Okay. I'm ready." Nodding my head trying to convince myself more than Athen, he grabbed me and hugged me tightly as we sailed down to the snow patch that was still hiding under the shade of the trees. I didn't want to let go. Catching that feeling, he didn't let go either.

"If you aren't ready, you don't have to do this," he whispered, the breath catching my hair like the many nights I knew I hadn't been alone.

"Nope, I got it."

Waiting for him to let me go, I got my nerve up. It had to happen sooner or later. Not expecting him to let go quite so quickly, my breath got caught in my throat, and before I knew it, the instruction had begun.

"So everything that you've learned about feeling where you want to be, or what you want to do is applied directly the same, except that you can't break concentration – at all. If you think of it with your climbing and jumping abilities now, you focus on a target, and you mentally end your journey before it has even begun. If it is the treetop that you are stopping at, then that is where it is. You have stopped before you started, essentially. Imagine never having an end point. Theoretically you could keep going, right?"

"You're trying to tell me that if I didn't tell myself the stopping point was the top of the tree, I would keep going?" There was no way I could hide my skepticism, but I, also, knew that it was exactly what he was telling me.

"Yeah, you're creating your own limits. You're the only one who can change that. You can create your boundaries, your stopping points, or whatever will get you to where you need to go. The speed will come. Don't even think about that right now."

"What about stopping, like landing? That seems like it would be a little dicey. But pretty important."

Arie and Cyril were making their way over to where Athen and I were standing. I was grateful for the idea of more people to possibly catch me when I fell from whatever mishap I was about to get myself into.

"Don't be worried, Ana! You're gonna do awesome!" I was extremely thankful for Arie's exuberance because I wasn't feeling it at all.

"When you're ready to land, picture yourself a few feet above the ground as a stopping point. It makes for an easier landing." Cyril did his best dive bomb motion to drive home the point, with a smile of course.

I was worried if I took my hands out of my pockets, it would be a complete giveaway for how nervous I was, but I still needed them to get where I was going. I'd done so much practicing in front of Arie and Cyril that I began to feel a little sheepish in front of Athen, especially with how graceful he already was with everything.

"You're gonna rock it, Ana. I promise," Athen said, winking at me.

And with that, I was off. I pointed myself away from the trees, arms stretched, and adrenaline pumping, reaching for a nothingness that was sure to hold my body weight. Feeling the energy build through my body, I sprung into the air, the promise of flight close enough to let the fear slowly drain from my system. I was above the earth, and there was no tree for me to cling onto for my next landing. I looked over to the left and felt my entire body shift to the direction that I was looking. I continued ascending higher and higher, matching my height equal to when I scaled the conifers. The pride in my ability was beginning to swell inside of me.

The freedom of what this meant kept me going, and before I knew it, Athen was by my side, following my every move as we floated through the sky with what felt like lightning speed but was only a fraction of our potential. Afraid to reach for him, I only smiled as we glided along the tree line.

"I told you my angel could fly."

"Only this time, I'm not harnessed onto the zipline, right?" I was afraid to say too much and lose my ability to control where my body was flying.

"Yeah, exactly," he said, laughing. "Who knew this would all be happening so quickly though?"

"Glad you think I'm learning quickly, but I feel like I'm only holding us all back. Especially with you barely returning to us and picking up where you left off basically... *showoff*."

"What was that? I couldn't hear you?"

It was pretty windy whipping around everywhere, but when I went to repeat myself, he rolled his eyes and sailed off, calling me over to follow him. I saw a fairly flat surface ahead of us and was hoping that maybe that would be where I'd attempt my first and, hopefully, not last landing. I wanted to end on a good note.

"Ready?" he asked. "Think above where you want to land," Athen said, landing as graceful as ever, walking into his landing more than anything.

Concentrating so hard on not landing on the ground but above it. I felt my feet searching for something that wasn't where I thought it was. I was sure I was only a foot or two off the ground at the most, but I was pretty certain that would hurt just as much. Kicking my feet frantically as I attempted to land, a squeal escaping into a scream exploded out of me, but not before Athen was there helping me down to a soft landing on my knees somehow.

"Oh my, god. I almost face planted." My heart was beating so fast. Here I'd been flying, literally flying, and could have created a catastrophe for myself when only dealing with the last three feet of landing space. "How long is the landing thing going to take? That seems kind of important." I asked breathless.

Athen was grinning, his eyes taking me in as if I'd achieved some sort of greatness that I could never understand.

"It'll come. Maybe another time or two, Ana - that's all." He was already praising me to Cyril and Arie, who had decided to come over and meet us with my backpack in hand from up on the mountain.

"Nice work out there, Ana," Cyril said, shaking his head. "I'm surprised, for sure. I thought you'd have mud stains, or something signaling some sort of run in with the dirt."

"Nice, Cy. Thanks for the support. Remind me to only practice in the snowy areas so you can't fault me for my landing techniques."

"No, kid. You did awesome. Really," he said, swatting at me and missing, grabbing Arie's hand instead.

"We don't need to take the gondola down, you know," she chuckled and hopped on Cyril's back as he began cruising down the mountain before I could object.

"Well? Hop on?" Athen said, reaching for my arm, spinning me towards him.

"Alright, buddy, but you better be careful. After all, you're the newbie in all this." Unable to hide my grin at the thought of being able to hold onto him for the entire ride down the mountain, I hopped on his back and wrapped my legs around his waist as we took off down after Cyril and Arie, who had surely made it down a third of the mountain.

Chapter Twenty-Five

The excitement level from my earlier adventures on the mountain was pretty hard to hide, but I did my best to help Arie make dinner as the guys went walking Matilda. We'd decided that this was going to be the last night we spent in before making contact with everyone in the village. Time was ticking, and we couldn't afford to be up in Whistler having fun that much longer before confronting some of the issues down below that had been brewing.

Besides learning what I had on the side of the mountain, I needed some time to absorb the idea of using my poor innocent friends as target practice for my shapeshifting lessons that were next on the agenda. It was hard to justify what I was going to be doing to Karen. Supposedly, even if I messed something up badly, my family could intervene and help to make the memories disappear. Karen was going to be my first attempt. Being that she was my closest friend in Whistler from before, and our comfort level was as close as it ever could be with me; she was my best shot.

Apparently after the skill was learned, it doesn't matter friend or foe, stranger or not, anyone can be fair game. When beginning, the comfort level needs to be there with the alleged target or victim. That's where poor Karen comes into the equation. Since I was close to so few people, she was the lucky one. Thankfully, she's already excited to get together tomorrow, which was half the battle. Arie promised to show me the end result with a stranger in the morning, but it was all me in the afternoon with Karen.

I was mindlessly chopping the garlic for the stew when I noticed Arie standing by the sink, blankly staring out the kitchen window. The sun had almost set, but the wooden blinds were still pulled halfway down, from the earlier sunshine.

"What's up?" I asked Arie. "Everything okay?"

"Oh, yeah. Totally," she said, shaking her head, trying her best to convince me that she was fine.

"Well, I don't believe it, so why don't you tell me what's going on? It's high time the world doesn't keep revolving around me. I'd like to know."

Arie turned to look at me, her eyes distant and reflecting something far different than what was on the mountainside only hours earlier. A frailty began to emerge that I'd never seen before from her usually bubbly self.

Pulling her over to the kitchen table, I cleared off a section of the groceries, we still had to put away, making way for whatever was about to spill out of Arie.

"Have you noticed anything off about Cyril?" she asked point blank, her eyes tracing mine for any sign of insincerity or answer to her unasked questions.

Startled by the direction of this conversation, I took a moment to gather my thoughts, thinking back quickly to all the times I'd spent with Cyril over the last few weeks and guiltily realizing how little time I really paid attention to much of anything besides myself and Athen.

"I... I don't know. I don't think so. Like what?" I uttered back, completely puzzled.

She was shaking her head, reaching for the grapes that were on the table in the fruit bowl.

"Don't know how to explain it... Shouldn't probably even be talking about it, really. I'm sure it's nothing. I..."

"You've got to talk to someone about it, right? That's what you're always telling me." I did my best to smile but was deeply concerned with her lack of discussion. Knowing the guys would be back soon, I knew I had to prod to get it out of her.

"Where's this coming from? Since when are you noticing anything? I'm not saying there isn't something going on, but I honestly have been too wrapped up in my own stuff, and for that I apologize. But you've got to give me some clues."

"I don't know. I really don't know," she reiterated again, shaking her head.

"Yes, you do, Arie. You wouldn't have said anything if you didn't."

She was quiet for several minutes, and I wasn't sure if I'd pressed my luck until I heard the sigh escape from her.

"It started right before Athen came back. I noticed that he had been more impatient with you. You probably didn't even notice with everything going on, but I did. I dismissed it though. Then he began to pull back from me a little. I'd start to talk with him, and he didn't want to hear it. Didn't seem to matter what the topic was. He changed the subject and... now, it's like he doesn't really want to be close."

"It didn't seem like that on the mountain?" I gently offered, not wanting to contradict what she was dealing with too harshly.

"No, you're right. Coming down the mountain was great, but have you noticed, it's not like he's been doing that all the time lately. I mean, come on, think about how he always acted with me when you first came back into our lives. It was like he and Athen were always competing to see who could be the better gentleman, or who could impress us the best. I know it sounds petty, and now that I'm saying it out loud, it doesn't even make sense."

"No, I kind of see what you mean. But, truthfully, I chalked it up to him not wanting to rub everything in my face with Athen gone for so long."

"Well, Athen's back, and the old Cyril isn't."

Keys in the front door signaled the end to our conversation. Reaching over to pat Arie's hand, I was at a complete loss for words and couldn't wait to see Athen turn the corner into the kitchen.

As if a direct page out of Arie's worst speculation, Athen came into the kitchen, letting go of Matilda and grabbing me up from the chair instead, swinging me around and kissing me on the cheek.

"Miss me?" he asked chuckling.

"You didn't give me enough time to," I whispered wryly, glancing over at Cyril who briefly touched Arie's shoulder before heading upstairs. Hoping she wouldn't notice that I caught the interaction, I buried my head into Athen's neck.

"Alright, that's enough. Dinner's still not quite there yet." Not wanting to push him away but doing so for Arie's sake, I spun around to grab the spatula and continued on where Arie left off. The conversation would have to wait.

***

The morning's sunshine was beating through the window as I was nestled in Athen's arms. Feeling the firmness of Athen's embrace, I wriggled in deeper hoping to stretch out the minutes that much longer before getting up to start the day's training activities.

Before going to bed the night before, we decided to get through the last of the training up here and feel out the situations before heading back to Victoria.

"Wanna get up?" Athen whispered.

"Umm, no. I'd like to stay right here, thank you." I pulled the covers up that much more for extra effect, loving the feeling of his skin next to mine.

"Yeah, tell me about it." He rolled over me, his arms surrounding my shoulders, kissing my forehead ever so gently. "We've got to squash these Legions. It's really interfering with us."

"Tell me about it." I rolled my eyes. "You know it actually is. It's like this nonstop chase is all I've known since coming back. I start to get comfortable loving you again, and something disrupts it. Never mind the poor people that they are trying to attack. It's all about me," I said laughing, throwing the covers off of me as I did my best to distract myself from watching Athen get ready for the day. Hearing about Arie's struggles the night before created an odd attachment to Athen, even more.

"Has your sister talked to you about anything recently?" I asked, throwing him his robe to take in with him to the shower.

"No, not like anything out of the ordinary. Why?" He had the shower running, probably not expecting a conversation to possibly turn the way it might if I fully brought up her suspicions.

"No reason. She seemed a little down was all." I did my best to brush it off as he climbed into the shower, and I decided to make my entrance into the world for the day by making the pot of coffee for everyone and escape the closeness the shower could possibly bring us.

Arie was already waiting in the kitchen, presumably for me, because as soon as I entered she pounced.

"I hope you don't think I'm imagining things or making something out of nothing. It's probably nothing," she said immediately.

"Trust your gut, Arie. Whatever it is you're noticing, it's wearing you out. The usual perky Arie has vanished since about 4 pm last night, and I'm not used to it." Grinding the coffee beans gave me a chance to formulate what I should or shouldn't say. I didn't really want to mention that I'd seen Cyril barely giving her the time of day.

"Not to sound ridiculous, but have you talked to him about it?"

"Yeah, actually. Last night I brought it up. Didn't go so well."

"Like how? He brushed it off?"

"I wish. He got angry, and he's never ever gotten angry over something petty like that. I only asked if anything was bothering him because he seemed tense, and for the first time ever, we went to bed not holding each other."

"I doubt it's anything that has to do with you. Something's gotta be bugging him and since you're the closest to him, he's taking it out on you. I know how much he loves you, and you do too. We'll get to the bottom of it. Where's he at now?"

"Went to grab some breakfast stuff from the bakery. Hope that's the only reason."

Seeing Arie like this was so painful. I never imagined her to be in this situation or even ever to have a worry or care in the world. I was going to talk to Athen about it. In case, he knew something we didn't. Hopefully, Cyril has opened up to him about something at some point.

"Are you gonna be okay with everything we are trying to stick in for today's plan? I don't want to press you to do anything. It can wait."

"Thanks, Ana. But you know as well as I do, it can't wait. We've got to get this last piece of training started. This is going to be the most difficult to get the hang of. Guarantee it."

The door from the garage opened, and I did my best to act normal.

"What are you two up to in there, huh? Scheming away?" Cyril asked, seemingly like his old self. I found myself watching Arie's every movement, rather than his. Maybe, it was her who began the cycle, and he can sense her discomfort or something. He seemed happy and completely like I was used to. The coffee maker beeped, letting me know that I could finally get my hands on the best wake up method I knew. Grabbing two mugs from the cabinet, I poured the steaming liquid into both, hollering to Cyril and Arie on my way out of the kitchen to help themselves as I headed back up to our bedroom to talk with Athen before we started our day in the village.

Shapeshifting seemed a little terrifying to say the least, but Cyril and Arie were set on showing me how to do it, so that over time I'd get the hang of it again. I was excited to see it because they had always kept this part from me. It's kind of terrifying thinking that they could be in someone else's body, and I might not even know it. Actually, it was frightening to think that I could be in someone else's body, never mind them.

Truthfully, I think they were trying to come up with things to keep my mind occupied and somewhat focused, rather than what I'd really like to do which was stare at a wall and think of Athen or, actually, stare at Athen and forget the wall.

Athen was pulling the wool sweater over his head as I closed the door quickly to our bedroom and placed the mugs of coffee on the nightstand.

"Okay, your sister is completely convinced that something is going on with Cyril. Have you noticed anything?"

"To be honest, I've been so occupied with eating up every second that I can spend with you that I haven't been paying much attention to them on that level." He kind of grimaced in embarrassment, exactly how I'd felt the night before.

"Yeah, that's kind of what I told her too."

Athen came over to me, wrapping his arms around my waist, the tie on my robe getting in the way of his hold.

"Are you after me or the coffee behind me?"

"Both!" he said, grinning and letting go to reach for the mug as I went to the bathroom to shower.

"The things she was mentioning kind of clicked as she spoke about them, but they weren't anything that I'd noticed until she pointed them out."

"Like what?" he asked, now in the bathroom sipping his coffee.

"Well, the level of affection or lack of it compared to normal. I chalked it up to him not wanting to make things worse on me while you were gone, but she said it's been since you were back too. I kind of saw it last night... I think. Or I could just be on high alert now that she mentioned it. Either way, she's really worried about it and focusing on it. So he hasn't mentioned anything to you?" The spray of the shower alerting my muscles to the previous day's activities, I stood in place letting the warmth penetrate me to my core.

"No, he hasn't mentioned a thing. I'll check it out though."

"Thanks. I thought we should be on the same page in case it actually meant something along the way. I hope not, though."

"Yeah, me too. I'll meet you out in the living room."

***

Arie was attempting to be back to her bubbly self, but there was no way she could fake that totally. A bit of her sparkle was definitely missing.

We had all ventured to one of the parking lots closest to the village where the day visitors often parked. Everyone thought it was best to show me the first of the shapeshifting with people who would be gone from here as fast as they came. The gravel crunched as we all found our way towards the back of the lot, near where all the RVs were sitting.

"So are you gonna pounce on the first poor soul who wanders by, or how is this whole training by example thing supposed to work?" I asked, completely perplexed.

"Probably the first person who wanders by," Arie said laughing.

"And they won't remember a thing?" I asked, not understanding the process.

"Not a thing." Athen stepped up behind me and rubbed my shoulders like I was getting ready for something myself.

The far off crunching began to reach us as we realized our first target was coming up quicker than we thought. Whoever it was they were blocked by all the cars that were parked up and down the aisles, so we had no idea whether it was male or female, old or young. The butterflies began stirring inside as their steps became louder and louder. I followed Arie's every move, watching for any sort of preparation that I might need to learn. As usual, there didn't seem to be any. She stepped out from where we were all standing to the major throughway of the lot, readying herself for her victim.

She smiled and nodded at the man who had stopped right in front of her. He seemed friendly and helpful. He was dressed in khaki shorts and a green polo, probably in Whistler to enjoy a day of drinking and hiking. I grabbed for Athen's hand right before the man began to look concerned.

Arie's entire body whisked itself into the man who was standing in front of her. It happened so quickly, the only thing my eyes could pick up was the odd expression the man had as his gut was pushed back into himself. Not really understanding what exactly I witnessed, I looked up at Athen for confirmation. He pulled me over to Arie, who was now inhabiting this man's body. It was that quick.

"Hey, what's up?" Arie asked, in a now deep, male voice. She reached around to hug me, but that just seemed creepy.

"I don't think so, thanks though," I said laughing.

She began placing her hands above her head and started dancing like we were all suddenly at a club, and it was funnier than I ever imagined. As she took this poor unsuspecting guy's body and began dipping her body to the floor and circulating her hips, I couldn't hold in my laughter in any longer. The topper was her bending over to shake her booty like she was totally getting down.

"Man, we've got some sick humor, huh?" I was barely able to get it out to Athen, whose eyes were streaming with tears by now.

"Not bad, right?" The stranger's loud voice began booming as she got back up to look at us. "I think that's enough for this poor guy. You all wanna move down the lot a little bit so it doesn't look like there's a mob of us staring at him when he comes to?"

We all started moving back towards the entrance to the village when, I felt the strength of the strange man's hand wrap around my wrist.

"Not you. I want you to see how it completes."

Looking at Athen, he nodded and kept walking. I stood my distance as the man's body began convulsing. It seemed like minutes were passing, but I was sure it was only seconds. An intense glow began escaping from the man's chest as she glided out of his shell as quickly as she squeezed into it. Doing my best to get rid of the alarm on my face, not knowing when he would reappear as himself, I stared at where Arie was standing, now about five feet from him. She was bending over looking like she was picking up things from her purse that had rolled under the car.

"Hey, miss. Is everything okay?" The man asked Arie, as she was picking up the scattered items from her purse that she, only moments before, spilled on purpose.

"Oh yeah!" she said giggling. "Just my clumsy self. Got it all now, thanks," she said, with her beautiful smile, surely melting the guy where he stood.

He hadn't a clue.

She stood up completely and walked towards me, grabbing my hand as we proceeded to meet the guys in the village.

"Seamless," I whispered.

"Pretty sweet, huh?" she whispered back.

"Yeah, now I have to only figure out what the heck you did." I playfully scowled at her before heading into the village.

***

We were sitting at a table in the far corner of the Dublin Gate, surrounded by the beautiful cherry wood booth and exposed brick wall, it felt especially cozy and secluded for the conversation that was bound to happen.

After we all ordered our pints, I looked around at everyone waiting for some sort of explanation, and none came. What I did notice, however, was Cyril's arm wrapped around Arie's shoulder.

"Okay, well, this is overly inquisitive. Not to be a pest, but you guys are expecting me to give it a go on Karen, and I don't have a clue about what I should be doing. Oh, wait. Lemme guess. I need to feel the target and pow. I'm there," I said grinning.

"You know how everyone has a first impression or a vibe they give off? It's kind of an essence of who they are? That's what we tap into," Athen said.

"Like Karen - what strikes you most about her?" Athen asked.

"I'd say her protective nature, but how would that create a way for me to go for it?"

"Check this out," Cyril said, nodding at our waitress who was coming over with our poutine. "What do you get from her?"

She put the poutine down and paused, looking at us a little curiously, and then giggled.

"Did I forget something? I feel like I forgot something?" she asked.

"Nope, we've got it all. Thanks," Athen told her and she spun away.

"She seems a bit goofy, fun spirited," I replied, sipping my Guinness slowly.

"So when she comes back, we'll keep her here for a sec, and I want you to really concentrate on her. Tap into that energy. That's what you can channel a bit. Get the feel for it," Arie whispered.

"I'll give it a go." Was all I could come up with as we dug into our appetizer. Slowly scanning the pub, I decided to pause on each individual to see how different the feelings were that washed over me. Not expecting that much of a difference from person to person, I was completely surprised at how vast the emotions were that I was able to pick up on. The one bartender had a darkness around him, a very pessimistic vibe. Whereas the other one was totally happy-go-lucky, kind of reminded me of Arie. The three customers who were lined up at the bar, each had something different to offer up too. Staring at the cast of characters in the pub, I almost missed that our waitress had returned to check on us. Next thing I knew, Athen's asking where she's from, and Arie started piping in all sorts of things.

Trying to not freak her out, I did my best to look past her rather than at her as I tried hard to tap into what made up her most human self. The colors of her soul began swirling through my mind, the spirit of her character becoming tangible. Feeling as if I could almost touch her beating heart, my head began spinning as I felt my own cells beginning to merge with hers. Something was beginning to happen that I wasn't sure was supposed to happen, at least at this very moment. A commotion began quietly as Athen began distracting me, and Arie stood up making the waitress move suddenly, disconnecting our connection. The waitress touching her head, began moving away from our table cautiously.

"Hey, guys. I'm actually due for a break so if there isn't anything else I can get you right now, I'll be back in about ten minutes," she said, rubbing her temples.

"Yeah, sure totally – no problem," Cyril said, quickly trying to dismiss anything as unusual.

Watching the waitress take off towards the back entrance, I was pretty certain something came over her that I hadn't intended.

"Is she okay?" I murmured.

"She'll be fine. Honestly, I can't believe that just happened." Athen seemed like he was about to jump out of his seat. He was more interested in me than the poor waitress.

"Wasn't that what you guys wanted?" I asked confused.

"We never thought it would go there, Ana. She's a complete stranger. You actually started to experience the shapeshifting. If we hadn't broken it up, I think you would have completed it." Cyril was shaking his head in complete disbelief, and that wouldn't have been the best spectacle in the middle of the pub.

"GOD, I'm proud you," Athen said, nestling his head into my hair, "You never cease to amaze me."

"Does this mean I don't have to do it to Karen?" I asked hopefully.

"You know, not sure you have to actually. What's the point? Right? Apparently a stranger is just as easy for you."

"Thank God! Between a room full of chains and blood, flying around a mountain top, and possibly entering into someone else's body, I think I've had enough action on my Whistler trip."

The tension completely left as I relished the idea of a restful and drama-free dinner with Karen tonight before we headed back to Victoria the next morning.

Chapter Twenty-Six

The viciousness and frequency of the attacks were getting worse. As soon as we got back to Victoria, we were dealt more of my visions. The last three restless nights left us with no options. An attack was on the horizon, and we had the chance to stop it. My family had begun to decipher the pattern, and we had decided to try to thwart the next one, hopefully sending a message. If it was me that Azazel wanted to fight, then it was me he should fight, not the mortals. They had no chance. The demons were obviously cruel by nature but knowing their true intent had nothing to do with the mortals made it that much more painful to witness.

Their next attack was going to be this evening at Witty's Lagoon. Again, they chose a park that was covered in Douglas fir trees and maples, providing plenty of shelter for them to hide and pounce on their intended victim or victims. Unfortunately, we were pretty certain that they were planning on attacking several tonight. There was a family reunion picnic planned, and that seemed to be their target.

As we walked along the long trail through the forest, the echoes of the Orange-crowned Warblers filled the air with their beautiful melodies. With spring's arrival, the delighted birds were welcoming the warm weather that would arrive in the months to come. It saddened me to know that such happiness and innocence could be located on the same ground with predators and evil lurking at every turn. I had one vision of this attack the night before, and the images in my dream pointed near a waterfall. As it turned out, Witty's Lagoon contained a waterfall. Things were beginning to fall into place.

"So are we heading straight for the falls or are we checking out the other places first?" I asked Athen. He squeezed my hand and put his finger to his lip. He was sensing something that I wasn't. My heart began to patter faster as I realized that a fight could happen at any time. I nodded at him and kept following them as we made our way down the trail. The birds fell silent, and things became suddenly clear as to why Athen signaled for my silence.

Ahead, where the black boulders were finally showing themselves, signaling the waterfall directly behind, I heard squabbling that was in no way any sort of human language. I reached for Athen's hand and squeezed it. Turning back to look at me, his eyes provided the comfort that I needed. The gentle green radiated warmth and reminded me of the strength that I'd been slowly accumulating and needed to keep building up. He let go of my hand and secured his black knit cap, readying himself for whatever might be on the other side of the boulders.

Following his lead, I secured my hair into a ponytail and took a deep breath in.

Cyril and Athen moved slowly up the closest tower of bark and pine needles to spy on our enemies. When they reached the top, I saw them communicating an attack plan. The adrenaline began pumping through my veins. I wasn't sure of what to expect but felt secure in the knowledge that we would be able to conquer this group. Before I realized it, Cyril and Athen were back on the ground behind Arie and myself. Athen wrapped his arm around my shoulders and gave me a gentle hug, reassuring me and helping the doubts that kept appearing to vanish. He let go and began pointing towards the right for him and I to go, and Cyril took Arie to the left. Waving feebly at Arie, I forced myself to buck up for the impending fight. We were going in for the attack, ready or not.

I followed closely to Athen as we made our way to the top of the waterfall area. The trail was steep and slippery, with exposed stones making every step a precarious effort. The tall rye grass rustled in the breeze leaving an eerie feel in the air. With every step I took, my fear diminished, and a strength stirred deep within me. Hopefully, the element of surprise would be in our favor as we fought these evil monsters.

Athen slowed his pace and turned back towards me signaling for me to slowdown and creep along the trail. My body began its usual twist as I lowered my body in position ready for a fight. The cackling from the creatures got louder with every step towards their hiding place. The evil that was ringing through the air filled me with the last bit of anger to ensure my success with this battle. I knew they were right around the corner, and I saw a glimpse of Arie down at the fall area, positioned behind one of the large, glistening boulders, which the splash from the falls had completely coated. Athen and I were going to initiate the attack, and any stragglers were going to be pushed down the falls towards Cyril and Arie.

Before I knew it, Athen had jumped toward the group of demons, surprising them and flushing them in all directions. The cackles quieted, leaving the rushing sound of the waterfall to reach my ear. Leaping onto the slippery rock, I quickly scanned who to attack first. Finding my target, I flew through the air, landing on the back of the demon who was fleeing the furthest. He crumpled to the rocky floor with a thud, collapsing back on my leg. Not wanting to show any sign of weakness, I wrapped my arm around his neck, snapping his head to the left. The weight of his body fell off my leg. His lifeless shell began its black mist ascent into the sky.

A stabbing pain stung my back. As I flipped around to see the cause, I saw a completely distorted female demon staring back at me, smiling with a callousness that I'd seen many times before. Not sure if my mind was seeing how she truly looks or how miserable her inner spirit was, I dismissed the horror that was looking back at me. Lunging towards her, I saw the red glowing metal that she was waving at me, which must have been the source of the pain. Not recognizing what it could be from, I did my best to stay far away from her weapon. Noticing a limb from a maple that dangled right behind her I jumped over her head, grabbing on tightly and spinning my body with all the force I could, shoving my feet into the back of her. Caught off balance, she tumbled towards the rocky falls, falling directly into the crashing water.

Athen was downstream where the majority of the demons were now forming a circle. When I saw Cyril and Arie jumping into the mix, I shot over to the group as fast as I could to help finish off the bunch. Athen's shirt was ripped, and he had a severe scratch on his chin, but I did my best to push my fears away and finish these creatures off. I hadn't wanted to look to see where or who Athen was fighting earlier, for fear I'd be distracted.

The ground began trembling with the force of all of our energy gathered so close together. The leaves began fluttering, signaling the last battle was about to begin. Screams began releasing into the air, as I dove toward the female demon who had been staring at me so intently as I flew down the mountain. Cyril had the largest demon by the throat, squeezing with all of his might as Arie had another one pinned down to the earth. Athen wiped at his wound and dove into the mess flinging flesh into the atmosphere with every swipe.

I tackled the glaring female, who whipped out a slicing piece of silver chain tearing at my flesh. I yanked on the end piece as hard as I could hoping to dislodge it from whatever it was attached to, unsuccessfully. Grabbing my neck, she began squeezing tightly as I felt my ability to take deep breaths diminished. The harder I pulled on the chain, however, the less power she was able to use when squeezing my neck. It was a bit puzzling why one would be connected to the other, but I did my best to continually yank on the metal. My strength was quickly waning. I began kicking her over and over again in an attempt to thwart her efforts. The pain around my neck was getting worse with every breath. I scanned to see where Athen was, and I couldn't place him among any of the figures. Arie was busy with a male demon, and she, too, seemed to have figured out to pull on the metal chains that dangled from so many of these Legion members. Cyril was shooting right towards Arie's opponent, ready to finish him off. A comforting sight, after the concerns Arie raised up in Whistler.

Whipping me back to the seriousness of my situation, the throbbing pain in my windpipe began to create a hollowness with every breath in. My time was limited if I couldn't figure out a way to defeat this creature. The wetness from my eyes began streaming down my face. The strength in the demon's arms began to lessen just enough for me to crane my head to the left, only to get a little glimpse of Athen overhead.

He was fighting one of the last remaining demons that we all had our hands full with. I was truly on my own. I closed my eyes and thought of Lilith. I'd use her to my advantage. Remembering seeing her hand brush against Athen's began the stir of hatred that I needed to build the strength to destroy this creature. I took the largest breath in that my weakened lungs could handle, raising my chest enough to create a gap for my hand to slip through and twist the demon's grasp away from me. Surprising her was to my advantage, and I immediately wrapped her dangling chain around my hand several times and yanked it down to the ground, slamming her entire body onto the boulder. Quickly placing my foot on the chain, I released it from my hands freeing them to go in for the kill. Athen jumped down from the rock above, finishing

213

her off as I let the anger of Lilith escape, along with the evilness of the creature now laying before me. I was exhausted, but it looked like we were finished. There would be no more cougar attacks for now.

Sitting at the base of the falls, I let my hands hang into the swirls of water, wondering if I'd been as close to defeat as I felt inside. The coolness of the water began to stabilize my thoughts and bring me back to the discussion of my family.

"What did you notice about all those demons?" Cyril asked.

"Besides their ridiculous clothing?" I chuckled.

"No, actually that was exactly it!" Cyril exclaimed. "They all had those silver chains dangling from them. What's up with that?" he asked, shaking his head.

"You know, I didn't even think about it at first, but that was weird. Even the one female who I thought didn't have a chain, actually did; it was tucked in her jeans. I saw a piece of it shining under her shirt right before I flipped her on her back," I announced, a bit proud of myself. Thankful that a tiny bit of confidence began to show itself.

"Huh. Yeah, I didn't really think about it, but you're right. They all had metal on them," Athen said, coming over to walk with me back up the trail.

"Well, with every yank, I think some sort of pain or something must have shot through them, because their grasp lessened, or the fighting capabilities slowed a bit, unless it was in my mind."

"No, I noticed it also. I didn't want to announce it; in case I'd made it up too," Arie said, instantly making me feel better.

"Another thing to file away, I guess," Arie said, as she climbed over the last of the shells who hadn't disintegrated yet.

"Guys, I'd kind of like to see the family who the demons had targeted. I think it would make me feel better knowing they are all intact and everything. That okay with you?" I asked, not exactly sure why I wanted to see the family.

Looking as disheveled and beat up as we all did, we shuffled along the forest line on the way back to civilization, hoping to run into no one, making certain to avoid the spattering of picnic benches with beach views, and hikers spread along the sandy beaches scavenging for purple star fish or whatever exciting find they might spot. The confidence and strength from this last win between good and evil created a sensation that I enjoyed. I took pleasure in destroying the demons, the evilness that they embodied. Everything about the process created a delight deep within my soul. My fear was beginning to be replaced with absolution. Certain that I could play a vital role in the battles to come, I vowed to channel my anger properly and make certain that human casualties were at a minimum.

Feeling a warm trickle puddle in the base of my ear, I reached up quickly to rid myself of the sweat or whatever had accumulated. Once my fingertip touched the warm, thick substance, I realized it wasn't sweat at all, but blood. I was bleeding and had no idea where from. Suddenly feeling like I was in a lot worse shape than I knew, I quickened my step to get the spying over with so we could get back to our place.

Once we reached the outskirts of the forest that was overhanging against the slight cliffs, I peered down to see the picnic area confiscated by what I suspected was the family reunion. Children were playing alongside their older family members, while the parents, grandparents, aunts, and uncles were spread out setting up food station after food station and laughing and enjoying each others' company. Even though there was a slight chill in the air, the warmth from seeing the love below was enough to warm us all up. Thankful for what I was seeing, and for what we stopped, I knew I was coming into my own. Nothing could compare to this feeling, knowing the family was now going to be all right.

Athen came up behind me and whispered something so quietly that I had to spin around to hear him repeat it. Cyril and Arie had started back towards our car, and I appreciated the alone time the two of us were able to share over a moment like this.

"I'm really proud of you," he whispered again, feeling his lips press against mine, I let my thoughts of the family below vanish, leaving me to enjoy Athen's affections.

Chapter Twenty-Seven

With the message sent to Azazel, and an attack thwarted, the point was bound to get across to him. The message was as clear as we could send to him. Hopefully, Azazel would begin to play fair and involve us and not the mortals.

Things had been quiet for several days from all the other families. The attacks had stopped. The Legions were obviously planning something, but we were hoping that whatever it was, it would be directed at us and not the humans. My premonition of the attack on us at our Victoria home had yet to occur, making me on edge. It was something we had to be on the lookout for, but nothing had happened. Only time would tell, however. The tension in the house had eased a bit. Cyril seemed back to his old self to me, and Arie seemed to be thoroughly enjoying his attention. I was even able to catch up on reading too, for which I felt incredibly grateful.

The little things in life that I'd become so accustomed to up in Whistler, before my entire reintroduction process, seemed to have gotten put on hold for awhile between learning my new world and chasing down Athen and preparing for attacks. It was like the normalcy of life was completely out the window, except for the last few days.

Athen came jogging into the living room where Matilda was sprawled out in front of the fireplace, with her quiet snores drifting in and out of range with each breath, and I was laying out on the couch, book in hand. Seeing his energy light up the room made me feel like the love I felt for him was going to lift me off the couch.

He came rushing over to the couch, sitting next to me and looking so amazingly gorgeous. It was hard to think of anything but what I want to do to him.

"What's got you so excited?" I teased him.

"Seeing you and everyone's gone," he murmured, as he hugged me tightly.

"I love you, Athen," I whispered in his ear. "I'll never stop loving you."

"I love you more, my angel." He scooped me up from where I was sitting on the couch, carrying me into our bedroom.

Laying me down gently on our bed, I couldn't wait for what was in store for me. He began unbuttoning my shirt slowly while I grabbed his black leather belt, pulling him towards me with all the strength I could muster. His lips met mine, his body slid onto mine as he quickly finished unbuttoning my shirt. I grabbed his grey t-shirt and pulled it over his head, kissing every inch of his chest as his shirt fell to the floor. He moved me up against the top of our bed, securing pillows around us both. His skin was warm against mine, his breath reaching new areas of my body, as I thought about how lucky I was that he was here with me, so soon. The time away from each other only made this moment more special. Bringing his lips near mine again, I looked deeply into his eyes, searching for answers.

As much as I enjoyed what I was experiencing with Athen, I couldn't help but wonder if she'd gotten to him in this way as well. The sweat of the moment quickly turned chilling as that last thought popped in my head. Athen caught my shiver pulling back slowly.

"Something's wrong. What is it?"

"Nothing, nothing. I'm sorry. I can't. I ..." He rolled onto his side, grabbing my chin.

"You think that the time apart led to things?" His eyes finding all the questions buried deep inside that I was afraid to ask aloud, in case they were true. "You saw the images during the Awakening. You still think we did?"

I nodded, completely unsure of myself.

"Nothing happened. It didn't." He held me, pulling the covers over us. "I'd tell you, and it didn't."

I turned on my side to face him, burying my head into his chest.

"I'm so sorry. I don't know what's gotten into me. She's been plaguing me for so long in all of my nightmares. The grin that I'd see cross her lips has made me ill in my dreams so many times I kind of assumed that ..."

"Don't assume. Much to her disgust, I wasn't as easy of a target as she hoped. I didn't know what was going on. I really had no clue, actually, but seeing you in the library that day, I realized something bigger than I could ever imagine was taking place. I had a pretty good idea whose side I wanted to be on and an even better notion that I needed to watch myself with that woman. I've loved you for thousands of years, Ana. Nothing has ever taken us away from each other's heart, and nothing will. You have to trust. You have to be brave in the face of us – what we represent. We have a love that no one can break, but you have to believe that too. You used to know that beyond anything. I know you will again someday."

"Thanks. I needed to hear it one more time. Everyday it was like a piece of me eroded bit by bit while you were gone, and only fear replaced the hole. I feel like I'm closer to filling it. I promise."

"I know, honey," he said, kissing me gently on my shoulder.

"On a different note, you're saying the library incident was a good thing? You have no idea the turmoil I caused myself – catching your glance. I thought that I'd ruined everything. Especially with you bolting out of there the way you did."

"Actually, I was pretty freaked. I won't lie. I didn't go home that day though. I rode around and stayed at a place where I didn't think she could find me for the night. I needed time to figure things out. In hindsight, I never could have figured this out," His smirk was reappearing, "without the memsors. But seeing your gaze in the library told me what I wanted to be near again, and it was you."

"Wow, you're incredible," I told him, letting the evening unfold into a brilliant memory that I would cherish for eternity.

***

There was a faint rustle in the blackberries. I prayed it was an animal – maybe a raccoon or something harmless like that. Matilda had finished her business and was already standing at the door for me to let her back in, but I wanted to check out the movement. I shined my flashlight towards the intimidating, thorny bushes seeing nothing. A low hiss began, one that I recognized all too well. It couldn't be her. Why now? The house was only a few seconds away back behind me. I could reach it with a quick sprint.

Knowing that I didn't want to turn my back to the thicket of hisses, I slowly walked backwards towards the porch, hoping I would make it to the steps before she began her approach. I had no idea which form I should be expecting, slithering or walking. It didn't matter. They were both despicable. I tried my best to communicate to Athen in the house. Hoping that I was getting skilled enough to channel who I was talking to rather than broadcasting it to anyone in our particular radius, I concentrated as hard as I could without losing track of her. Not turning around to look behind me, I realized someone inside must have turned on the living room light as the glow bounced off the shrubs on the left side of the house. My spirits began to lift a bit at the thought of strength in numbers. I had no idea what her intention was. She knew fully that Athen was back with us. There was no chance of turning him onto her dark side. She had another reason for being here.

The bottom of the front door scraped the floor as it was swung open, letting me know that my family was now with me.

"What seems to be the problem?" Cyril's voice booming as ever.

"We have a visitor. I just don't know if she's slithering or crouching," I yelled back to him.

Athen stepped to my side, grabbing my hand and squeezing it.

"My guess is she's slithering around. She never really made a great-looking human," Athen said, making my heart sing.

Athen reached down and grabbed a handful of rocks.

"Check this out," he said, as he was tossing one after the other into the thicket of thorns, taunting her.

I tried getting outside of myself but was loving every second of this torment. Eventually, her anger would get the better of her, and she would appear.

Arie and Cyril were directly behind us, waiting like we were for Lilith to show her face, and she didn't let us down. The thorn-bearing branches were thrown to the side as she stood up quickly, glaring at us all. Stepping forward, her hissing became more constant, making her look especially ridiculous.

Letting go of Athen's hand, I took a step forward.

"Is there something you wanted or did you just miss us?" I asked her.

"Azazel got your message. He wanted me to tell you myself, since we have such a connection," she said, her lip curling over her gruesome smile, with her sharp tongue ready for anything I was going to throw at it. "You and I."

"There is no connection, Lilith. Don't flatter yourself. Athen and I have always been and always will be."

"What makes you think that's the connection I was referring to?" Her serpent eyes were glaring at me as if the others didn't exist.

"That's the one that came to mind, I guess, whatever." I refused to show any curiosity whatsoever as she waited for my reaction.

"Well, it's good you have each other because you'll need each other's strength as the fun begins. In fact, it's starting right now. Look, see off in the distance? Isn't it beautiful? By the way, Azazel feels it is far more intriguing to keep the humans involved regardless of your wishes." In that instant, she was gone, leaving us looking towards the harbor where her eyes had last been, leaving us to deal with a horror we weren't prepared for.

***

The flames were shooting straight up from the ferry. Smoke was creating a low, covering cloud, hovering right over the doomed vessel. The screams for help were shaking me to my core. In the sky, the large black creatures, with wingspans twice the length of their bodies, were circling around their victory. The creatures were swooping down onto the ferry picking up the people and dumping them into the water as if they were ragdolls. The fury was building inside of me. Those were innocent people, and the demons were destroying countless lives and families. We had to stop them. I knew it was the demon's direct invitation to us. The humans were the bait, but we were the target.

The black, soulless creatures continued taunting us with each dive-bomb onto the ferry. We had no time to deliberate. These winged-beasts couldn't be seen by humans for now, but it was only a matter of time before that would change. The demons in this form were not visible to mortals unless the humans were evil themselves, and death was upon them. Otherwise, humans couldn't see them.

I looked up at Athen unsure of my abilities, but I knew that didn't matter. It was a trap that the demons had set for us, and we had to participate. I knew this going into it, but I couldn't let innocent people perish because I was worried about my own safety and Athen's. The fear began building as I thought about the lack of training or anything, really, that Athen had since he came back to us. I, also, knew he wasn't going to be on the sidelines.

"I love you, sweetheart," I whispered into his ear.

"I love you too," he whispered back, kissing my neck as he backed away.

"Now's the time, Ana. You've practiced enough. I know you can make it to the ferry," Cyril said.

Before Cyril's last words left his lips, my body had already begun the process of forward motion. The mist was hitting my face like tiny shards of glass, but I arrived so quickly onto the ferry, the images were all a blur. I felt Athen land right behind me. Thick smoke was creating a wall that I couldn't see through. I heard the coughs of victims, guiding me to them. I felt for the first body, which turned out to be a limp mess of a woman. I grabbed her and threw her over my shoulder, when I heard a whimper from a small child. I steadied myself with the weight of the woman on my shoulder and knelt down feeling with my hand until I reached the hand of a child, probably this woman's daughter.

"Come on, sweetie. You're going to be okay." I tried my best at speaking without inhaling.

I grabbed her, closing my eyes and concentrating on the shore that I'd so quickly left behind, hoping I would make it back safely with my added cargo. My body tensed up, and I pictured myself on the rocky shore. My body began its lightning-speed journey only to crash onto the beach in mere seconds. I dumped them off, knowing help would get to them both. I needed to get back to the ferry. I saw Cyril and Arie releasing the boats onto the waves, helping the passengers as best they could into the boats. I hoped Athen was doing okay since not all of his abilities were completely at a hundred percent.

I looked back up into the sky, watching the winged creatures hovering over us as we attempted to help the survivors. I was thankful, at least, that the humans wouldn't see these monsters. I didn't understand the demons' intentions. I knew it was only a matter of time before we were their next targets. We were falling into their trap beautifully.

Taking a deep breath in, I started back to the ferry. I found myself back in the cabin. My search began for people who may not have made it back down to the lower ferry decks for the evacuations by Cyril and Arie. The smoke burning my eyes made it almost impossible, as I felt for anything that didn't feel like it belonged where I was stepping. I could see Arie and Cyril whipping around the ferry dropping people into the boats. To the human eye, it would look like the survivors were jumping into the floating boats themselves, but that was impossible. Arie and Cyril had made sure the boats were far enough away from the burning ferry, and there was no way a human could land that.

"Athen?" I hollered. "Are you still here?"

Tears were streaming down my face from the pain that was unrelenting from the thick air. Athen's energy was warming me. I knew he was near me.

"Are you okay?"

He came up behind me, feeling around just as I'd been doing for survivors, and grabbed my waist.

"I think there are only a few left." His voice muffled as he spoke into his shirt, trying to keep the thick mess out of his lungs as best he could. "I've gotten several to the lifeboats."

"Hello?" I hollered out into the cabin, choking on smoke. Silence.

I began my way down the other side of the cabin when I kicked something soft. I felt for the person's arms and swung them over my shoulder. This time, I decided to try to drop them in one of the boats that Arie and Cyril had released into the sea. The closest one to the ferry was already full, so I found a spot in the next one to drop off the man.

Heading back to the ferry, one of the demons suddenly barricaded me. Hovering directly in front of me about five feet, he attempted to stop me from moving forward. Knowing that my range was limited with the other creatures still flying overhead, I shot to the left waiting for the creature to follow me through the ferry's car deck. Knowing my best shot for victory was if the demon couldn't use his wings, I hoped that the demon would be forced to relinquish them due to the tight quarters of the car deck. Landing smoothly through the steel opening, I gained my composure before I felt the black soulless creature arrive behind me. He was perched on the metal framing, surveying his options. Relief flooded me, as his wings were sucked into his back as if they never existed. The victims on the ferry needed Cyril, Athen, and Arie more than I needed them. I would need to finish this creature off on my own. I was actually looking forward to it.

A screech echoed through the air, bouncing off the metal walls alerting me of his intentions. My body was hovering in the air, as I did my best to blend in with the dark smoke that was getting thicker by the second.

"Come here. I'm ready for you," I hissed.

My veins were pumping with excitement at the thought of destroying this demon and anymore that made the mistake of coming towards me. Another message needed to be sent. I was stronger, and I was ready for whatever Azazel wanted to send at us. If I was the reason behind these battles, then I would ensure that I would make my presence known.

A sudden black streak darted towards me as I dropped to the floor, leaving a steel support beam in my wake behind me. The demon crashed into the steel, slinking to the floor, which gave me the opportunity I needed. Jumping up, I extended my leg, quickly kicking him in the spine, pushing him back towards the steel beam, his jaw cracked on the metal. He spun around, reaching for my neck with his hand and missing, but not before grabbing my hair and slamming me down onto the metal floor.

Looking up, the smoke made his features indistinguishable, but I could still see what I needed to continue the fight. Playing lifeless, I let the demon bend down to continue his attack, attempting to step on my neck, but not before I was able to rotate my body underneath the nearest car. Imagining myself back on the cliff, throwing the boulder over the edge, I knew what needed to be done. Letting my mind imagine the weight of the cold metal car above me, I grabbed onto the axles, squeezing as hard as I could, becoming one with the machine. The rage that had been building since stepping foot on this ferry took over, and I rolled the car on top of the demon who was waiting for me to roll out. The scraping of metal on metal overshadowed the demon's shrieks of pain as his body was crushed by the weight of the car that I toppled onto him. The adrenaline was still pumping, and I was experiencing a high like no other. Defeating the demons was becoming my drug.

Athen was dropping off another lifeless victim into a lifeboat as well. A man, dressed in a beige suit now covered with black soot, who was probably rushing home to be with his family. The fury would not stop building inside of me. I hoped that help would get here soon. Athen looked exhausted, which wouldn't be unusual since he only recently had begun using his skills again. I nodded at him before I began my rescues again. I knew there were more victims in there. My job was to find them before it was too late.

Cyril was yelling to Arie to go to the car decks and begin searching inside the cars, and that was when I realized the ferry was beginning to sink. We didn't have much time left. There were still people on this boat, most unable to make a sound, and who weren't able to move from the mass amount of smoke inhalation.

I focused as hard as I could, placing my thoughts in Cyril, Arie, and Athen's heads telling them that the boat was sinking. We had to hurry. Otherwise we, too, could get caught up in the ferry's final resting place. I shuffled my feet, using the tables and seats as my guide, searching for anyone. Cyril and Arie's thoughts came rushing into my mind telling me that we probably only had five minutes at the most to try to rescue whoever else we could. I still hadn't found any other bodies in the cabin, but I felt they had to be here. I didn't understand why I couldn't find anyone else. Arie summoned me to the car deck, and I agreed since I couldn't find anyone where I was at.

I sprinted to the stairwell and attempted to open the door. It kept bumping into something, so I wiggled it more, and it only gave way a little bit – not enough for me to open and get through.

"Athen," I hollered.

I knew he wasn't able to carry any more bodies to safety but would be able to help me, at least, get the door open. His strength was failing, and we still needed some to be able to leave the ferry unnoticed and be prepared for the demon's next surprise.

"Athen! I need help!" I used all the energy I had hollering and communicating through our mind network.

"Ana, Ana. I'm on the other side of the door. People are in the way. They are collapsed onto each other. I'm moving them right now," he yelled through the door.

I could feel the pressure begin to release from the door as it gently started to swing open.

"Oh, my God! There are like ten bodies here. Are they still alive?" I asked, bending down to the first one that was propped against the steel walls – a man with his head hanging down, and his chin resting on his own chest.

"Yeah, they are still alive. I think we'll be able to do it," Athen uttered as he was throwing the first two bodies over his shoulders. "We've got to hurry."

He ran down the stairs. I knew he didn't have the strength left to be doing this. I knew I didn't. I grabbed one woman and tried for another when I realized that I didn't have the strength to carry both. I carried the woman and ran into Cyril who directed me to Arie, who was carrying the two Athen had brought her. On my way back to the stairwell, I darted out of Cyril's way as he was carrying two more from the stairwell, this time two large men. Athen had one man right behind him. I used what little energy I had left picking up the last two women I could find, who seemed to be barely breathing.

A low whisper from one of the women startled me beyond all belief. "Where's my husband?" she asked again. I hoped with everything that one of the men we had already brought to safety was her husband.

"He's okay. He's in a boat already." I gave her directly to Arie, along with the other woman.

The sound of the metal creaking and echoing into itself began getting louder as I realized our side of the ferry was the only piece of metal that was sticking up in the ocean. We needed to get off this thing. A thunderous shudder began as if all the metal was about to explode.

Athen and Cyril had the last three men and were carrying them to the ledge when the ferry began to quickly fill with the crashing of ice-cold water. They began to slip backwards, and Cyril nodded at Athen, and instantly, they both shot off the deck. I was stunned. I didn't know how Athen had the strength, and before I knew it, Arie grabbed me around my waist. We left the ferry that was now completely encircled by the rescue boats. We didn't leave them many to have to rescue.

While Arie was trailing Athen and Cyril, I looked up into the sky, seeing nothing but the ominous starless sky. The winged creatures were no longer circling their prey.

"Where did they go, Arie?" I hoped she could hear me with the wind swirling around like it was.

"Hopefully not waiting for us. As exhausted as you and Athen must be, we can only hope for the best. Only time will tell though, huh? You did an incredible job of fighting off that demon, Ana."

"Thanks. I am drained, and that wasn't quite the answer I was looking for." We all landed on the shore with a thud. My body completely crumpled with the weight of itself. I reached for Athen who quickly fell to his knees and began hugging me.

"Do you think we got everyone?" I asked, looking over Athen's shoulder at Cyril.

"I do. You guys did amazing. You really did," he said, patting my arm that wouldn't let go of Athen.

I was so afraid of releasing myself from Athen's embrace. The comfort his touch provided me was beyond anything I could explain. I just couldn't let go.

"You did wonderful, sweetie," he whispered into my ear.

"No, *you* did. Carrying two people over and over? You, at least, could fly to the shore after everything! Arie had to haul me off the ferry, or who knows what would have happened to me," I said, only half-joking.

I realized, by this point, that Athen and I were literally propping each other up. The amount of fatigue was unlike anything I'd experienced in any of my fights or training so far. Athen must have felt the same way.

"So, Cy, isn't there like a power up or something?" Athen asked, laughing as he tried his best to steady himself and move backwards so we could both sit on the ground. I really didn't want him to back away, but I didn't want to appear as clingy as I felt.

"Well, I wish it was as easy as that. It's gonna take good old-fashioned rest. You'll be surprised."

"Let's hope nothing is waiting for us back at the house though, right?" I announced, rolling my eyes.

"You know? Come to think of it, I think we should hang out in public for a little while. Try to rest up a bit before we head back." Not wanting to admit that I was actually terrified at the thought of having to expend any more energy on anything.

"Sounds good." Arie plopped herself of the ground.

I finally exhaled and felt all the air escape that I'd been apparently holding in this entire time. Looking up into the sky, thankful, I didn't see any of the winged creatures any longer. I fell fast asleep on the grassy hill.

I'd only been out for a matter of minutes when my mind became emblazoned with images of an impending attack on us. It was at our home in Victoria. I forced myself to wake up. I'd seen everything I needed. They were waiting for us, or they would be waiting for us. I needed to be able to tell everything to my family before it was too late. It had matched my earlier dream. The attack was coming. Waking them all up from their rest, I began relaying what I was certain was waiting for us at home.

Chapter Twenty-Eight

Everything looked like we had left it, but that was little consolation. Since when we were expecting them last, they toyed with us making their presence known, only to be missing in action. Something told me the demons were here this time or were about to arrive.

"Guys, I don't think we are alone or won't be for long." I was finally understanding my role in this family. I had to communicate. I'd learned my lesson the hard way.

Cyril opened the door slowly, letting the living room light cascade onto his shoulder and out onto the porch. In our hurry to the ferry, we hadn't turned on the porch light, making tonight's return a little more intimidating. I squeezed Athen's hand, hoping for comfort. I partially wanted the demons to be waiting for us, because at least we were alert and ready for action.

We had a couple of hours to refresh and restore our energy from the ferry battle. Unfortunately, the majority of the burden was left in Cyril and Arie's arms. They were the strongest and most skilled in fighting.

Cyril looked over his shoulder and nodded at us. We were going in. Athen positioned himself in front of me as we walked into the foyer. Always trying to save me, I guess. The house was quiet – not unlike the other night. How many times could I be wrong with these visions...

Matilda wasn't coming out to greet us, which was a little unusual but not unheard of. She often slept through our arrival. That was my hope now; although, I didn't hear her snores.

Arie and Cyril headed towards the kitchen and the back part of the house, while Athen and I went to the bedrooms. Knowing what I saw in my visions, the bedroom might be where they were lurking, preparing themselves for a battle.

Everything looked okay in Cyril and Arie's bedroom as Athen flipped on the light switch. I peered into the closet, and there was nothing. Athen and I checked the office. It was just as we had left it earlier. The last place to check was our bedroom. That was where I saw the initial attacks. I grabbed on to the back pocket of Athen's jeans. He could sense my tension and slowed a bit.

"Matilda is out back!" Arie yelled.

That was all I needed to hear to know we weren't alone. We would never leave her outside, and she would never go outside on her own.

There was a sudden urgency to her voice. We were all on the same page.

The draftiness of the house became more evident with her words. Each chill was sending a new message. Matilda came running down the hall to greet us, followed by Cyril and Arie.

"This is the last room to check." Athen looked at us all.

He pushed the door open. Our room was empty... actually empty. Free from creatures lurking, and anything else that once had a home in this room. Our bed was gone, the nightstands, the chest of drawers. This was truly bizarre. Unfortunately, it fit my dreams perfectly. The images of me huddled in the corner ran through my mind. I was in the corner, not the chest of drawers. Things were beginning to fit like a puzzle, one that I didn't want to solve.

"They are coming. They must be on their way." I exhaled all of my breath that I must have been holding in since we came in through the front door. "This is what I saw."

"You mean no furniture?" Athen asked, a bit puzzled.

"Yeah, exactly. I was actually huddled in the corner," I said, pointing to the far right corner of the room. Everyone's eyes shifted.

"I can tell you, I'm going to do my best to stay out of that particular corner," I murmured halfway, hoping they didn't hear what I said.

Athen wrapped his arms around my shoulders. "We aren't going to let it end that way."

He knew what I didn't tell them. It was my goal to make sure that it didn't happen like my dream either.

"So, I guess we wait?" Cyril looked at me like I actually knew the answer to this.

"Guess so." I wanted to get this night over. They weren't in their human form, which frightened me that much more.

"Why would they have put Matilda outside?" Arie bent down petting Matilda, who was still feeling slighted from being left outside. She was a girl who wasn't used to such treatment.

"Just to mess with us. Guess they don't have much else to do." I don't know why I was taunting them. Maybe my fear was turning to anger. I hoped so.

Athen started towards the living room to get the fire going, for which I was super grateful. The house seemed especially cold at this moment.

"It's because they were here, Ana," Arie said. "The fire isn't really going to help."

Since the ferry, I realized I'd never shut off my ability to communicate with them all with my thoughts. I cursed myself for not remembering something so important. There were things I didn't want them to know about my visions or my decisions.

The house began shuddering a little bit. The vibrations weren't coming from the ground, like when Athen appeared on his Ducati. No, it definitely wasn't that kind of feeling. I looked up at Athen and Cyril – they felt it too. The flicker from the candles started dancing quickly off the walls as if a breeze was causing the flames to stir. There was no breeze. Our lights began flickering a little. There was no storm outside. Arie came from the kitchen, her face ashen.

"You guys feel that?" she asked, Matilda at her side.

I nodded my head. At the same time, the lights went out. They didn't come back on.

"Good thing we have our candles going for ambiance." Cyril tried to add some humor to the situation. I was grateful. Arie started walking to the office with Matilda following right behind her. We decided we were going to put Matilda in there for safekeeping. It was the best place we could think of.

The vibrations were getting stronger. The paintings and photographs on the wall beginning to make slight shifts. The anxiety inside of me was starting to build. I knew what I saw in my dreams, but I knew seeing it in person was going to be far worse. They were the same creatures that were circling in the sky over the ferry.

The air began to get very stuffy. Each breath felt like I was inhaling dead air. Almost like I couldn't get enough oxygen. I looked around at the others, and they were feeling it too. I could tell the way their chests were moving. I was actually thankful for the dim lighting at this point.

"Alright, so we have our plan. We can win this one." Athen was a pretty good motivational speaker. I had to give him that – especially in light of his most recent situation.

The thunderous noise off in the distance was getting to us in the same rhythm as the vibrations. The stronger the vibrations, the louder the rolling boom became. Feeling like we were bait wasn't something I liked – stuck in between four walls. This didn't seem right.

"Hey, what if we changed it up a bit?" I asked to a room full of glares.

"I don't think that's a good idea, Ana," Cyril said, as he was steadying himself from the shaking that was becoming more violent with every minute that went by.

"Why not? We began the fight inside in my visions, what about beginning outside? Throw them off a bit." I had to holler over the noise that was coming our way.

"You're coming up with this now?" Arie was a little incredulous.

"Didn't want to put anything out in the airwaves, you know?" My heart was pounding with the thought of guiding us in the wrong direction. Obviously, she was feeling it too.

Athen grabbed my hand and squeezed it. He was in. Cyril and Arie nodded at us too.

"Let's do it. They're almost here." I had to flush the images of the winged beasts out of my mind while we ventured to the backyard.

They were almost here, and I had to prepare myself for the second battle of the night. I began feeling that desire to defeat these beasts. I needed that high again.

Chapter Twenty-Nine

The air's chill was like we were in Antarctica. The demons were almost to us. Arie leapt into the air, and in a flash, her body flew away to the nearest fir tree. Even with my eyes conditioned to see us in our other forms, I couldn't immediately spot her. Cyril jetted to the front yard, my guess was to prop himself in the maple tree. Athen wasn't budging. He knew what my plan was. I knew I wasn't letting any of my thoughts escape so he just knew because he knew, and he wasn't going to let me do it. He stared intently at me, grabbing my arm, pulling me towards him. I felt him shove something in the back pocket of my jeans.

"We aren't going to keep doing this. It's not your turn to vanish on us. You aren't going to be bait, Ana." The smirk that I adored surfaced as if he had won a victory.

"Who said that was my plan?" I asked.

"What do you mean?" He let go of my arm and stared at me, as I looked up into the sky seeing the first demon begin its decent. As the wings of the creature began their final push of air, I looked back at Athen and winked at him. We were going to be bait.

I readied myself for what I wasn't sure of, but whatever it was, it had to be ended with us as the victors. My fear had completely subsided, and I was ready to fight. All I felt was the anger of being taken away from Athen for over half of a century, and then him being taken away from us. The lifeless bodies on the ferry were an added accelerator to my anger. The demons did us a favor by laying that trap. They just didn't know it. I was angrier than I'd been for a long time. With that last thought, the first winged creature swooped in, attempting to knock Athen over with his unfolded wing as he landed. To the demon's surprise, Athen shot into the air towards the second winged demon that was emerging from the clouds.

I looked the demon straight into its eyes. The creature looked back at me waiting for my move. I did nothing, which only angered the lifeless eyes that were staring back at me. Another demon converged onto the roof, kneeling down, surveying the land. We weren't giving them the fight they had anticipated. I was expecting three more demons to make their appearance. I didn't know if I'd be able to hold off the fight until then, but I was going to try.

The creature in front of me took in a deep breath, making his chest appear as if his lungs might be at capacity. It was hard to believe that we shared the same air. I shook my head at him and took off towards the sky. My skin burned as it glided into the atmosphere. His eyes were tracking my every movement. To my relief, the other three demons emerged below the fog, ready to engage in the fight they thought had already started. I smiled as I watched the demon, my demon, take off after me unaware that one of our own was going to pounce.

Arie dropped out of the Douglas fir tree, graceful as ever, landing directly on top of him. A glistening piece of metal was sticking out of her boots, scraping his flesh as she landed on him. The screams of pain began to make their way through the yard. It was exhilarating. I looked up and saw Athen darting around the winged creature he first went after. My heart began pounding with worry, hoping that he could handle it.

Something grabbed my ankle and pulled me to a stop. Looking down, I saw the demon who had been on the roof, now holding on to me with his gnarly fingers wrapped around my flesh. Arie had almost finished the demon that I'd come to know in my short time waiting, so I felt like if help was needed she would be there for me. Athen would have to wait for assistance, not that I knew if he needed any, actually.

I somersaulted backwards, kicking towards the sky releasing the demon's grasp, surprising myself as the demon went flying towards the sky. Either my strength had grown tremendously, or the demon wasn't very strong. I would like to think it was the first assumption. Before I was able to get too cocky, the demon came barreling towards me. My hand searched my back pocket for what Athen had shoved in there, feeling a closed knife, I was thankful, even with as tiny as it felt.

I flung it open, releasing the blade, barely in time, as the demon arrived in front of me hovering and laughing. I charged toward the wretched being, blade in hand, as he moved quickly to the side dodging me and my attack. I swirled around, quickly gaining my bearings, and shot myself directly towards the creature, only to dive upwards where Athen was located. The demon was chasing after me, but I knew I could make it to Athen before it got to me. With my blade exposed, I shoved it directly into the back of the demon Athen had almost finished off. My knuckles had gone in so deep that the warmth of his insides were drooling over my hand. I unstuck my blade and hand, releasing the creature to fall to the ground.

Thankful that I'd lured the other demon with me, I watched as Athen grabbed the demon's wing, throwing himself onto it and crushing the stem that he was sitting on. The tiny cracks from the cartilage breaking from Athen's hands began calming my fears about this battle. The demon was wincing in pain, and I knew this was my opportunity. My blade would do little to quicken his demise at this point. We had to wear him out first. Our odds were better if we paired up with our lack of strength compared to Arie and Cyril.

I flew behind the demon quickly and wrapped my arm around his neck in a chokehold, doing my best to crush his neck. His energy was getting low. I could feel his strength slowly begin to deplete. I kneed him in his spine, hearing success as he howled out into sky. Athen crushed the wing he had been working on, and it crumpled as nothing was left to support it.

Now was the time. I stuck my already dripping blade into this demon's back. I didn't understand what was coming over me, but I found myself wiggling the blade back and forth for extra effect. It was gratifying thinking this creature was suffering with every twist and tilt of the metal inside his body.

In that moment, I realized there was a fine line between good and evil. I was doing this for good, yet it was a really bad thing to do. I liked it. They probably liked it just as much. Our justification was to eradicate evil. They didn't need a justification. They only acted on their impulses. The adrenaline was pumping. An addiction had formed. I promised myself to stay on the right side of that addiction as I pulled the blade from the inside of this creature.

That made three demons gone that I knew of. Arie took care of the first one. Athen and I had managed to down two. My excitement level began building as I realized, Cyril probably had taken care of one as well. I finally spotted Cyril, now on the side of the house, fighting one of the larger creatures. Cyril looked exhausted. His shirt was tattered with claw marks. His face hadn't missed the claws either – blood had already dried up on his cheek and forehead. Arie jumped onto the creature, and I knew instantly that they were going to be okay. Not seeing any other demons, a sigh escaped signaling for Athen to come over to hug me. His eyes were evaluating the same scenes as I.

"I think we would be a nuisance at this point. Don't you?" Athen asked, hugging me tightly.

"Yah, I think we would probably screw it up. I can't believe it, but I think we actually defeated these Legion members, and we're pretty unscathed, I'd say."

"We probably shouldn't be tooting our own horns. But I think you're right," he said grinning. The welcomed chilly air was finally because of the weather and not the impending doom that I'd been worried about.

A crushing sound reached me, and I spun around seeing the last demon crumble to the ground, wings folded ready to disintegrate. Athen and I ran over to Cyril and Arie who both looked amazingly well for what they just went through. Besides Cyril's clothing and scratch marks, it was pretty hard to tell he just defeated a towering, winged creature that was twice the size of any of us. I was thankful Athen and I had only the little ones to defeat – if there was such a thing.

"You guys did phenomenal!" Arie exclaimed, her excitement level bubbling over.

A sense of pride started swelling, and it was nice to hear that someone else thought we did well too. Athen kicking butt didn't surprise me considering everything else he never really let go of, but I didn't know how I would fit in the battle equation. The yard looked like a mess, with one of our tiny birdbaths broken into pieces, and a wooden bench that looked like it was turned into many little, wooden daggers.

"I think I'm going to go start some tea water. How does that sound?" I asked, breaking free from Athen's grasp.

"Sounds perfect," Cyril said, reaching to pick up some of the broken pieces of cement that the birds would no longer be frolicking in.

As everyone began spreading out to pick things up in the yard, it occurred to me how odd this life was. I was beginning to get used to switching back and forth between conversations in public, but battling demons in one instant and picking up yard debris from the aftermath the next was really hard to grasp. I bounded off towards the house as everyone else was left gathering any evidence of mass obliteration to toss in the trash.

I put a kettle of water on in the kitchen and decided to go take a look at our bedroom, which was still furniture-less. I was really intrigued as to where the furniture went. It wasn't in our yard; at least, that I saw.

I opened up the office door to let little Matilda out, and she began growling and staring at the wall in between the room she was standing in and our bedroom next door. The fur on the back of her neck was on end. I closed the door on Matilda and quietly moved back into the hall leading to our bedroom. Guess I can't change the sequence of events entirely surrounding premonitions. I took a deep breath in of the ice-cold air, letting it hit my lungs, signaling the visitor who was waiting for me, exactly like my dream. We didn't destroy them all. No matter how I tried to avoid it, my visions were still leading me directly to intended destiny.

I opened our bedroom door where a creature, not unlike the ones we destroyed earlier, was standing before me. His wings were spanning the entire room, and his eyes were twice as cruel as the others. Victorious laughter filled the room.

Chapter Thirty

The soulless creature stood before me, waiting for me to enter the room entirely. I closed the door behind me without locking it. My family had been filled in on my entire dream, and it looked like they would be participants in the reality of it. No matter how much I tried to avoid this encounter. There was no need to keep the door open. It would only clue the demon into when they were coming down the hall.

I took a deep breath in, letting the air fill every part of my lungs as I locked my legs into place, ready for a fight. The demon nodded at me and lunged towards me. With a speed I didn't know I had, I dodged to the left, leaving the demon to crash into the wall. The thud made Matilda bark even louder in the next room, only adding to the anxiety that was building up inside of me.

"Is that all you've got?" I chided, as I barreled towards the monster, twisting my body as if it were a horizontal cyclone. My own nails becoming weapons as I grasped onto his flesh, attempting to rip any part of it to shreds. Feeling overly victorious, I jumped off the demon, ripping his shirt as I went.

Answering my question that I now wished I hadn't asked, the demon grabbed my arm with one quick movement hurling me across the room. My bones crushed into the wall as I slid down into the corner. I did my best to get out of the foggy state that the creature had so suddenly thrust me into. I reached my arm behind me, hoping to prop myself up, ready to fight again, when I realized this was exactly like my dream. I was now cornered in this room, squatting. All I could do now was hope that I could change the outcome that I'd seen so many times before. Doing my best to concentrate on what I thought his next move might be from my dream sequence, I leapt from my stance, tumbling over his head, landing with a thud. I didn't have a knife in my dream. At least, that was on my side.

A warm trickle began making its way down my ear, knowing it wasn't sweat, I wiped it with my arm, leaving a rusty, brown mark on my sleeve. I wondered how badly it was bleeding. The demon lunged at me, carrying a force behind him that was going to be hard to avoid. I ducked towards the ground, barely missing his fingers trying to grasp my neck.

Grabbing the knife out of my pocket, I reached my arm out, stabbing at his spine but missing completely. In the background, the teakettle began its wild ride of chirps and whistles, alerting us all that the boiling water was ready. I prayed my family outside would hear it, knowing that was probably my only hope of surviving this fight. Seconds continued to pass by as the demon took a piece of my flesh out with his nail while tossing me completely across the room again. The kettle continued blaring, and Matilda's barks became more aggressive. I knew Athen would be here any minute. I only hoped it wasn't too late.

The strength in my legs began to resurface as I became angrier with my inability to fight off this creature as easily as the ones outside. I was waiting for the bedroom door to open any second, and unfortunately, I think the demon was too. I flicked open my knife again, completely determined to use it as I jumped at the demon with the blade ready to slice his grey flesh open, landing close enough to tear through his cheek. The pleasure began building up deep inside me as the demon reached up grabbing at the hole that was now left by my handiwork.

The window shattered into a thousand little pieces as my family tore in through the small square. Athen reaching for one of the shards of glass, lunged at the demon who was taken completely off guard as the glistening edge tore jagged bits and pieces through his skin. Athen wrapped his legs around the neck of the demon, somersaulting back into the wall as Cyril took another large piece of glass, jamming it into the stomach of this soulless creature.

The body slumped to the ground, wings completely contracted and unidentifiable as such, with Athen hopping off and tossing the glass to the pile of shards.

"I can't stand that sound!" Arie flung the door open and bounded down the hall to turn off the tea water.

Athen looked over at me, holding out his arms as I ran right into them. Feeling the comfort of his clutch, I buried my face into his chest. Not wanting to see any of the devastation that was left in the room or on my body, I closed my eyes shut as tight as they would go. I felt like such a burden had been lifted having him back again. The crumpled demon's body was now beginning to dissipate into the air.

Matilda's paws were scratching frantically on the door in the next room. No more being cooped up for her. She was making that clear.

"Nice job, Ana. I mean it," Cyril said, over his shoulder as he went to let Matilda out.

"This is getting really tiresome, Athen. Is it always like this?" I murmured, before slumping completely in his arms, not hearing his answer.

***

I was obviously not in our home in Victoria. First of all, we had no bedroom furniture there at the moment, but secondly, there was a beautiful view of the harbor right outside the window. Everything around me was so plush and grand. I reached my arms out from under the covers, feeling my body stretch the way it only does after an amazing night of sleep. Athen wasn't in bed, but I had a sneaking suspicion he wasn't very far off. I wiggled my way up out of the comforter and did my best to try to figure out where we might be, when it hit me we were at the Empress Hotel. Porcelain clanking in the other room alerted me that Athen was on his way in.

"Hey, sleepyhead," Athen said smiling, carrying in a tray of tea and cookies. "You kinda slept through the whole afternoon tea thing downstairs, so I thought I'd try to recreate it a little up here."

I couldn't believe I'd slept so long, since the last thing I remembered was being in Athen's arms the day before, after the fight.

"Have I been out that long?   Since yesterday afternoon?" I was so embarrassed.

"You are the one who has most recently been brought back, and I'm the one who is exhausted? This makes no sense."

"Come on, sweetie.   You'd been gone for half a century – I was only gone a couple months, if that. I don't think I ever truly left."

I grabbed the teacup, which had such tiny pink flowers all over it – perfect for the setting at the Empress, wondering what kind of delightful flavor I might get to sip on.

"So did we leave poor Cyril and Arie to take care of everything?"   I felt a little guilty, knowing the answer already.

"Yeah, pretty much. I'd say when everything is back to normal, we are going to owe them pretty big." His grin said everything.

Nodding my head, I took in the warm, gold liquid, coating my throat on the way down to comfort my belly. The tea hinted of oolong, and I hoped it would perk me up enough to get back to normal.

"It's kind of nice that our room gets destroyed, and then, we wind up at the Empress Hotel."   I was so happy to be alone with him, I couldn't even hide my grin.

"Yeah, not a bad place to have to hunker down at for a while," he said, flipping on the television as we snuggled, and I sipped my tea.

"Do you think this thing that's happening is as big as it feels?" I asked Athen.

"I think it's bigger, Ana. This is personal for Azazel. Why he chose now out of all the centuries that have come and gone to begin his disturbances, we may never know, but we've got to make sure we are all prepared. I don't just mean us either. Our network is moving as swiftly as his is. We'll be ready when the time is right."

"How will we know?"

"There won't be any missing it."

"I've gone over all the memories that have slowly been rebuilding, and I don't think I've come to anything that resembles what we could be up against. Is that right?"

"True, there's been nothing like what this threatens to become. The key is knowing how many false starts and mini-battles we are going to have to contend with until the one that counts occurs."

"Kind of felt like they all counted." I began snuggling into the back of him, hoping for maybe one quick nap, so I could count myself as fully recuperated. The last several days had really created an exhaustion that seemed almost impossible to shake.

***

Waking up next to Athen was literally heaven on earth. Seeing that the light was still shining outside, I was thankful I didn't completely sleep the day away. I rolled in towards his beautifully defined body, placing my head on his chest. I grabbed the sheet, which was the only fabric left on the bed, and pulled it up around my shoulders, feeling the warmth of his skin next to mine. Having Athen back in my life was incredible. I felt complete again. My soul no longer ached. I moved my body on top of his as he began kissing my neck, his breath sending a chill throughout my body.

"There's a possibility, you know, that this is heaven. Right here," I whispered into his ear.

I closed my eyes, thankful that the serpent-eyed woman was no longer present in my dreams. She was quickly becoming a distant memory. She might be back to fight us with the rest of the Legion, but she couldn't steal his heart from me and that was the most important thing.

"I think we've had a piece of heaven for quite some time, my love," he told me, raising my body up. I felt his lips against my skin, tracing his way back up to my neck.

Hoping that we could stay here forever, I let myself fall back down into his arms. His hands reaching down my back on the way to grab the sheet once more to cover us up.

***

We were both overlooking the beautiful view on the lawn. The temperature was on the verge of freezing. The air was signaling a thunderstorm was on the horizon, but I didn't care. Springtime thunderstorms were actually quite gorgeous. If this was where Athen wanted to be, then this was where I would be, outside, standing next to him. The months that we had been apart had torn at me from every single direction. At times, I wasn't sure if I'd even make it, especially knowing there was someone else vying for his attention. That someone, also, happened to be an absolutely beautiful being, as long as she stayed in her human form.

Seeing the boats off in the distance with the fog hovering off the water, created the wonderful contained feeling I so loved about the Pacific Northwest.

"This place is amazing, isn't it?" Athen breathed out a deep, long breath.

"Truly, but I'm so grateful I'm able to share it with you again. Coming here by myself, remembering all the times we had here together, created a loneliness that I wasn't sure I could handle." Never wanting to admit my emotions aloud, I was surprised at my willingness to give him a glimpse into my more dark thoughts.

"Ana, don't ever lose faith in us – in our ability to love forever. Our bond is something that can never be destroyed. They can't force a future on us that we don't want. I know you're all I want. She never had a chance."

"I'd like to tell you I always believed that, but I'd be lying. Seeing the visions of you two together and knowing you'd been spending so much time with her made me doubt a lot of things. Things I didn't think I'd ever waver on."

"Sweetie, we'll make things right again. Those feelings will be a distant memory, I promise."

"There was even a moment, Athen, where ..." I could feel the tears beginning to make an entrance and forced myself to knock it off.

"What? It'll make you feel better if you just get it off your chest. I'll understand, no matter what it might be."

Knowing that for a brief second, I tried to con myself into believing I didn't need Athen, made me sad beyond belief. I was disgusted with myself, wishing those thoughts would forever go away – but the guilt was something I couldn't shake.

"When I realized the severity of things and what we might be fighting for and who we are fighting against, I felt that my feelings for you were obviously getting in the way of my ability to act with any sense." I was scanning his eyes to see if any of the hurt that I was spewing on him was reflected. There was no such look.

"I actually thought about trying to stay away from you," I whispered.

"Ana, you're my angel. Remember that, regardless, of who or what tries to separate us. You could do no wrong. Besides, I'm pretty irresistible. I don't think you could have stayed away no matter how hard you tried." My heart completely melted. How could he be so understanding and so very forgiving –and so completely correct?

Athen's hand wrapped around my back as we headed back to our room. Before I knew it, he scooped me up and brought me through the doors leading into our hotel room where he laid me down ever so gently. Bringing his lips closer to mine, I felt the warm, softness glide along my own, parting only slightly as he began kissing with a passion that was uncontrolled and brilliant.

We had nothing left to lose - our inhibitions were gone. I had no more secrets bottled up. We had been separated for decades, only to come together briefly again, before being separated yet again, and in all that time, we never lost sight of one another, even if it was on another level of consciousness. We knew deep within our souls that we were not whole until we had one another in each other's embrace.

As the comforter slid off the bed, I felt for the edge of his shirt to pull off as fast as I could. The beauty of his body was purely magnificent as he fell back on me, sending me to an utterly glorious place. I no longer needed to worry about the outsiders who had so often frequented my mind. Athen was mine and I was his. We were meant to be one for all eternity.

Chapter Thirty-One

I'd been avoiding Athen all morning. We were back at our home in Victoria. Cyril and Arie did an amazing job cleaning everything up for us, but the thanks we gave them over and over was about to be blown away into a million pieces, knowing that I'd seen visions that were going to disrupt our entire family. The most horrifying images had woken me up time and time again. I didn't want to believe any of the dreams, but they were all so real. I'd learned my lesson, once already, to not ignore these dreams. I knew deep inside I had to take them seriously. What it meant for the future of our family, I didn't know, but I had to voice them to Athen. He had to know.

I was out at the bakery closest to our home trying to gather up enough courage to tell Athen what my visions had shown me and, maybe, soften the blows by bringing home croissants for us to share as I was telling him things that I didn't think possible.

After I was through my second Americano, I knew I had to go home and face what was before me. Grabbing the brown paper bag containing our breakfast, I took a deep breath and pushed through the door letting the bell signal my exit.

I somehow managed to appear at our front door. The spring wreath did its best attempt at making my mood lift a tad. I wasn't sure if I should go in and just start telling Athen or, maybe, divert his attention first by way of a croissant. I hoped that as soon as I opened the door, the answers would come, and they did. Cyril and Arie were not home.

"There is something I need to tell you ..." I felt faint knowing the words I was about to utter could possibly change our family dynamics forever, and they could be wrong – my words could be wrong, but if they weren't, they needed to be said.

"I think Arie was tapped into something in Cyril that she didn't even realize." I could barely speak the words.

Athen's striking green eyes searched mine for answers, and I wasn't sure I was going to be able to have enough info to completely stop the destruction. I didn't want to believe that one of us could be tricked into turning against what we believed in.

"You've got to tell me, Ana." I knew he was right, but I didn't want to believe the images that woke me up the night before were true. There was no way one of us would purposefully betray any of us, but I saw it. Not knowing if it had already happened or was about to, I knew I had to tell Athen everything.

"It's Cyril - he was approached by Azazel, and he didn't make the decision I thought he would."

"What are you saying? That he went to the other side? Are you joking?" My worst fear was beginning to happen. The rift was already beginning. The thought that our family could be broken apart made me ill, and I didn't want to believe it either.

I looked up at Athen seeing the pain deep within his eyes. A coldness crept over the lenses as he looked back down at me. I knew the coldness wasn't directed at me. He was beginning to build the same emotional wall against Cyril that I'd attempted when I thought I should distance myself from Athen. Athen grabbed my hand and pulled me towards him. I felt the comfort of his arms, something I needed now more than he ever knew.

"It's true, isn't it?" he asked.

I didn't need to answer. My tears said everything.

***

Our croissants stayed untouched on the coffee table as we impatiently waited for Cyril and Arie. We both knew the best thing to do was get it out in the open. My mind began wandering back to what Arie was trying to tell me earlier. Could she have sensed it before I did? Does Cyril know?

The living room door opened to Cyril and Arie laughing as Cyril's arms were full carrying more bags of whatever else she could find to buy. The lightness of the moment was something I wanted to inhale in and never lose because I knew what we were about to discuss was going to change everything, possibly forever, and in our world, that was a very long time.

Athen and I, obviously, didn't do a good job of hiding what was going on. Their laughter stopped as soon as they saw our faces. Cyril placed the bags on the floor, and they came into the living room for a discussion I never thought possible.

***

"It's too dangerous to stay together. I didn't think I'd ever be saying that, but it looks like that time has come," Cyril announced. He was taking this as seriously as the rest of us. I wasn't sure if that made me more nervous or less. I guess I was hoping for him to completely deny that anything like that could happen, but that's not what I got.

Athen grabbed my hand. I knew this was hard on him too. He was so worried about his sister, especially with the visions I told him about, but this was our best shot. We had to divide and conquer and try to thwart whatever might happen with Cyril. I didn't want to believe my visions, but with my track record, I knew I had to tell Athen. I hoped with all of my heart that he would tell me that what I saw was impossible and persuade me that it was rubbish. Unfortunately, that wasn't what happened at all. Instead, we came up with a plan to switch things up a little bit. We weren't going to let Cyril be taken to the other side.

Arie nodded her head. With as dizzy as she may seem sometimes, she had a strength about her that I hoped to emulate one day. She wasn't just the bubbly, fun loving girl I loved so much. She knew when to turn it on and off. Right now she was all business. Cyril was pacing back and forth, confusing Matilda who wanted to follow his footsteps, which, any other day, would make me chuckle. Instead, I focused my gaze on Athen.

"We were thinking that maybe we should split up between Kingston and Whistler. Ana and I don't have a preference as to which one we should go to. You guys tell us."

"I'm thinking, we'll go up to Whistler. I don't think there is a right answer to this one," Cyril said, the anger building in his voice.

He didn't want to believe my visions anymore than any of the rest of us, but I think deep inside he actually believed it more than any of us, which was scary. I wasn't sure what gave me that vibe, but I knew it to be true. Things could turn very dark for our family if there was even an ounce of truth to my premonition.

"Well, I think this house, and Victoria has seen enough action to last a lifetime. I'm ready to get a move on it. The sooner the better to get this crap over with." Cyril shoved a magazine off the shelf closest to him and headed down the hall. This was a side I hadn't seen before. Searching Arie's eyes, I knew this wasn't a side of Cyril she had experienced either.

"It's gonna be okay, Arie. I know we can make this go away. I'm sure I'm wrong, but better to be safe than sorry, right?" I searched her eyes for forgiveness. Guilt was coming at me from every direction. I felt responsible for creating this new Cyril. What if my images were all wrong, and I put us all through this for nothing?

"Yeah? Well, what if you didn't tell us, and we weren't prepared. What if they are correct? Imagine if we experienced the ending to this scenario because you didn't want to mention it?" Athen replied to my thoughts aloud. I totally forgot to shut him out of my mind with all the drama surrounding Cyril, but was kind of grateful he heard my thoughts. He made me feel a little better.

"I know. Believe me, I know. But there's a part of me that wonders if I'm wrong."

Arie walked over and sat next to me on the couch, hugging me as I began to feel my eyes fill with tears.

"You did the right thing by telling Athen. Really - it's just a lot for us, any of us, to handle. Don't blame Cyril. I can't imagine what he must be going through. Knowing he could never commit such an atrocity, yet having just enough doubt creep in to shake everything you believe in? This isn't his fault, and this isn't your fault, Ana. We'll make it through this." Her hand reached for mine, squeezing it. "Azazel will not get to him. I guarantee it."

"Thanks." Was all I could utter.

***

None of us had that much to pack so we were done pretty quickly. It felt odd knowing that we would be leaving this house in separate directions. It was hard to comprehend us as separate pairs, preparing for a fight that we knew nothing about. Arie had reached out to all of our friends, and to none of our surprise, they saw the Legions' activity strengthen in their regions. It was clear that we would be coming together at some point for a battle, but none of us knew exactly when. We were all too busy trying to get our loved ones back or help squash the little uprisings that the Legions had begun starting with the humans to worry about when the main battle was going to begin.

I was thinking back to all the road trips we had taken with Cyril and Arie and the happy times those always brought. Whether we were driving from Whistler to Seattle or to Kingston with a car full of snacks, pillows, and Matilda stuck in between us somewhere. Now, we are leaving each other, hoping for the best and preparing for the worst. Matilda was jumping up on her hind legs, resting her front paws on my leg, hoping for any sort of scratch on her head or an ear tickle. I was secretly relieved that she was coming with us. After being without her, when Athen was gone, it had made me become even more attached to the little girl.

Our goal was to be down to Kingston before sunset, and at this rate, we would be very lucky to achieve that. None of us really wanted to say goodbye. Athen made the first move, by loading the last bag into the Jeep and setting Matilda inside.

"Alright, man," Athen said, grabbing Cyril. "Keep an eye on my sister. She tends to get herself in trouble when we aren't all together."

Cyril obviously appreciated Athen's lighthearted goodbye as he let go of Athen and nodded.

"You got it, man, but you've got the klutz. You should be more worried about her."

"Alright, I'm happy everyone is able to feel better about things at my expense but come on! I'm not that bad. Especially lately, right? You've seen my moves recently. Pretty impressive right?" I almost didn't want to hear the answer, because I thought I'd actually been doing pretty well; all things considered. Granted, I did have a shapeshifting accident, but that could happen to anyone.

"Yeah, Cy. You got me there." He rubbed my shoulders as if that would make me feel better versus his words as we all left our home in Victoria to go our separate ways.

***

I woke up in a dead panic. I hadn't felt this level of fear for quite sometime. Athen shot up in bed beside me, flipping on the lamp on his bedside table. We had only been in Kingston a short time.

"What's wrong, sweetie?" His eyes were full of concern. "Did they get to Cyril?"

"No, it's not that. It's something else. They've started something else." My fingers were running along my temples. My head was pounding. I wasn't certain of what I saw, but the images were beyond terrifying.

"Who has started?" Athen already knew the answer since he was getting out of bed, heading for the phone. "Fill me in."

"They're lighting fires." I ignored his question. I couldn't help it as a lump began to form in my throat. "Surrounding Whistler."

Athen had already dialed Arie's number. We thought we had made it through the biggest hurdle with Cyril, not realizing more was to come so quickly.

"What did you see, Ana? Give me all the details you can." Athen was waiting for his sister to pick up.

I'd already grabbed my notebook and begun writing. I liked to keep track of things since I was still learning the ins and outs of everything. Trying to write in words and condense the images that had haunted me minutes before seemed almost impossible.

"Yeah, hey," Athen began. "Ana's visions led her somewhere pretty horrible. Here she is." I stared at him not really wanting to take the phone.

"Hi, Arie. So fire is going to be their main weapon, and it's directed where you guys are. They are going to attack Whistler." I let my mind wander to what I'd dreamed minutes earlier, doing my best to let the images reach Athen, Cyril, and Arie. I felt the images would speak louder than anything I could relay in words.

Closing my eyes, left me with the latest images I was attempting to place in their minds, those of the streaks of fire streaming down from the sky. No one would see it coming. Humans would think it nothing more than lightning strikes or human error with a campsite. Unfortunately, those were events that can be handled pretty simply in the scheme of things. There can be an end to those kinds of flames. What I didn't see with these images was any sort of immediate end to these events unless we stopped them. Every time one fire was extinguished, it looked as if the demons had started another, trapping everyone up in Whistler. The images formed of the thick, green forests being turned into charred remnants of sticks and twigs. Smoke was filling up the beautiful skies, confusion setting in for the tourists and residents of the most quaint village the Northwest had to offer. I did my best to shut off the images before letting them all escape. There were some I couldn't let them see. I didn't want to believe them.

"So, I think you guys need to leave." Was all that escaped over the phone as the last of the images found their way into them. "Now."

"Ana, we can't leave everyone up here. We've got to help. As soon as I hang up, I'm gonna let everyone know. We have to stay, you guys. We can't leave."

Unfortunately, Athen and I already knew they would say that. It would be so much easier to think that they would be self-serving first, but of course, they weren't. Athen took in a deep breath and let it out slowly. It must have been loud enough for Arie to hear because she uttered something quickly into the phone, I almost didn't catch it before she hung up on us.

"Guys, we'll be fine. We'll call you after we contact everyone up here." Hanging up the phone, Athen wrapped his arms around me but not before whispering quietly into my ear.

"Why don't you tell me the images you didn't want any of us to see, sweetie?"

Chapter Thirty-Two

Cyril, Arie, and the entire Whistler community were cut off from all contact. The forest fires had begun. Of course, everyone thought it was the unusually dry spring, and the lightning strikes. If only it was so simple.

We were glued to the news, but truthfully, we were able to get more information directly from Cyril and Arie who were constantly communicating to us. The demons' attempt to cut off Whistler from aid was a success. The hillsides were either a charred mess of ash or brilliant new flames that the demons had set ablaze. It was an absolutely sickening sight. The beautiful wildflowers, which had only barely begun to bloom, were now fighting with fleeing animals, flames, and firefighters to maintain their beauty.

Miraculously, there had been no casualties, yet. Unfortunately, that could change in an instant, and we all knew that. Cyril and Arie were meeting nonstop with all our fellow counterparts in Whistler trying to gauge damage and next steps. The flames hadn't gotten to the village but rather had cut the town off completely from help. The smoke was too thick for air support. Help was working its way up from the backside and the upper mountain to get the flames to a manageable level, but unfortunately, the demons were laying in wait to start them up again.

I felt completely helpless and was riddled with guilt. If I hadn't told anyone about the dreams I'd been having, none of us would have separated, and we would all still be together.

Athen flipped off the television and slid the remote across the table at me.

"I think I've had enough for the moment. Between the reports from Cyril and Arie and that, I don't think I can do it for another second."

"Why won't they just leave?" Knowing the answer already, I wasn't sure why I asked it.

"Listen, I'm just as worried about them as you are, but to your point, they can get out of there if they need to. They just don't want to leave all of those humans. I think they feel they can somehow stop this before it takes any human lives."

"Do you believe that?" I asked Athen.

He reached for my hand across the table. His was cold as ice.

"If anyone can pull off something like that, they can... But they are going to need our help."

I nodded knowing that it was only a matter of time before Cyril and Arie were going to call us up there. They had been working with the other families up there, figuring out what method would work best to evacuate the humans if needed or put an end to the flames. As of now, neither alternative seemed very plausible. Then again, I hadn't been exposed to this type of thing recently.

"Evacuations would be more risky. Pulling something off like that without any humans figuring out seems almost impossible. We would have to help their memory out, and in those numbers, I'm not sure we could do it as timely as we would need to. I honestly think that we'll be up there to attempt to extinguish the flames. I think that's our best bet. I'm just waiting to hear that from Cyril. I've already contacted about seven hundred of us locally who could get up there and fight."

"So, we are going to have to *fight* to get these fires to stop?" My stomach began twisting in knots. This kind of battle seemed far larger in scale than anything I'd dealt with before. Sadly, I knew it was nothing compared with what we could be facing in the future, but regardless, it frightened me. A huff escaped, alerting Athen to my worry.

"There will be a lot more of us than them, sweetie. I promise. We wouldn't attempt it if we knew we couldn't win it." His calming, green eyes immediately began to soothe my worries. "Plus, I've seen your sweet fighting skills, hun. You're better than all of us."

"Haha, very funny!" I said, taking my hand back.

"I kind of feel like this is my fault," I blurted out.

Athen's eyes were full of confusion. I knew on the outside of it, it might seem like a stretch that I was responsible, but it seemed pretty matter of fact in my world.

"If we hadn't split, they wouldn't have been up there alone. The demons might not even have attacked." It was hard for me to say it aloud.

"Regardless of location, they would have found a way to get to us."

Athen had gotten up and moved to stand behind me, hugging me from behind. I needed that comfort so badly. I didn't even realize it until his arms continued to keep hold of me.

"This will be over soon, my love," he whispered so quietly, I almost didn't even hear his words, the very words that I needed to hear.

Closing my eyes, I did my best to focus on the needs of our family, feeling as blessed as I had in a long time. Having Athen here was everything I needed to maintain my strength, and I began planning for whatever might be in store for us.

"So do you believe Cyril when he says he hasn't been approached yet by Azazel?" I asked Athen.

"Yeah, I do. I don't think what you saw has happened yet."

"So there's hope we can divert it or change it somehow then?"

He nodded his head in agreement as his cell began receiving text after text, giving us the signal that the time has come.

***

The amount of smoke that was hovering in the air was beyond anything the TV images showed. How many blazes the demons had been setting was unclear, but it had to have been a ton. We had called in help from everyone in the Northwest who could come as quickly as possible. The fires hadn't been burning for long at all, but so many were being set the destruction was building. We didn't want to waste anymore time on their plan.

Being in the presence of the demons' wickedness put everything that was ahead of us in perspective.

Because of the work that the fire teams were able to achieve, the road back up to Whistler had been opened so the evacuations were beginning rapidly. However, since our goal wasn't to evacuate but rather go in and fight the true source of the flames, we knew we wouldn't be able to take our car. We were going to have to get in by our own abilities. We left our car in Squamish, and Cyril and Arie were meeting us along the railway tracks so we could plan our next steps.

It was such a wonderful sight to see Cyril and Arie land together, holding hands. Obviously, my visions didn't set them apart. Hopefully, it made them only stronger. We had to protect each other no matter what.

"Arie!" I squealed, squeezing her with all of my might. I was so happy to see her again.

"Are you doing okay?" I asked.

"Yeah, I think. We've been working nonstop up there making sure the flames wouldn't get near the village. We've been on watch so whenever a new fire was started, we were able to put it out immediately. It's getting really tiresome, though. We're all worn out. That's why we need you guys and the back-up."

Nodding, I grabbed Athen's hand, completely understanding their exhaustion.

"Well, we're surrounded. They are waiting for the word from us to swoop in, so to speak," Athen said grinning. "How many of the demons do you think there are?"

"I honestly don't think that many." Cyril stepped in. "I think they're just quick. I'm guessing no more than seventy five or so."

"Really. That's good news, because there's about seven hundred of ours waiting for our call."

"Nice. Let's get on it," Cyril echoed. "We were able to figure out where they were all congregating at. That's what took us the longest, and why we didn't want to call you up here too soon."

"Awesome, then let's just do it," Athen announced.

Hearing those words began to send fear through my body. I hadn't met up with this many demons at once before. Knowing we had the numbers we did, waiting for our directions should have calmed me, but it didn't. The fear of losing Athen again was beginning to overwhelm me. I focused on the gratification that I had gotten so many times before when fighting these creatures, hoping that would replace the fear.

"Honey, you're going to be fine. I'm going to be fine. We've got this. Don't let your mind go there." I nodded, knowing he was right.

"Let's get going shall we?" Arie asked.

I watched her take off towards the heavens, with Cyril following right behind her. Athen let go of my hand, and he shot into the air next, pausing only to look back at me and call my name. The adrenaline began pumping throughout my body as I let my body head towards the treetops as well.

I heard Athen's call go out for all of our fellow comrades. I wasn't sure if he was channeling it to everyone or if it was actually going through the airwaves. It was intense as I began hearing all the responses coming back directly to him as well. The many octaves of voices signaling their participation in the expected battle was exhilarating.

We were only moments away from the camp that the demons had made. Not all would be here since they were still starting fires as fast as they could, but

Cyril and Arie had our friends back in the village ready and waiting to scope out where the stragglers were at, so we could pounce.

The air was thick with smoke as we began our descent back towards the ground and our target. They had a makeshift camp set up, and it looked like their plan was to spend very little time in it. We circled the camp one last time to gauge the activity, when one of the minions came flying from the north readying himself for an attack against Cyril.

I directed my focus on my new target, flying as fast as I could to reach Cyril's side and do my best to fight. Seeing the chain dangling from the minion, I yanked on it as hard as I could, allowing a scream to escape into the air, alerting the camp below that they had visitors. Ripping the chain out of the minion, the black mist immediately began releasing into the air.

"Nice work, Ana," Cyril said, as he shot down to the ground to begin the battle.

The wind was shifting behind me as I felt our support arriving. One after the other, they began landing in the campsite, immediately demolishing whatever and whoever was in their range of sight. I took a deep breath in as I attempted to land myself without wiping out or causing a disruption. Right before my feet hit the ground, a minion slammed itself into me, ramming me into the hard earth.

The minion had my hair pinned back on the ground, ripping each strand as I attempted to move. My legs kicking at the creature as I scanned for the piece of metal that I'd become so accustomed to seeing. There didn't seem to be any this time. Seething in anger, I reached my hand over the minion who had now begun grinding his foot into my shoulder, creating the perfect opportunity for me to grab his ankle. His other foot lightened its hold on my hair, so that I was able to roll my body far away from my attacker. The drug of victory was now pumping through my entire body. He came barreling at me, and my body lifted over his as his arm reached into the empty air. Spinning around in the air, I landed on his shoulders, snapping his neck. Feeling his body crumple to the ground, I knew I was in for another bumpy landing as I crashed to the dirt below.

Standing up to gauge our success, I saw hundreds of our kind landing and squashing the minions as quickly as they came. Athen came up behind me, scoping out my victim, turning to me completely impressed.

"Nice. He wasn't like the others," he said before taking off again.

"Tell me about it," I yelled after him.

The minions were being discarded as quickly as they appeared. Arie had let the others in the village know of our success, and they began attempting to flush the stragglers back to the camp. This win was close to being ours, it was only a matter of timing.

***

We were in our home in Whistler, trying our best to rest up a bit from the day's feverish activities. The Hemlocks outside were lightly swaying with the breeze that was beginning to come up. Now that we had defeated the minions and their efforts, the last few remaining fires were being put out. On our way back up to the village, I was amazed at how little of the forests leading up to the village had been harmed. Compared to the images on the news, what was right before me, looked like a little brush fire. The larger fires were set off in the hills, and that seems to be where the news crews were able to get with their helicopters.

Even though it was spring, I had one of our throws wrapped around me. The chilly mountain air was never truly gone, regardless of the season. Cyril was making us some tea before Athen and I headed back home. We left Matilda back at the house, knowing we had to get back to her the same day. In hindsight, Athen felt far more confident about our victory than I realized.

"You've got to come back down with us. Ana's got more to tell you. Azazel's ready to meet with her - with us. It's gonna be big." Athen told Arie and Cyril.

"Should we really though? With her other visions?" Arie asked.

I wondered that myself but told myself that knowing what was lurking in the shadows for Cyril was half the battle.

"I think for this, we should all be together. She has seen Azazel come to her in her dreams."

I nodded my head in agreement to what Athen was relaying from my dreams.

"Okay, well. I guess we'll drive you back to your car in Squamish and meet you back down south," Cyril announced, his grin as large as I'd seen it in a long time. I think he felt better knowing we were willing to trust him by our side and not be as plagued with worry that he was going to turn against us like my vision.

"I've got some girl items I want to talk with Ana about anyway, so I think this was perfect timing." She looked at me allowing a few of her thoughts to slip over to my mind, none of what I expected to hear.

I shook my head in agreement, fearing what she might be wanting to divulge.

"Awesome! I'm glad we are back as a unit," I chuckled, throwing a pillow at Cyril.

Thankful that they were coming back down with us, I decided not to mention that my vision called for everything to happen tomorrow. Since Athen didn't mention it, I decided I wasn't going to either.

Chapter Thirty-Three

The clanking and clashing began getting louder and louder with every moment that whipped by. I was hoping my family would arrive soon. I knew who I was about to meet. I wasn't sure I was as ready for it as I needed to be. I had no idea how to prepare for it in the first place. Instead of the usual ice-cold temperature I was so used to experiencing with the arrival of the Legion members, an intense heat began to surface alongside of my body. The rumbling and clashing was beginning to vibrate the ground I was standing on. The earth was beginning to shift and give as he got closer and closer. As I was scanning the beach, boulders, and mountainside looking for this creature, I wondered what I should be expecting – just one creature or several?

I looked down at my legs, realizing I still had the black leather leggings on from the woman I shapeshifted on earlier as practice. I still hadn't completely gotten the hang of things. Sure that she was probably wearing my outfit, I wondered how on earth I could be caught dead in this mess of a look - the black leather leggings were only accentuated by a wonderfully tacky silver top, and black stiletto boots. I was certain some could pull off this look, but I wasn't meant to, especially on a beach. I did my best to distract myself from the overwhelming amount of fear that was beginning to surface by wondering what Athen would think of my new look.

A loud buzzing, like an amplifier hiked up too loud, began rattling my eardrums. It matched the same rhythm as the clashing and clanking that I was growing accustom to. The disorienting effect washing over me created an uneasiness that would only be solved with the arrival of my family.

To my horror, I finally focused in on Azazel. He was flying low enough beneath the clouds now that I could see he wasn't alone. He looked as wretched as I feared. My heart fell with the realization that he was going to make it to me before my family did. I glanced quickly over my shoulder one last time to see if by any chance Athen was there to help, knowing I wouldn't dare turn my back on this monster once he arrived.

Azazel swooped down to the beach, walking before he even touched the sand, his silver hair swarming in the wind. He was dressed in an all black leather trench coat, dripping in silver metal chains, I did my best to push down the feelings of defeat that were already surfacing. As he came closer, I realized that the silver chains were attaching minions to him like stray dogs. Those other beings I saw in the sky were these poor chained-up beings. It was utterly disgusting to see. Standing only a few feet from me now, I began to feel the tiny beads of sweat beginning to form at the base of my neck from the overwhelming heat that was rolling off of this demon. Now was my time. I could no longer play the innocent.

"What is it you want, Azazel?" I stared directly into his black, hollowed eyes.

The desire to fight him was building in my veins. I wanted a fight. I wanted to destroy this demon and all the creatures connected to him.

"The kiss of death. How does that sound for romantic?" His voice raspy, yet strong and exuding victory before I even had a chance to be defeated.

"From who?" I asked, repulsed by the being that was standing before me.

"I think you know the answer to that one, my Ana. If I couldn't have your mother, the way Remiel, your father, did. Then shouldn't I get the next best thing ...her daughter - don't you think, Ana?" He paused for several seconds like he was debating whether or not to utter the next few words. "Your sister, Lilith, agrees with me."

The anger was rising beyond anything I could control. I chose to ignore his Lilith comment. I knew I couldn't defeat this demon by myself, not with my lack of experience compared to his – not yet anyway. The chemicals had been fully released, and I wanted to satisfy my craving.

I needed a fight.

Of course, he had planned it this way by destroying me fifty years earlier, making my family run in circles trying to bring me back to them. It wasn't the humans who were pawns in this world he created. It was us he had been playing games with. It was me. Countless families losing loved ones all because of me. I was no longer going to be a pawn in his depraved game of chess.

"You won't get that satisfaction, Azazel," I hollered at him, wanting victory at this very moment.

"I think we both know you could come with me right now and solve this entire little problem we have here. Don't you agree? You are even dressed for the occasion - black leather and silver. How perfect can you get? Some things are meant to be."

I truly cursed my utterly lacking shapeshifting ability now.

"You know, Azazel, what I can't believe is that you would let a mortal woman have that much control over you - thousands of years of hatred building for a woman, my mother? That seems pretty pathetic. You don't strike me as someone who wants to be seen as pathetic. I get that you never forgave my father, Remiel. But his falling in love with the same mortal woman who loved him back actually saved you. Don't you think it is punishment enough that my father is stuck in between worlds? You were saved from that atrocity because you were never with my mother!"

"You don't understand revenge very well do you, Ana?"

The weight of mankind's possible destruction was a crushing feat to digest, all because of my father and mother's love affair.

"I guess I don't." The longer I spoke to him the better the odds that my family would arrive. Azazel's minions were getting restless. I knew they were hoping for a fight. I knew they were hoping for blood.

"Say I come with you. Then what? The fight's over? I doubt that very much. What assurance would I have?"

Azazel's fingers were as gnarled as all the others - his nails tinged brown and dreadfully long. Getting impatient, he began rubbing his hands together.

"So, Ana. What's it gonna be?" he seethed through his clenched teeth. He didn't answer my question.

"I think you know the answer to that one. You don't understand revenge very well do you, Azazel?" I smiled. My family was near and so were others. I could feel them.

"If you don't come with me, I promise you that a war like no other will ensue."

"I'm willing to take my chances."

They had arrived. Thousands of them. He was surrounded. The hillside behind him was a constant landing strip for my kind, one right after the other. To my right, hundreds of Fallen Angels marched through the sand to come stand by my side. Taking in a deep breath, I felt Athen's hand rest on my shoulder from behind. My family was here, and they had brought friends.

"Was there anything else you wanted to tell us? I know we would all like to hear it. Wouldn't we?" My glare was as icy as it ever had been.

The minions surrounding Azazel were suddenly cowering. The obedience I'd mistaken earlier for strength allowed me to see a victory like never before.   My appetite had been wetted and only victory would curb it.

Azazel let out a loud bellowing sound as he flashed into the air, with his chained minions dragging behind him.   He suddenly vanished, releasing the chains allowing the minions to remain. Sure he would return, I looked around the beach as more of our fellow Fallen Angels were arriving, I felt deep inside that this was a war that could be won.

It was a war that needed the right leader, and I knew I was that leader.

Chapter Thirty-Four

How many thousands of us there were, I'd never know. I didn't need to know. I could feel their souls. I could feel their intentions. We were all acting as one - here for a single act.

The wind was blowing harder than it had all spring, the rain coming in sideways as it pelted us, picking up speed from the ocean. The weight of my drenched clothes was nothing compared to the burden I felt deep inside. As the wind howled over the cliffs and through the trees to finally reach us all where we stood, there was a vigilance it brought with it. I was leading us directly into victory, and I was leading us directly into defeat. Some of us wouldn't make it. Some of our family members wouldn't make it. That was known well before anyone decided to join us.

We were an army. They never saw it coming. Standing in the front row, I felt for Athen's hand and squeezed it. Looking up at him as he stood stoically, hair completely drenched, clothes stuck to his body, I knew we were all miserable - miserably waiting for a fight that would drastically change things to come for both our world and the mortal world. Looking to my left, I saw Cyril and Arie, hands interlocked, looking straight ahead, waiting for the same thing as all of us – a sign of the enemy.

I let go of Athen's hand, stepping forward and spinning around to see something I'd been telling myself not to. Partially worried that the numbers I'd see wouldn't meet my expectations, I didn't want to psych myself out. Instead, what I saw was countless rows and rows of our fellow Fallen Angels, lined up side by side, hands interlocking, ready to face whatever we might encounter in this first of many battles.

The entire beach was lined with being after being with the beautiful green eyes that I took so much comfort in. The lines of Fallen Angels went as far as I could see, circling beyond and behind the jagged cliffs. The sight was more magnificent than anything I could have thought up in my own mind. Catching Athen's eyes, I felt tears begin to surface because of the overwhelming support that was going to accompany us into victory.

Nodding at me, he took a step towards me, spinning like I did to look at the numbers who had gathered to support us.

"Wow, Ana. This is incredible," he whispered.

"Isn't it? If only it weren't for the reason that it was, I might be able to revel in it all."

Doing my best to wipe off the rain droplets that were continually running down my face, I shrugged off the chill that was trying to present itself deep within in my bones.

"More are coming, aren't they?" I asked Athen, as I did my best to make out the images I was seeing come down one by one, making their way to the end of the lines that my eyes could no longer find.

Nodding, he stood back in line, and I followed his lead. The evil ones were on their way. I could feel it. Facing forward, I raised my arm up towards the sky and circled my wrist, with a finger extended. It was time to listen.

Straining to hear past the torrential downpour and crashing waves, I did my best to concentrate on the vibrations that I'd learned so recently to pick up from the demons. I steadied my breathing in hopes that it would help pick out what I needed to hear before the others.

I felt the shift, everyone had noticed my signal. Row after row of warriors, like myself, were stiffening, preparing for an unknown. The vibrations began to set themselves into motion. A light pounding began off in the distance - the intensity rising with every beat. Closing my eyes, I did my best to distinguish the beats. With every thud echoing through the air, I knew that it accounted for an army not that dissimilar to ours in size.

The cracking sound began reverberating through my eardrums. They were here. The sky opened up, pouring more on us than dampness as the deathly images began dropping down on us one by one. Thousands of minions, dripping in chains were like puppets dropping from the sky, only coming to life once they hit the ground.

The battle had begun. Letting go of Athen's hand, I heard his whisper reach me telling me that he loved me just in time. He rocketed through the air meeting his first opponent. Forcing myself to turn away from him, I was determined not to let our love hinder my performance; rather, it was there to strengthen it. I felt the first blow of the sharp, metal chain as it hit my back, sending my body to the wet sand with a force like no other.

As I felt the tiny granules of sand enter my mouth, I commanded myself to get up. Everyone was looking at me to lead us to victory. I couldn't let them down, especially within the first seconds of fighting. I jumped back up, readying myself to take out the creature that sent me into the earth, only to see a towering figure hovering over me waiting for my next move, laughing as if he had already won the fight.

I moved towards the figure, who I didn't recognize, darting to the right at the last moment, grabbing the chain that I was certain was the one that whipped me, pulling it with all of my strength. A shriek ran through the air, as the demon was flipped onto his back, my heel burrowing into his neck. Tugging on the chain, another shriek came barreling out of the creature. Finishing him off with one last quick stomp on his neck, I followed the chain as it led to his body. Assuming that the chain was hooked to the demon's clothing, I was horrified when I felt it lead its way to his hip. Pulling up the shirt, I realized the chain was buried deep within the monster's flesh. The sight was repulsive as the metal edges were barely visible as the chain snaked deep under the skin.

The shrieks and screams from the other minions, as they were being thrown and caught by their chains was an encouraging sound. As the demons and minions continued to land, I was able to estimate there were at least three of ours to every one of theirs. For now, the numbers were working in our favor. I knew it was crucial to not let myself become overconfident because that's when mistakes could be made.

Scanning the beach, I saw the demons being overtaken by our own. I did my best to channel my findings to my family. If we target the ones with the chains first, we would be able to eliminate quite a few in a very short time. It felt too easy. I couldn't see Athen, Cyril, or Arie so getting confirmation that they received my message was comforting.

Looking in the crowd for Azazel, the disappointment began building as I realized this wasn't the battle he was going to participate in. This was the preemptive battle that was our test. The fury was building inside of me, knowing the battle would not be ending today, but rather, this was only the beginning. My desire to destroy Azazel was only growing stronger with every trick and trap he set for us all. It also answered my question that I had buried deep inside on whether Lilith was going to show up for this one either. My disappointment would have to wait for another day; instead I had to channel my anger into the fight before me.

Diving into the crowd of minions to continue my fight, I was determined to finish them off quickly. This was a waste of time and resources. It was disgusting, and there was nothing I could do about it other than participate and make it end.

Snagging chain after chain, causing dreadful squeals of pain as I tugged from one evil creature to the next, destroying as many as were in my path, gave me the strength to keep going. Catching Athen's eye quickly, he nodded, letting me know he captured all of my thoughts earlier, which brought a huge amount of relief. They are on the same page. We needed to get this over with and quickly.

It was painfully obvious that we were the victors in this match, but unfortunately, we had to ensure that we had taken care of every minion left standing. They wouldn't stop until they were destroyed. The dark mist was being released into the air from the mounting pile of minions. The mist could easily be mistaken for a wicked winter storm. I stood in the far corner of the beach surveying our victories and watching our side fly away to wherever it was they came from after they finished their last victims off. I'd never get to say thank you or meet all the individuals who came to help us fight. The fallen angels were leaving as quickly as they had come, never receiving anything in return. I was staring in utter disbelief as I saw the piles of minions we had destroyed.

Feeling the slash of a chain hit my neck from behind, I turned around quickly, only to be hit again. Grabbing the chain and yanking it as hard as I could, while I watched the wretched creature's skin stretch in the direction of each tug, I collapsed alongside the last minion. Seeing his body crumple to the beach, satisfaction began to swell through my body until the pain dropped me to my knees.

Athen was immediately by my side, picking me up. Not understanding why these injuries, compared to any of the other lashes I had received, were worse, confused me. I honestly couldn't fathom why the last lash that I was dealt would have done this to me. My mind was becoming quickly cluttered as I tried hard to concentrate on Athen's face, his lips, anything to get my mind focused.

"What if our love is the downfall?" I whispered.

My arms were wrapped around his neck as he carried me from the pile of bodies spread across the beach.

"Never. It only makes us stronger." He was out of breath, and I didn't understand why until he dropped to his knees, letting me roll out of his arms onto the pebbles below.

"Athen!" I screamed without realizing what was happening, watching him begin to fall forward. "No, Athen!"

I searched his body for any sign or clue. I didn't understand what was happening. My fingers felt over every crease and crevice of his skin and clothing. I felt nothing. The tears were streaming down my face, I was unable to catch my breath. We had defeated the Legion. It was me who had gotten hurt, not Athen.

"Sweetheart, please...please. I don't understand. Don't leave me, please." My wailing had to catch someone's attention. There had to be someone left on the beach. I prayed someone would hear because I couldn't move, not with my injuries. I began to feel serenity envelop my body. Holding Athen, I slowly scooted myself to be closer to him. It was as if his body was making me calmer. The ocean air began to get deep within my lungs, as I did my best to focus. I had to communicate with Cyril and Arie. I tried my best calling for help.

The confusion set in. We won, and now, Athen was lifeless in front of me, and I can't use my legs to get help. A sense of hopelessness began to invade my thoughts as I did my best to concentrate and beg for Cyril or Arie to help by way of thought. The steady beat of the waves crashing, washed over me as I, too, met the same darkness as Athen.

***

Somehow I was in our bed – we were in our bed at our Kingston home. I opened my eyes and saw the familiar colors surrounding me along with the wonderfully comforting sound of Matilda snoring. I reached for Athen's hand, clasping it as tight as I could. He slowly began to tighten his hand around mine. Remembering where I last was and the inability to move my legs made me shudder. Cyril and Arie must have gotten us both back to our home.

"How are you feeling?" Athen muttered into my ear, turning on his side to face me. Remembering that I couldn't move my legs from the injuries, I turned my head to face his.

"Good but awfully confused." He looked completely unscathed. "Come here!" He moved closer, and I began kissing his neck frantically. I couldn't stop. I thought I'd lost him, yet again. I felt his breath whisper down on my forehead.

"You've got to explain! I was the one with the injuries, and then you collapsed?"

"Um, well. I was doing my best to try to heal you. I was just trying to do it too fast, and it depleted my resources so to speak." His eyes were sparkling as if I should be pleased with this answer. "Move your legs."

I curled them up and realized they really did move. Happiness flooded through me.

"Are you serious? You can do that?" I completely flipped over now, not having any fear of pain radiating through my spine or legs.

"Yeah, depending on the injury. We've all got our talents, you know?" He tried to play it off.

"Seriously? That's your special talent?" I asked tickling his ribs.

"One of them," he replied before coming over to grab me and take me under the covers with him. Completely exhilarated by the idea, I happily followed as he slid me down between the sheets. I couldn't believe that I was still relearning so much about this life and, truthfully, Athen.

***

The sun was drying up every cloud in the sky - a welcome sight for the Northwest. Athen and I were still at our Kingston home, just us two. It was incredible to be able to spend this time together, alone. I couldn't get enough of his newly-created sparkling, green eyes. It pained me not to see them for those several months that seemed like an eternity. Understanding more and more what fifty years of waiting for me must have been like, I felt like I could never reach that same level that he had been on, no matter how hard I tried.

Feeling Athen entering the bedroom, I spun around to greet him. Seeing his smile, my body rushed his, jumping on him as he lifted me up.

"Whoa! What's gotten into you this fine morning?" he asked, hugging me back tightly.

"I just can't believe how lucky I'm to have you. That's all," I said, not wanting to let go.

"Well, I feel the same way, sweetie," he said, letting me go to slide back onto the bed.

"Yea, but you know how lousy I feel about my patience? I only went months waiting for you and was thinking of some pretty drastic things. The amount of desperation I felt when I thought I couldn't have you or wouldn't have you made me act in ways I never would have thought. I had no control. You managed for fifty years to have your act together." I told him, somewhat sulking as I relived how awful of a soul mate I might actually be.

His finger tilting my chin to look up at him, he spoke the words that I'd been hoping to hear for so long – forgiveness.

"Ana, you didn't have someone chasing after you the way I did. I didn't have to deal with the thought of someone else possibly getting you. I don't know how I would've responded. Somehow, I think I might have been on the same track. You've got to let go of all of that. It will eat you up. That's one thing I'm sure of."

"Do you really think you might have had some of the same thoughts?"

He stared deeply into my eyes, brushing my hair from my face.

"Yeah, I think I'd rather have lived in oblivion than think someone else might have become the new me. Better to wander around knowing you aren't missing anything, than knowing you're missing everything, but someone else has it."

"Thank you, Athen. Thank you. I needed to hear that."

He was holding me tightly, and I believed he was telling me the truth. Maybe, I wasn't that horrible after all. Maybe, it could have happened to anyone.

"It's been wonderful being down here, only us two. I know it's coming to an end though," I said, the seriousness of our latest victory still fresh in our memory.

"Uh, before ya know it," he said, ruffling my hair as I jumped on him, pretending to attack.

"When do you think they will get here so we can all say our goodbyes?"

"Way too soon," Athen mumbled. "Way too soon."

"Do you really think this is what we're going to have to do for the next while? It seems like we sent a pretty good signal to Azazel and his followers."

"Yeah, he got the message alright. He knows that on that beach we were united in our pursuit for the good of mankind. But it also told him something else - that the fight has barely begun."

"So you think he's only going to step back for a little while before starting up again?"

"I think you know the answer to that better than any of us," Athen said, referring to my latest premonitions.

"I know, but it's hard to fathom that separating from Cyril and Arie is the best thing for us now."

"You and I know both know that the threat Cyril poses is still great. We aren't out of the woods with him turning against us. We all know that. He could still become trapped with Azazel's plan, unable to refuse." My heart ached at the sound of those words hitting the air. I also knew that I was part of something larger that I couldn't tell Athen. Arie had made me promise, and this was the only time that I would ever follow her wishes by keeping a secret.

Hearing Cyril and Arie arriving, we both readied ourselves to say our goodbyes to them, for as long or as short as it may be. Our plan was to spread out to places where we would be less obvious. All of the

Fallen Angels around the globe were leaving the comforts of their homes, not knowing when any of us would get to return. We would be doing our best to not use our typical way of communicating between each other, no telepathy, so to speak. We would actually be using cell phones so that it would just blend into the other chatter of mortals. Our goal was to try to stay off the demon grid awhile so we could all regroup and establish our networks and plans of attack.

It didn't help that the lingering images of Cyril being tapped to join Azazel hadn't been executed. If it was something that we thwarted, at least, we could check it off the list, but that hadn't even happened yet. There had been no attempts. It was still a viable problem. Arie had been a nervous wreck and asked me to participate in a plan that she had devised to possibly stop the entire vision from happening. She thought being the sister of Athen would work in her favor as long as I played my part in it. Arie was certain she had a remedy for Cyril's possible predicament, and it was me who had to keep the secret buried deep inside, waiting for the signal. Knowing everything they had done for me, I felt it was only natural to help in any way I could, even if I didn't necessarily agree with it. Only time would tell if we did the right thing.

Chapter Thirty-Five

"Will they find our hiding place? Will they find Cy and Arie?"

"Not a chance," Athen replied flatly. He had something on his mind, and he was doing an incredible job of hiding his thoughts and not divulging anything. I was getting more antsy by the minute as I continued to hide my soul secrets as well, lightly cursing Arie for putting me in this position in the first place.

"Do you think it could be true or are you only being extra vigilant because of everything else going on?" I hoped with all my heart it was the latter. I could feel my entire body tense up as I scanned our surroundings. It was actually warmer than I expected for this time of spring, especially considering we were out in the middle of nowhere holed up in a carved-out piece of rocky Mt. Rainier. As far as caves go, this would probably be considered a pretty spacious one, but it certainly wasn't somewhere I hoped to live for long.

Athen had managed to create quite a little cozy home for us three, somehow. Not knowing the length of time we might be on the run made things very difficult to cope with. Nothing like this had happened before in the realm of the underworld - a family possibly turning on itself? Impossible. Unfortunately, we were not the only family it was happening to. After we told Arie, she refused to believe the claims at first. She was hysterical and didn't believe my visions – until we heard from the other families around the world. We weren't the only ones. The demons were trying to divide us as best they could. The Legions were almost complete. We had already experienced some of them. We had been expecting the wrong kind of battle. We had been preparing for the wrong kind of war.

The Legions were threatening harm to family members of the Fallen Angels if the chosen victims didn't do as they were told. Continually involving mortals only added to the mix. If the persuasion techniques continued to fail, the demons had begun to lure the family member into their world with more promises of terrible things that would rip the families apart, but it all seemed to imply some sort of mind trick. That was the scary part. That technique hadn't ever been mastered between demons and our side. We were only able to persuade humans, not one another in the underworld. The underworld usually had a fair balance of power and abilities, this could swing the world in a way that it never had been before. Unequal distribution of power was frightening, especially when it was possibly favoring the darker side.

A slight draft began sneaking its way through the boulders that Athen had packed in so tightly to create one of many barriers between us and the outside world. It took both me and Matilda, judging by her quick movement, by surprise.

"Wow! Where'd that come from?" I got up from the rock turned recliner to grab some of the wool blankets we had available for a moment just like this.

"A storm is coming in." Athen was shaking his head. "Wouldn't you know it?"

"Yeah, kind of fits our luck."

Matilda climbed up on the pile of extra blankets, apparently claiming the rest for herself. Having the items that Athen grabbed from our Kingston home made this feel a tad less peculiar as we tried our best to create a sense of normalcy. The stockpile of food in the corner did little to bring comfort. I would rather think we weren't going to be here long enough to eat that all up.

"How was Arie before we left? Had she accepted it more?"

"With the specifics that you were able to give from your visions, I think that sealed the deal. She knew in her heart that this wasn't something to take lightly. You did the right thing."

"Not that I don't think this piece of real estate isn't great, but I don't feel like things are so 'right' at the moment."

The longer we were in the cave, the more the dampness from the earth began to make its entrance. Athen grabbed another wind-up lantern and placed it in front of us as he sat down next to me, pulling the blanket around him as well.

Not knowing where Cyril and Arie were, made me really nervous. It was for the best. We promised each other no communicating for the first while in our normal sense between minds, cell phones only, and that was only in an extreme emergency. Our families were in far more danger being together, being a family. We needed to stay apart and possibly for a lot longer than any of us might ever realize. Arie would be able to get hold of us if anything went wrong. The thought of something going wrong made my stomach turn. The kind of wrong that would result in her needing to find us was something I didn't want to think about. Having one of us turn was something that seems incomprehensible. Yet, it appeared it could be a real possibility. It had already happened to other families.

"Is this going to work?" I asked Athen, hoping he would hold me and tell me everything was going to be okay.

"I hope it will, sweetie. Only time will tell." His energy was so nervous. I hadn't seen him like this in a long time, if ever.

Matilda began her grunting as she snuggled tighter into a ball as the chill began to get worse. I think she was actually sensing our fear more than the weather.

The flickering light was making me drowsy, but I was determined to stay awake. I couldn't let Athen face the first night alone. Either we were going to both be up, or we were going to both be sleeping.

"Is there a chance to get your loved one back, once a turn has happened?" I knew I didn't want to know the answer but had to ask.

"It's doubtful."

We both laid against the stone wall, letting the coldness reach through our bodies, reminding us gently that we were still alive and thankful to be next to each other. Knowing everything that Athen and I'd been through the last several decades, made me so grateful to be in his presence even if we were in hiding for awhile. Our story was still unfolding; our history wasn't completed yet, but here we were, now hiding in a cave, waiting to figure out our next steps. The others were waiting word from our family, and it was up to us to lead us all into victory.

Our eyes closed, we continued to lean against the cold stone, listening to the wind begin its howling concerto, when the worst noise invaded our peace. The cell phone began ringing. The call that we had been dreading was happening, and so quickly. Athen let the phone ring and ring. As if answering it would somehow make it a reality, while letting it ring let the fate be undecided. Looking into Athen's eyes, hollowed by worry and fear, made me realize that our world had forever been changed once more. A loss had just occurred that none of us could ever understand.

The sorrow I felt was nothing that I could explain. Our goodbyes might have meant something far more than anyone of us had ever realized back in Kingston. I looked over to where Matilda had been curled up, and she was gone. She was nowhere to be found. The process has begun.

Athen nodded, reaching for my hand with his left, and touching the screen of the cell with his right.

"Arie, what's wrong? Where's Cyril?" His voice calm and deliberate, as he spoke into the speaker phone. We already knew the answer.

"Athen," began Cyril's voice, "she's gone. Arie was taken."

Dropping the phone, to the dirt floor, Athen collapsed in my arms. He had never prepared for this, and I wasn't prepared to tell the secret that would change everything. I had promised her I wouldn't.

**AVAILABLE NOW
CATACLYSM**

BOOK 3 OF THE WATCHERS TRILOGY

ABOUT THE AUTHOR

Karice Bolton lives in the Pacific Northwest with her awesome husband and two wonderfully cute English Bulldogs. She enjoys the fact that it rains quite a bit in Washington and can then have an excuse to stay indoors and type away. She loves anything to do with the snow and seeks out the stuff whenever she can.

LONELY SOULS

Book 1 of The WITCH AVENUE SERIES

It's two weeks before Triss turns 18, and her world is about to change into the most magical one imaginable as she readies herself to enter The Witch Avenue Order... that is until her mother's disappearance.

Determined to find out what happened to her mother, Triss uncovers cryptic messages that lead her to the dark side of magic that she never wanted to believe existed. Forced on a journey that may not give her the answers she was hoping for, it's up to Triss to not fall victim to the realm of Lonely Souls.

G — 210

M — 380

A 250

J —

Printed in Great Britain
by Amazon.co.uk, Ltd.,
Marston Gate.